Dance in an Empty Room

Novel
by
Derek Bates

Inspired by the young people whose lives have been transformed and made extraordinary by the work of Dance United.
www.dance-united.com

Published by Reflective Productions LLP

Reflective Productions LLP.
Jindabyne
Moonhills Lane
Beaulieu,
Hants
SO42 7YW
drb@reflective-productions.com
www.reflective-productions.com

CHAPTER ONE

The Reverend Belari mounted the steps of the pulpit in the village church and stood in front of the lectern, looking out over the congregation. Methodically, he placed papers and what looked like a rolled, glossy magazine in front of him, while the congregation waited for him to speak. His thin, emaciated body shook with emotion as he grasped the lectern with white knuckled hands and stared with his eyelids reduced to slits. Several people coughed nervously, in anticipation of the tirade which they felt sure was coming. At a time when congregations were declining, the Reverend Belari always attracted a full church.

In the quiet Cumbrian community of Loriston, where there was little in the way of entertainment, Belari filled the role of a stage actor.

He held the congregation in his stare for several minutes while throats were cleared and those with uneasy consciences tried to look away.

Ponderously, he picked up the magazine and slowly and methodically descended the pulpit stairs. The congregation waited, wondering why their priest was not speaking to them from the pulpit as he always had done.

He walked backwards and forwards across the aisle, waving the rolled magazine before stopping on the steps in front of them and staring while they waited for him to speak. When he spoke, his voice was little more than a whisper, but a whisper that could be heard clearly throughout the church.

"You will be wondering why I, a priest who normally addresses you from up there - closer to God than you are, have come down amongst you to deliver a message from our Lord."

He looked around so that his eyes seemed to be resting on each one of them, looking deep into their souls, causing them to shift uncomfortably on the hard wooden benches.

"It is because of sin," he continued, first in a clear whisper then at full volume, "SIN!!!"

He stopped while the echo of his voice died in the corners of the church. Then he continued in a stage whisper. "Yes, Sin! I see it everywhere in this town, with its undeserved reputation for tranquillity. The town is peaceful and lovely, except for you and your evil." He pointed his finger and slowly moved it around the church, seeming to cover all of them. "Those to whom I am addressing these words from God will know in their consciences who I mean. I suggest that you think about it. Decide when and where you have sinned. You know! Each one of you knows the Commandments and His words. 'Thou shalt not sin'."

He stopped and looked at them with his jaw clenched. "But I know that you ignore his word. I see the evidence when I stand in front of you here. I see it when I walk amongst you in the streets of this otherwise lovely town. I see it when I visit you in your homes." He raised his hand and again waved the rolled magazine over their heads. "You may wonder what is in my hand; I will tell you; it is a magazine of the Devil. It is just one of many such magazines I have seen; magazines of filth, depravity and lewdness that I have noticed in your own homes. It is not an old magazine, either. Look!" He pointed with outstretched finger at the magazine. "If you look closely, you will see it is dated May, 1934. One of you has bought this lewd magazine recently and has been reading it in your home. Yes, in your very homes, homes which should be filled with the sanctity of prayer. Homes which I should be able to enter and feel uplifted, when instead I feel degraded."

In the congregation, dumpy, greying women looked sidelong at their menfolk as the priest reached into his cassock pocket and pulled out another rolled up magazine. He placed it in his hand with the other magazine and waved them both menacingly in the air in front of the congregation. Suddenly, he brought them down into his outstretched palm, with a violence that made them all start.

"These are just two of those filthy papers. I picked one up from a dustbin yesterday. The dustbin was outside the house of one of you here. I will not say whose house it was, but you will know."

He held one of the magazines up.

"My friends, I have looked through this paper and it disgusts me. If this unclean paper was unique, I would worry less for your souls."

He waved the magazine above his head and once more slapped it loudly against his outstretched palm.

"But it is not unique. I have seen it and others like it in other places. I have seen them in homes where there are children. Fortunately, all your children are in Sunday school, otherwise I would not wave this venomous filth about, for fear that they would be corrupted. And yet some of you," he waved the magazine slowly over the head of the congregation, as though it were a weapon, "some of you have these things around where our dear children can see them. God's message is that you should be ashamed;

ashamed that you could risk corrupting even your very own children." His eyes lined up along the magazine as he waved it at them, and he noted with satisfaction the bonneted heads of some of the wives turning suspiciously towards their spouses.

"Sinners!" his voice boomed over them, echoing off the stone walls of the church. "Some of you have forgotten that God created man and woman for the sole purpose of bringing children into the world. And when the family is complete, any thoughts of union of bodies should be put aside. The purpose has been served. God is satisfied with you and you should devote your lives, as I have mine, to the glory of our maker."

His voice dropped to a whisper again, "Repent and pray to God for your souls. Even though I am ashamed for you, you can be sure that I will also be praying for your souls because the Lord would welcome you back, if you would only change your ways and repent."

Sitting at the back of the congregation, Grace Belari, his daughter, would have liked to stand up and reject her father's claims. To tell him and the congregation that they were being fed nonsense; that the dilemma of man's purpose was far more complex than they were being told. She had long been unable to share her father's single-minded convictions, and found his sermons so exaggerated that she would often feign illness just to get out of going to his services. She could hardly bear to listen to his distorted and over-simplistic preaching to his unquestioning congregations. In reaction to his beliefs about a wrathful God, she had found herself becoming increasingly agnostic, shielding herself from what she considered little more than a naive attempt to explain the inexplicable forces of Nature.

4

Suddenly feeling unable to stay and listen to his vituperation any longer, she silently rose from her seat at the end of a row of pews. With relief, she opened the door and quietly left. The air was fresh outside and she breathed deeply, glad to leave behind the musty smell of the church which, for most of her twenty one years, had filled her with dread. After walking for five minutes, she looked back, knowing that she would not be able to see the church, now hidden behind tall beech trees. The lane took her past the high privet hedges concealing the vicarage where she had lived with her parents almost all her life. She knew that he could not be there but still walked hastily past the house. Even when he was absent, the house seemed to be filled with his lurking presence with too many dark corners which she could not enter without a feeling of foreboding. As she walked quickly away from the place, the fog that always clouded her mind within the walls of the church began to lift, as she breathed the scents of the countryside.

Driven by her need to get away from him, and all that he stood for, she was impelled to get into the hills which lay some distance off. Here she knew she would escape from a father who required unquestioning conformity to his own ideals, without regard for her thoughts and feelings. She could also leave behind the uninspiring town and the people of narrow experience and narrower aspirations who lived in it.

In the hills and in the fields, she was able to find harmony with her spirit of freedom and a creative urge, so powerful that it seemed to produce a pressure in her brain. The pressure made her head ache with desire for a life that she knew too well she would never find in Loriston.

When she was alone and the house was out of sight, she would begin to sing, softly at first, directing her voice around her as she moved her body slowly, dancing to the rhythm of the music. She was singing to the trees and to the birds, but most of all, she was singing to the undiscovered self inside her head.

As she danced, her mood changed from depression to euphoria, and she was able to forget the suspicious glances that followed her into every corner of the rectory. As the memory of those dark corners left her, she was able to convince herself that she was destined to take her part in a world where religion was irrelevant, and art, music and philosophy were the only topics discussed.

In that state of euphoria, her thoughts often turned to imagined young men, attractive, with interesting minds; men concocted from novels she had read, or even to real young men seen in bars and restaurants during a brief period of her life spent living in Paris. In Loriston there were no such men. The few that she had known as she had grown up were now living in cities and could be reached only in her imagination. In Paris, although she had had a short liaison with an artist, she had never known the romantic love which so often dominated her thoughts. Thinking of what such love might be like, when she finally experienced it, set her body trembling and gyrating to the rhythm of the music in her head, which gradually took control of her.

The wind, often wild in that empty landscape, was driving her to dance more violently, accompanying her in and out of the trees scattered around the hills. She was intensely aware of the grass beneath her bare feet, and of the wind clutching at her flimsy dress. It almost seemed to her that she was twin souls, the one, detached and observing, watching her own movements, the other violent and possessed by an un-worldly force which seemed to take her to the edge of sanity.

She had seen the influence of mind-enhancing drugs during her time in Paris and felt disgust at their effect on people. Such was her father's influence that she had never even considered taking drugs herself, but when she danced, the uninhibited wildness of her movements made her feel as though she had been drugged. It had been several weeks since she discovered her special tree, slightly stunted and sad-looking, seeming to be lost and struggling to survive in the wind- blasted country. It seemed so in need of friendship that she felt compelled to dance round it, to show that someone cared. She had danced so many times that it had become a silent friend to her.

In the field, there was a scooped-out hole almost nine feet wide. When, exhausted from her exertions, she finished her dancing; her exhilaration was such that she would feel convinced she could leap from one side to the other. She had never managed it and always landed awkwardly on its sloping sides. She would fall to the ground, worn-out but happy, lying for blissful minutes with her mind running forward to a creative future which she was sure she would have.

The exhaustion was not only physical. Dancing set her emotions racing; sometimes with such turbulence that she became fearful that she was being taken over by them. She seemed almost to possess an alter ego from some other world. She knew from her time in Paris that artists sometimes felt this way when they came back to work begun years previously. The work would sometimes seem to have developed a personality and the artist become aware of illusions which had been buried in their sub-conscious minds or had been forgotten.

After her dance, she would lie on the grass, looking up at the sky for such long periods that her clothes would become damp. Eventually, when the damp and cold ground became uncomfortable, she would get up, shake her skirt to remove odd bits of grass, and reluctantly make her way home. Gradually, as she walked, she would return to reality, but still changed by the violent sensations of the dancing, so that, even when her heart stopped racing and her energy had returned, she would still remain ecstatic.

Without knowing why, she felt as though she were being guided by the same benign force that had controlled her dancing, to wander back along a different road to the one that led to her parent's house. The road passed a wooded area and she turned down an overgrown path leading off the road. Her way was blocked by tortuously-shaped undergrowth which seemed almost to want to prevent her passage. Although filled with apprehension, she continued to make her way over fallen trees and brambles, which tore at her dress. Finally, she came to a clearing and, with some surprise, realised that she had found the deserted house that she had heard people talk about, the home and studio of the artist, Artemus Ruane. Reputed to be an almost feral creature, who had had a series of women living there with him at different times.

With difficulty, she pushed aside the undergrowth with a stick she had picked up, and eventually reached the entrance to the house. Filled with anxiety, she waited outside for some time before feeling able to push open the door which was not locked. Inside, she was surprised to see how light it was, and looking up, she saw that most of the roof was glass. Even though the glass was partially obscured by the plant tendrils snaking over it, light still streamed into the room. Covering one wall was a painting of a landscape, with mountains so high they passed beyond the top of the canvas. In front of them were strange creatures that seemed to be looking down at her. Although at first they filled her with apprehension, when she examined them more closely she saw that the painter had somehow managed to impart a sense of humour in their eyes, so that the strangeness disappeared. She then saw that in the corner of the painting was a figure of a young woman in shadow, sitting on a fallen tree. She was facing the animals with her arm raised in a manner that made Grace feel that she was in control of them.

The scene was so powerful that she began to feel part of it as though she herself were the shadowy figure in the corner. After gazing at it entranced for a long time, she turned her eyes away and looked in the right hand corner of the painting, and saw the name 'Artemus Ruane'. Grace smiled to herself; the date beneath the name was in the year she had been born. She began to study the painting more closely; the colours, the careful brush strokes, the general composition and the confidence of the artist, all filled her with delight and amazement.

She remembered that her mother had talked about this painter, had known about his life and referred to him as a man who always seemed alone even when surrounded by admirers. She had heard that at one time he had fallen ill from suspected food poisoning which, it was rumoured, was really a mental problem. He had been taken to hospital but, when he was only partially recovered, had put on his clothes and walked out of the hospital, and had not been seen in the town until many months later.

She looked around the room she had entered and saw that the internal walls of the house had been removed and the building, apart from one small bathroom, consisted of just the large space in which he would have eaten, slept and painted.

The furniture seemed to be scattered where he must have left it and, as she looked round, she saw that this man had had a sense of fun and had arranged objects in what seemed to Grace to be the style of Marcel Duchamp. He had painted vaguely human features on a turnip, given it a hat and placed it in a flower pot.

She almost laughed aloud into the silent room when she saw that on one large cupboard, a hand had been painted with its index finger pointing at the catch on its door. Almost against her better judgment, she crossed the creaking floor and did what the hand seemed to be asking. As she opened the cupboard door, it sagged down on rusty hinges.

Inside were several other paintings; some of them loosely rolled and others still in simple frames. She took them out and carried them one by one over to the light, which filtered through the fronds covering the glass roof. The first painting was of a woman, lying nude on a couch, looking at the painter with such tenderness that Grace was sure that she must have been the painter's lover. She turned the painting over. On the back was written 'Zelda, the only love'.

Several other paintings were of people who held no interest for her and she put them aside.

At the back of the cupboard, she pulled out the last painting and, as soon as she saw it, became transfixed with the image of a young man, also nude, but seated sideways on a chair. His hands were across the back and his head, turned to the viewer, resting on his hands. The figure was about quarter size but was so lifelike that the young man seemed to look straight into her mind. She had never seen any creature so

10

beautiful and could not take her eyes off his extraordinary face. The longer she looked at him, the more real he became. The painter's skill was such that he seemed to have built the person from the inside, so that she felt that if she had touched the image, the body would be warm. She turned the painting over and could just make out, grimed over with dust, the name 'Edward Alleyne, Paris'

She recognised that what she immediately felt for the man portrayed in the painting was what the romantics called love at first sight; love that was both physical and emotional. The sensation overpowered her and made her feel weak. She propped the painting against the cupboard and knelt in front of it, and after a few moments, began to feel her eyes fill with tears, not from sadness but from a happiness she had never felt before. She stared at him for so long that she began to feel that she knew him, and that if she talked to him, he would listen and understand.

This intensity of feeling was a new experience for her. Her life had so often been spent alone, looking out at the world. Whenever she was in the company of others, she talked, laughed, listened, but felt different from them. There seemed to be a force inside her which others did not have, nor, seemingly, even recognise. When she was face to face with other people, she felt inhibited, and the contact lacked the closeness that she experienced with people she saw in passing, who were not even known to her, and whom she had not even spoken to. It was as though she had built the unknown people into composite personalities. From the age of ten, just by looking at them, she seemed to be able to understand other people, their doubts, their fears, their loves and their philosophies. She noticed that she was most able to do this when she was in the presence of the people she knew she would never meet - at a concert when the music flooded into her body, or, when she was walking around paintings in an art gallery and, as well as looking at the paintings, observed the other viewers. At such times, she would look at people and feel so close to them that she was afraid they would notice that she was looking into the minds behind their faces, able to interpret their thoughts so intimately that they would feel invaded. She had read widely, fascinated by books on any subject, but particularly those on philosophy and she was captivated by the attempts man made to rationalise the often confusing world around. The Greek religions, based on their many gods, particularly charmed her. She had read of the Delphic Oracle, the female Pythia of Delphi who would sit beside a hole and become intoxicated by the gas issuing from it. In her drugged state, she behaved so strangely that her words were considered to come direct from the Gods, and it was thought that she had the god Apollo inside her. Grace felt more affinity with this ancient mythological life than with the often mundane world around her.

Her ability to understand the minds of strangers made her feel that she also had the spirit of a god inside her. She felt that she had power and, like those the Greeks called 'shamane', was able to contact the gods. In her wilder moments, when she became almost intoxicated with the ramblings in her mind, she felt she was drinking from a river in which the whole of human sensation was dissolved, which was entering her own body, liberating her spirit.

But her liberated spirit remained trapped in the small town life she led and she was desperate to find release and a way of expressing herself. She could not believe that reincarnation of people was a reality, but she was sure that her thoughts were a reincarnation of the ideas passed through her from earlier generations.

In the state of aloneness in which she normally lived, and which only disappeared when she danced with nature, she would lose herself in her reading. She had been intrigued to read how with Dionysian, orgiastic dancing, the Greeks were able to cure many mental problems, which in modern times would either be treated with drugs or considered incurable. In these Corybantic rhythms, people suffering from mental stresses danced until exhausted, when they would fall to the ground in deep sleep. For some ailments, the music of particular gods was used.

CHAPTER TWO

Much of Grace's learning had been gained from books taken from her grandfather's library, which had been moved to the rectory on his death. She had read them sitting under the shade of trees in the fields near her home. In one of the books, she read that in South America, dancing to exhaustion was still part of the culture. Poor people were more able to live with the dreadful poverty of their lives by using the exhilaration of dancing to distract their minds from the grimness of their surroundings.

It was partly this, and her own love of dancing which took her into the fields, to the freedom of the natural world to release the suppressed spirit hidden inside her. She had danced as far back as she could remember, usually in secret, but until recently, never in the countryside. There was a room in the rectory where it was her custom to go, shut the door and, in harmony with the music that always filled her mind, she would dance, sometimes slowly and sometimes violently. In her childhood days her movements were simple, but later in her life, after finding a book in her grandfather's collection on Isadora Duncan's dance revolution in the Paris of the 1920s, her own dancing became like the American woman's - freer and more extreme.

The dancing spirit she discovered in herself made her feel released from the narrow confines imposed by her father, who wanted her to be as pious as himself and thereby to expiate what he considered were her sins.

She had gained what at the time she thought was permanent freedom from him by persuading him that she needed to learn the language of his forebears, knowing that he had always wanted her to speak French fluently. Her loveless mother agreed and without her husband knowing, had offered to pay. With a sensation of flying in sunlight, Grace had left home for Paris. The reality proved to be less romantic and she had been unable to survive. In a state of numbing depression she had reluctantly left the city where she felt she had finally found a home and returned to find her father triumphant that she had failed. After that, he became even more demanding and convinced that his way was the only right way. Without consulting his daughter, he arranged for her to have singing lessons with a teacher in small town, ten miles from Loriston to encourage her in what he called 'right thinking'.

As soon as she got onto the little train and it pulled away, she would be overcome by a feeling of elation as she watched Loriston and the presence of her father disappear behind the hills.

The train deposited her in Upper Iston, which looked down onto a winding river at the base of steeply rising hills. As she walked to her teacher's house, Grace would look up enviously to the top of the hills, sometimes shrouded in clouds. She would imagine throwing off her clothes and dancing alone, hidden from view by the mists with the moist grass pressing up between her toes and the long buttercups brushing across her legs.

The thought so pleased her that when she arrived at the little terraced house of her teacher, Miss Dorothy, she would be in a mood of intense happiness which would last throughout the lesson, even though her father had so organised what she sang that it was obvious to her that he was trying to control her.

"The Reverend has sent me a letter this week about the sort of music he wants you to sing. He thinks you have had enough time with the psalms," Miss Dorothy said on her first visit, reading from a letter in her hand. "'Abide with me', 'Onward Christian Soldiers', 'Morning has broken' and then some parts of Handel's Messiah are the first few." She looked over her glasses, "Do you like these?"

"I'll learn them. They're quite good in themselves. But I want to learn others. I want to learn modern music."

"What do you mean by that?"

Grace opened her bag and took out a sheet of music.

"This sort of music. It's music to dance to. It's got rhythm. When I hear it on the radio in my room, I can hardly keep still."

Miss Dorothy looked startled at seeing the music. "Mm," she muttered in a non-committal way, "I've never spoken to your father about your lessons but, from his letters, it doesn't sound to me that he would like this sort of music. Put it away and we'll start with a few scales, we'll look at your music when we've done what your father asks."

In spite of her annoyance at the control of her father, Grace sang with pleasure and found she enjoyed her lesson with Miss Dorothy. The older woman surprised her with her attitude. When Grace had met her, she seemed typical of a confirmed spinster but, as they got to know each other at successive lessons, Miss Dorothy would begin to talk about herself when they stopped for tea and cake.

"Grace," she said, as she filled the cups, "You're an attractive young woman. You remind me a little of myself when I was your age." She turned and took a photograph from a drawer in a side table and passed it to Grace.

Grace nodded. "Yes, there is some similarity between us, isn't there?" she said, admiring the young woman in the photograph and comparing it to the lined face of the woman who sat in front of her.

"I was considered beautiful, as I am sure you are. I had many male friends." She smiled at the frown on Grace's face.

"Yes, you may wonder where they came from in this small town. It wasn't always like this. When the mines were operating, the place brought people in from all over the world. Many became very wealthy and built big houses. You can see some of them from here." Grace followed her as she stood up to look out of her little house.

"They are empty and deserted now; always seem like the skeletons of dead generations to me, having the same shape but without life. There is one at the end of this street," she said, nodding slowly, "A beautiful house, which I knew very well."

"How was that?" Grace asked, as they returned to the table and she drank her tea.

"An American came to the town," Miss Dorothy continued. "When he arrived, he had very little money, but he was clever and...," she breathed out with a quiet sigh. "Very good looking, you know. He was a geologist and understood about strata and the formation of the earth. One of the mines was abandoned but he discovered something that every one else had missed and the mine, which had been considered exhausted, was re-opened. After that he

17

was in great demand and made a lot of money. He bought Ely House at the end of the road." She nodded towards the house.

"But how did you get to know him and the house?" Grace asked, sitting forward on her seat.

"Someone told him about my music and he sent a note asking if I could teach him to play the piano. I went to visit him in the house and he showed me the music room he had just finished. In it there was a Bechstein grand piano. He asked me if I would play it. He listened to Chopin for an hour or more and never said a word." She took the photograph of herself from Grace and stared at it then, looking up, said, "He listened so attentively and kept asking for other pieces of Chopin. He asked for the 'Revolutionary', which, if you know it, you'll know is very difficult to play, but something about him gave me inspiration and I played it better than I had ever done." Miss Dorothy looked over the top of her glasses and smiled wistfully. "When I had finished," she paused, obviously overcome with her memory, "I knew I was in love."

"With the Bechstein?" Grace asked, knowing that that was not what Miss Dorothy meant.

"With the piano, yes; it was a beautiful instrument. But I meant with Jack. That was his name. Jack Tarreden for me was even more beautiful than the piano. What's more, he was powerful and I was always attracted to powerful men. Partly that was because my father was a strong and dominant man."

"My father is like that too," Grace said.

"Yes, I know, and that is partly the reason I am talking to you. Jack learned all I could teach him about the piano in six months. He was competent but not talented and I wanted to tell him that the piano was not right for him. But, you see, it was that which brought him to me and it was that which formed the bridge between us. During those months, we got to know each other well." She looked up at Grace, "Do you know what I mean?"

"Yes, I do," Grace replied. "You mean sexually, don't you?"

Miss Dorothy inclined her head slightly and briefly cast her eyes down. "At the end of six months, he had become tired of this town and wanted to sell up and go back to Chicago. He wanted me to go with him. I asked him if I could take that as a proposal of marriage. He said that he did not believe in marriage but if I loved him as he loved me, I would understand and leave with him."

"And did you?"

"I loved him so much that I would have done anything but…"

"Your father? Is that why you are telling me all this?"

"Because of my father, yes. My mother left him because of his temper. When I told him what I wanted to do, he screamed that my life would be wasted and sinful; that my children would be bastards." She stopped, obviously overcome. When she continued, her voice was quavering, "My father, as I said, was very powerful mentally, and physically. He started to hit me - so many times that I was bruised and bleeding before I managed to get away."

Grace stood up to comfort her but Dorothy gestured for Grace to sit down.

"When Jack heard about it later, he wanted to murder my father, but I stood in his way, thinking that was the best thing to do. But Jack saw it as showing that I preferred my father to him."

"He left?"

19

"Soon after; he went back a wealthy man. The house was never sold and I have not seen Jack since he went back to Chicago."

"Did he write?"

"I wrote and tried to explain, but by that time he was back in his own community. He replied, but in a formal way. That hurt more than if he had just ignored my letters," she said, her voice shaking. "So that is my story. It's why I am living here in this little house which my father left me. He died almost ten years after Jack had left."

"How very sad. Did you not want to leave this town after he died?"

"I stayed because of loyalty to my friends and family, and that's why I'm telling you all this. Your father seems just like mine was."

"You mean...?"

"I mean he could destroy your life like mine was destroyed. I sit here, quietly day after day, waiting for the only pleasure I get, which is the interludes when pupils come. You are different from most of my other pupils, my dear. Many of them just want to be out and have no real love of music like you have. You are different in other ways too." She opened Grace's case, took out the Ragtime music and turned the pages. "I share your fondness for this type of music, you know."

She tried to carry on with the lesson but they were both too overcome. They sat in silence until Miss Dorothy went to the piano, put Grace's music, 'Alexander's Ragtime Band' on the stand and played with such delight that Grace was driven to dance around the room, in and out of the chairs while she sang the words out loud.

When she had finished, Grace threw her arms around the little woman who had just come to life and said. "I would never have believed you could play that. How do you know it?"

Dorothy turned to her, her eyes glowing and said. "Jack."

"Jack?"

"Yes, that was his favourite piece of music. I played it for him often. He once took me to London with him – I told my father I was going to listen to a piano recital. We danced to Ragtime, can you imagine me dancing? I couldn't believe my eyes when you showed the music to me."

Grace embraced the little teacher and kissed the top of her head. Dorothy looked at the clock and reminded Grace of the time. Grace collected her music and dashed out of the house, turning to wave goodbye to the lonely woman standing in the window of the little house.

When she returned to the rectory, she crept quietly in and found the room where she danced, silently waiting. She shut the door, took the book about Isadora down from the bookshelves and folded it in her arms, clutching it tightly against her breast. In front of the large mirror she began to move to the music in her head, slowly beginning to dance in the empty room, but gradually dancing more and more violently. As she became hot in the summer heat, she threw off some of her outer clothes. Suddenly, she was startled by a sound behind her. Her movements froze and she turned aghast, to see the greying, slightly stooping figure of her father, wearing his priest's collar and walking slowly towards her. He stopped several feet away from her with a look of anger and contempt.

"What nonsense is this you are doing? And what is this book you are holding against yourself? Are you reading it - one of the books from that old scoundrel, your grandfather, no doubt?"

Grace looked down at the floor.

"I asked you what you have been reading. Tell me," he demanded once more, becoming even angrier.

Grace opened the book at the page she had been reading. Her voice when she spoke was quiet as though she did not want to be heard.

"I was reading about the way the Greeks cured illness by dancing," she replied in a low voice.

"That's nothing more than sorcery."

"But in South America, they still believe that dancing can take peoples' minds away from the poverty of their lives."

"And you, I suppose, think that you can escape from the disciplines of this life by such rubbish. There is only one salvation for us, my girl, and that is to follow God's path. Thinking on God and His works can work miracles."

Her father walked the few paces towards her, snatched the book from her fingers and flung it across the room. Grace's eyes watched in distress as the book smashed its spine against a wall. Her eyes turned back to her father as he shouted.

"I have wondered many times if I was right to have spent so much on your education, Miss. And this is the best it has done, reading drivel. I don't want to catch you reading that nonsense again and I don't want to see you swaying around in front of a mirror like a Bantu native. If you want to learn by reading, and I see very little evidence of it, I and only I, will show you which books to read. My library is full of uplifting books."

He turned away and walked from the room, slamming the door behind him. Grace continued to stare at his receding figure with a look that expressed her dislike of him. When he had gone, she picked up the book, saw that it was still intact and placed it against her face, taking comfort from its hard cover. Going to the shelves, she pulled out several books, putting the one she had been holding behind them where it would not be seen. She stood for a few moments, with her hands against the shelves, composing her feelings, then left the room and took herself out of the house. As she shut the front door she looked around to check that she was unseen as she walked away from the large, gaunt Victorian building.

At first she moved slowly and cautiously, constantly looking to right and left into the shrubs along the drive of the house, as though expecting to find her father watching her. Gradually, she quickened her pace. After a while she stopped, turned round and with a look of relief, saw that the house was obscured behind trees. She tried to think of music to which she could dance, but the incident with her father had distressed her so much that she could not throw off its memory. Feeling free of the house, she sat on a fallen tree and looked out across the countryside which always brought peace to her mind. She was in turmoil thinking about her father, and ways she might escape. What Miss Dorothy had told her about her own life had had a profound effect on Grace.

It was getting dusk before she felt calm enough to go back.

CHAPTER THREE

Back at the house, she returned to the same room where her father had discovered her dancing.

She now felt like an intruder in the room she had always previously treated as her own, because of her feeling of guilt when her father had seen her doing what she knew he would think of as sinful. To him, emotion and love were symptoms of a weak mind. Strength, decisiveness and his form of discipline were all part of being the pious adult he wanted her to be.

There had never been a proper parent-child relationship between them. To Grace, it seemed that he regarded her as a necessary but expensive part of being married. Tenderness was absent from his make-up. Up until the time he had discovered her dancing, she had pushed her relationship with her parents out of her mind so successfully that it had never really concerned her, but, after his anger at seeing her dancing, she found she could hardly tolerate the thought of being near him, or even of being in the same house. She decided that she would still make herself go through the motions of being a dutiful daughter. She would live in the same house and continue to tend to his needs on the many times when her mother was in bed and unable to do the household work. As far back as Grace could remember, her mother had always suffered from an ill-defined ailment, which seemed to have grown gradually worse under the hostile gaze of her husband. There was never a time in Grace's life when she had known her mother to be completely well; never even a time that Grace could remember when her mother had been happy. At least, her father, as far as she knew, had not resorted to the physical violence which she had often read about in newspapers. The violence in him was one of indifference and pre-occupation, apparently so worn down was he with the pressures of his parish and the 'tending of his flock' that it never occurred to him that his wife and daughter also needed tending.

After the upset with her father, Grace put a smile on her face when he looked at her, but the smile was empty, nothing more than a moving of her lips. The confrontation with him convinced her that the rectory was malevolent, pervaded by his disdain even when he was away. They still ate together as a family, and she still listened to her father pouring out his troubles, but for her it was nothing more than a ritual. Imprisoned deep in her body was a soul desperate to be liberated. She knew that it would never find release as long as she lived in Loriston, and that she would have to leave the place as soon as she could arrange it but with the difference that this time it would before good. Only then would she find liberty, and it would be with someone she had yet to meet.

As she, with a slight nod of here head, politely acknowledged her father's talk about his parishioners, her mind was elsewhere, wondering if her release could come from the young man in the painting. The possibility filled her with pleasure. His image was so vivid that even while she sat at table, she could recall the effect the painting had had as clearly as when she was alone in her room that evening, after her return from the empty house.

As soon as she could leave the meal table, she would herself to go to her room, saying she was going to read one of the books her father had put there. When the light was beginning to fade, and she beginning to tire, she lay on the floor, smelling the odour of dust that rose from the rug covering the scrubbed wooden floor. It had lain there all her life and probably for decades before that. Looking up through the skylight, she would pass into a dream-state. In her dream, she met Edward Alleyne, looking as he did in the painting, and walking in a city that she recognised as Paris. It was Paris where she had first been happy, but then desperately unhappy, when the man she had lived with there became violent.

In her dream, Edward smiled his greeting and took her hand in his as they walked together along the streets which she remembered from the time when she had lived there. She would awake in a state of euphoric arousal, her spirit having passed to France, unaware that her body remained in the Rectory in this Loriston which she found so uninspiring.

She roused herself from the dream-like state as she was about to get into bed, suddenly filled with a conviction that someone else might get to the painting and take it before she could see it again. The thought kept her awake and, after a few moments, she decided that she would have to go to it. Taking a paraffin light from a cupboard and putting on a dressing gown, she went down the stairs and silently opened the heavy front door. She stepped outside closing the door softly behind her. As she walked, she felt a chill against her skin. The night was cool and she realised from the damp beneath her feet that she had left without putting outdoor shoes on. The moon was full and from its light she was able to retrace her steps along the lane, past the tree, now clad in silver moonlight, where she had danced. The moonlight helped her to find once more the overgrown path leading to the artist's house. The branches brushing against her face and clothes made her feel that her way was being barred. She began to feel fear and for a moment hesitated, aware that what she was doing was ill-advised. But she was unable to stop herself, driven forward by a force outside her control. Finally she found the house, moonlit and looking more menacing than it had during the day. The door seemed harder to open, but she threw her weight behind it and crashed into the deserted house. With a smile of relief, she saw in the moonlight that the unframed painting was still where she had left it. She picked up the frame, pulled the canvas free and put it under her nightgown. Without stopping to shut the door, she ran fearfully from the house, holding one hand up to screen her from the undergrowth along the path. As she ran, she was almost screaming in terror but it was mingled with the exultation of securing the painting, now clutched safely against her breast.

Back at home in her room, she placed it on the floor, propped against the side of the bed in front of her. Feeling strangely overdressed in her nightclothes, she slowly removed them, and sat on a chair beside Edward, in a similar pose with one leg wrapped under the other. She turned over the painting, which was only about two feet square, to see if it was dated. There was some writing on the back, but it had become moulded over and, in the dim light, she could not make it out. She rubbed at it with a moistened finger. The dust was gradually removed, but the date was still indistinct.

In the quiet room with only moonlight for illumination, she rested her eyes on the young man's image. Propping the painting against a chair, and driven by some external force, she began to dance around it, slowly at first, but gradually getting faster. For her, the dance was like no other. She had always danced to an unknown future but this dance in the

27

empty room seemed to be inspired by the knowledge that she had finally found a purpose. It seemed to take her over so that she performed sublimely, her body being thrown into contorted shapes which amazed her as she saw herself reflected dimly in the large mirror on the wall. She seemed to see herself as an outside observer would: a young girl suddenly awakened, given a reason for living. She just knew the man in the painting who watched her dance was alive and was waiting for her. She moved in a dance of new-found love, a dance which also contained an element of worship.

Quietly she said, "Edward, I shall be with you."

She stared so long at the painting of Edward that she began to enter a state of hallucination and, as she looked, the image misted over and she felt that Edward was in the room with her. In her loneliness, she talked to him.

"Edward, can you listen to me, listen for a while? Help me to see what I must do with this empty life I lead. The day starts and the day ends and all I see is a wall in front of me which stops me, stops me so that time is flowing by but does not touch me."

In her mind she heard a voice, distant and clouded. "We live the life we make for ourselves. There is no other way, Grace."

"I know you are right, Edward, but I don't know which way is best for me. I know you are talking through my own mind, Edward, but that means I can tell you things that I can tell to no one else, because I am alone in this dismal great house and in this empty town, where I have only the trees to dance with."

"But you are lucky, Grace, you have a mind like few others. You can leave the drabness around you and create your own life, your own illusions."

"But what can I do? My father hates me, wants to turn me into a saint or something. I am not a saint. I hate sanctity, which seems to be only a way of preventing human beings from becoming real people, so that they just skate across the surfaces of reality. I cannot be the obedient saint my father wants me to be."

"Grace, tell me your choices."

"You mean what I want to do?

"Yes, tell me what you want to do with yourself."

"Before I decide, I want to do one thing. More than anything else, I want to find you," she said, her voice quiet and almost imperceptible.

"Where will you go?"

"To Paris, of course! That is where you are, isn't it?"

"For now, I cannot help you. Now that you have decided, you must make your own way. But I shall wait for you to reach me."

The next morning, she woke very late to a loud knocking on the door of her bedroom.

"Are you still lazing in bed? Get up and come to my study at once."

Something in her father's voice struck fear in her. She washed and dressed hurriedly and, shaking with despair, stumbled down the stairs. Reverend Belari was standing with his back to the fire as she went into his study.

"I want to speak to you, my girl. I have made it a habit to position the latch on the door in a particular way. When I came down this morning, I found the latch had been moved. It would not have been your mother who touched it, she is unwell again. You must have gone out through the door last night. Can you

29

explain to me why? I hope you were not seeing anyone during the night." His raised voice became menacing, his eyes narrowed in anger.

Grace felt her face going red.

"I was so hot last night that I couldn't sleep. I simply went out to get some air."

"Why do you look so guilty then?"

"I don't know. I have not done anything wrong, I swear to you."

"I hope that is true. If I find that it is not, you can be sure that you will be punished severely. I don't want you leaving this house again at night,"

"Very well, father," Grace said and as she spoke her voice trembled and she started to feel tears welling in her eyes. Suddenly, she turned and ran from the room. She found herself in the breakfast room, her hands gripping the table for support. She waited until her breathing was calmer before she sat and tried to eat the cereal which she poured into a bowl in front of her. The cereal and milk seemed tasteless in her mouth.

After she had forced the food down, she sat staring out of the window. A clock chimed in another room and roused her. She looked at her watch, stood up, went into the piano room and picked up her music case. As she walked past her mother's room, she saw her sitting up in bed with the curtains drawn, so she called out,

"Goodbye, mother, I'm just off to my piano lessons."

CHAPTER FOUR

Once outside, she cycled to the end of the drive and saw a young man cycling along the lane, hurrying to catch up with her.

"Carlton," Grace said, "Are you following me again? You always seem to be around when I am going to my piano teacher, haven't you got anything better to do?"

"I just like to see you, that's all, and the only time you seem to come out of the house is when you go to your lessons."

"I don't like to be watched, it seems creepy. But, as it happens, today I am pleased to see you."

"Why, have I done something you like at last?"

"No, I just want the company of a friend," she said, as they cycled together along the lane.

"Do you mean any friend, or do you mean me?"

"I just want to talk." Grace said, ignoring his question.

He smiled, put his hand on her saddle and pulled her bike to a halt.

"Have you decided you really do love me after all, then?"

"No, Carlton. I wish you wouldn't be so silly. I do not love you and I never will," she said emphatically. "I am fond of you, but it's no more than that."

"Oh," Carlton said, pretending to be dejected. "Why did you want to see me then?"

They began to ride off together and she replied, "It's my father."

"What; is he being difficult again?"

"Is he ever anything else? He still treats me like a naughty five- year old," she said, shaking her head despairingly. "I don't think I can take much more. If I stay here any longer I shall go mad."

"As mad as him?"

"Oh, don't joke about it, I'm serious."

"So was I, Grace. Honestly, I do sometimes think he's mad."

Grace stared at Carlton in surprise.

"Do you really mean that?"

Carlton nodded. "Yes, I think he is mad. Not in a loony type of way but he certainly seems to be driven, a robot under the control of a master." He looked at the clouds scurrying by, driven by high wind. "He only responds to forces - like those clouds do." He turned to Grace as they freewheeled down a slope. "Don't you think that's quite profound?" He grinned at her. "I know how you like profundity."

Grace smiled weakly. "Yes, but that doesn't change anything, does it?"

"I didn't mean it like that, I've always believed in a God but mine is different from his. My God gives us freedom to behave in our own way not rigidly like your father wants. When you are with him, I see that you can never please him; that's why he makes you suffer. It surprises me how you've put up with him all these years." He put his hand on hers as she gripped the handlebars of her bike. "I think my father was a bit like him – his principles applied rigidly to everyone except himself. Isn't it time you did something about it?"

"What choice have I got?"

"Well, it's very simple to me. You leave home. You are old enough. You could have been to university and never returned home again."

"Father wouldn't pay for me go, said it was a sinful place and would corrupt me." She paused, "You know I did go away for a few of months. I told him I needed to become better at French. Of course, his family is French, even though they were originally from Italy and he had always said he wanted me to be fluent in 'the beautiful language' as he called it. He said he couldn't afford to send me but mother has her own money which he doesn't know about so she paid for my trip, although he never knew. I was working in the Doctor's reception, he just thought I'd saved enough from my wages."

"So you now speak good French," he said as they pulled to a halt outside the high hedges of her teacher's house.

"I learned a lot of the language, much more than I ever could by being taught but I also learned about life." She flicked her pedals idly backwards. "But, I found out how naïve I was. All I knew about what goes on between a man and a woman I had learned from books. What Paris taught me most was what real living is all about."

"You would have learned a lot more from me with my experiences."

"Carlton!" she yelled, "Stop it, will you? I don't want to hear any more about your 'conquests'. You've told me about them too many times. I just want you to listen to me for a change."

"Well, try talking to your mother. That's what they are for," Carlton said sulkily, as he started to ride away.

"Carlton, don't go." Grace called after him.

She caught up with him and put her hand on his arm. "Sorry I shouted at you just then. It's just that I'm upset, that's all; it's not you. I have tried talking to mother, but somehow we've never had any contact. When I got back from Paris, at first she seemed so glad to see me, but then she changed and drew away."

"I'll bet your dad got at her."

"That's probably it. He was not at all pleased to see me go, and. I reckon, even less pleased to see me return. But in those first few days, mother wept and kissed me for the first time that I could remember, even though I'd only been away for a few months. Then one day, when I came back from walking, I could hear father screaming at her behind the closed door to the downstairs room she uses as her bedroom, ever since she became ill. I couldn't hear what they were saying, and I wouldn't want to anyway, but after the argument, mother returned to the way she always was. You know, almost a zombie."

"That's the effect he has on me. There's something about him that just seems to turn a tap and all my energy drains away. I don't know about the sin he is always talking about; something that he seems to see everywhere in the around him. Sin's a word I never use. His type seems to think that any pleasure is 'sin'. I can't think what he would say to me if I told him what we used to get up to in university. We never did anything which I considered to be 'sin', but it was just great to get away from family; to be able to please myself, and," he grinned, "Do a bit on my own."

Grace ignored what he was implying.

"Oh, I wish, I wish, I wish I could have gone to University. I'd love to study art and literature. I've often wondered, Carlton, why you ever came back here when you got your degree. You always told me you did so well; you could have got a job in London."

34

"Because of you, of course," Carlton said, jokingly.

"No, tell me."

"No, you're right, I never did want to come back, but it was just the family business. My mother couldn't run it on her own since my dad went off with his secretary. So my life is here in drab Loriston, and will be for as long as I can see." He took Grace's hand again, "I would be happy even in Loriston with you though, Grace."

"Don't be tedious, Carlton. You're a nice person but I've told you so many times that I can never be anything more than a friend to you." She started to cycle away. "I've got to get to my lesson," she called over her shoulder.

Carlton caught her up and said, "I'll see you when you finish."

After the lesson, Carlton was still waiting. Together they went down by the river and sat throwing stones into the water, watching the ripples spreading out on the slowly moving flow.

"It's so nice here in the country," she said. "I know I'd miss all this if I did go away - I did when I was in Paris," she frowned, "Carlton, what can I do? You've always got such good ideas."

"I told you before," he said, standing up and throwing a stick into the river, watching it float away. "Just leave; it's your life you are wasting by staying in that house."

"Leave?" she said. "But where can I go?"

"Hastings?"

"Hastings, I hardly know where it is. Where can I go in Hastings? And why should I go there? I'd just get lost."

"My sister Dusty lives there."

"Dusty lives in Hastings? But that's no reason why I should go there," she frowned, "You told me she's lives a wild life that you find shocking and you never liked her."

"That's right, too. And I don't think you'll like her either. She has a life with weird people. Charitable people might say she is eccentric; one of those eccentrics for which Britain is famous. To me, she is just bizarre and it seems the only thing she lives for is for men and to make money. She certainly has made a packet but even that hasn't made her happy, at least, as far as I can see. But what it has done is to make her lots of contacts with important people and she has house and flats that she lets out. You wouldn't want to have anything to do with her but you could stay in one of her flats as a start and I'd come and stay with you at week ends."

Grace stood up, folded her arms, looked into the water and after a moment, said decisively, "I'll go."

"You will? When?"

"In a few days, as soon as I can organise it."

Carlton had stood up and was throwing another stick into the water. When he heard what she was saying, he slipped and almost fell into the water himself.

"You mean it don't you?" He said looking Grace in the eyes.

"I mean it," she said, returning his stare.

CHAPTER FIVE

When she got back home, Grace felt freed by the decision she had made. She wanted to shout it out to the world, and decided that she must tell her mother. Without any more thought, she went into her mother's room to tell her. The door was closed, which surprised her, but she knocked and went in. Inside, she found her father sitting by the bed in which her mother spent much of her day. The curtains were drawn, because her mother found the daylight too bright for her eyes. Grace sat down in an armchair facing them both. Neither of her parents said anything or even acknowledged her presence. She felt as she had always felt; an intruder in their private world, and waited for them to speak but when they said nothing, she broke the silence. Her words seeming to echo around the loveless walls of the room. She sensed their hostility, obviously upset at her intrusion. In her mind, they seemed almost like waiting vultures.

She lowered the tone of her voice so as not to show her agitation and told them of her unhappiness. The silence in the room filled her with unease as they looked at her unseeingly, making no sign that they had even heard her. She knew they had always thought her strange. Neither her father nor her mother had ever made any effort to understand her. They seemed to look only at the face and the body which she inhabited, not at the person inside. Neither could see the woman she had become in the years since she had left childhood behind. As she looked at them, she knew that the spirit inside her body was beyond their comprehension. She waited while her mind went back to the many times her father had ridiculed her. She could hear his voice telling her that her fondness for modern things was wicked and that her life should be devoted to being a God-loving daughter.

"I... wanted to tell you how I feel. I have never asked for much but I do need your understanding, I am not happy," she said, and saw with some pleasure that her mother responded by sitting up in bed as though she wanted to speak. But, even as she did, the Reverend Belari put his hand on her shoulder and slowly pushed her back.

"You say you are not happy. Our lives are not given to us for such trivial feelings. They must be devoted to God. I have never known happiness and you will never know it; it is only the delusion of fools. Now," he said, standing up, "Your mother is tired." He walked to the door, opened it and waited while Grace got up. "If you have anything to say which is of any interest, you must leave it till later."

As he closed the door behind her, she thought she could hear her mother weeping and wanted to rush back in and confront the insensitive man. She turned to push the door open to see what was wrong but, as she did, she heard the key turn in the lock.

On the verge of tears herself, she went up to her room and stood silently, waiting to control herself. For some time, she tried to read, but her thoughts kept going back to the hostility in the room below. Her father's treatment of his wife, and his anger at the dance in an empty room, had crystallised her dislike of him. It was obvious he thought her dancing was just a little girl's play; he would never recognise that dance was her way of saying, 'I have become a young woman, a woman with freedom to do as I please when I am alone.' His wanted her to be a repeat of himself.

She tried to read the book she had started and which normally would have engaged her interest, but found she was reading mechanically without understanding.

When she heard her father leave her mother's room, go into his study and shut the door, she put down her book and decided it was time to explain to him the despair she felt and her inability to be the inhibited, conventional young woman that he obviously wanted. She knocked quietly on the door of his study and went in after he had called out,

"Yes."

As she apprehensively walked in, she saw him closing a drawer in what she thought was a furtive manner. He nodded towards an empty chair and she sat, waiting for her racing heart to slow down. He turned his swivel chair towards her and she saw from the look on his face that he was in one of his moods, when he made it clear by his silences that he wanted to be left alone.

"What do you want here?" he asked, making it apparent that he wanted her to leave him. Her eyes were cast down, avoiding his gaze as she spoke,

"Father, I know I am sometimes a disappointment to you. I know you would like me to hide myself away from the temptations that exist in the world. And I do feel, as you do, that many of those temptations are wicked and will only cause suffering for me and for you and mother. I have tried to behave in the manner you want but I have reached a stage where I know that I need to find out for myself what life is about. I need to have some freedom. I must find myself. I have no idea what sort of person I am; whether I am a good person, whether people will like me. You see, the only image I have of myself is the one you gave me."

Her father's jaw tightened, "That is a parent's burden, my girl. It's something you will not understand because you have never had any responsibility. I have always seen it as my duty to shield you from wicked behaviour because I know the sort of person you could become. You are like your mother in many ways."

"I don't understand. What do you mean by that? My mother's behaviour is not wicked in any way," Grace frowned, "In any case, I don't think I am like her. Why do you say I am?"

"You don't know and you won't ever know. You certainly won't hear it from me," he said, his voice becoming agitated as he stared at her accusingly.

"But I have to know why you say that, and why you look at me like that. You make me feel as though I have committed one of the sins you keep talking about," she shouted in frustration. "Tell me what you mean."

"I have no intention of telling you anything!" he shouted back. "Your mother has caused me enough suffering and I am not opening up those wounds again. The subject is closed." He turned to his desk, and picked up a book lying in front of him. "I want to ask you about this," he said, thrusting the book in her face. "Mrs. O'Brien was cleaning your room and she found it. She knew you must have taken it from the library where it is normally kept. It was one of your grandfather's and it is quite unsuitable for you. It contains nothing but stupidity; it is full of philosophical nonsense. It is this sort of book that corrupts young, impressionable minds. I do not want it in the house. It is only fit for burning." He held the book in front of her for long enough for her to see that it was the Greek play Lysistrata. He strode over to the fire, raked over the ashes until they flared up and threw the book into the

40

flames. Then he turned to his desk, picked up a card and his keys and stormed out of the room.

As soon as he had gone, Grace ran over to the fire, picked up the poker and dragged out the book. She was relieved to see that only the cover had been damaged. In triumph, she held it above her head with outstretched arms as she heard a car door slam and through the window saw her father drive off at a furious speed.

The injustice of his action made her so angry that she could think of little else. She became incensed with his treatment of both her and her mother, who had become little more than an automaton, a virtual prisoner with no freedom to act on her own free will. Holding the charred book to her chest, she screamed at the receding car, "Where they burn books, they will one day burn men!"

To calm herself, she sat down and examined herself in the mirror. As she did, she noticed the reflection of her father's desk and saw that, in his rush to leave, he had left the key in the lock of the drawers. For some time she battled with her conscience, wondering if she should open the drawer. With warring emotions and against her better judgment, she went to the desk, took the key in her hand and pulled the drawer open. Inside were papers and photographs. She turned them over and stared in horror at what they depicted. In only a few moments, she had seen enough to make her feel ill. Slamming the drawer shut and locking it, she ran from the house and lay down beside an oak tree, trying to suppress her revulsion, her mind a storm of disgust. She was still trembling violently when cold and exhausted, she returned an hour later. Carefully, she turned the front door handle, shut it slowly behind her and walked quietly along the corridor past her mother's room so as not to disturb her. The door was open and, as she passed it, her mother's voice called out.

"I'd like to talk, Grace, can you come here?"

Grace wanted to be alone but at the sound of her mother's voice, she turned and went in to the darkened room. Her mother was lying on the daybed and remained quiet while Grace sat beside her feeling awkward in her presence and began to shift in her chair. To break the silence, she said, "It's sunny out, mother, you should let some light in. Shall I pull the curtains? It would make the room much more cheerful."

"I used to like the sun when I was younger, Grace, but now I find it depressing."

"Why should that be? It always makes people happy."

"When I was young, I used to play tennis in the sun in Harrogate. After the game, we would go for walks and we would sing. I suppose that now I can't do all those things, I don't want to be reminded of those times."

"I think it's such a shame. You ought to get out more; I'm sure it would make you feel better."

"Perhaps I will one day. I used to enjoy the Harrogate I grew up in and I had lots of friends there. My parent's house was lovely. I often wonder what the people who rent it from me are doing with it now. When I was your age, we had parties with lots of interesting people. That was before I met your father. Gregor, everyone called him but he liked to be called Greg. He was different when we met and I thought he was so nice."

"Was that when he sent you that Bible inscribed with 'To Elsa with my love forever' on the inside cover?"

"Yes, he seemed to be so romantic then." She smiled to herself. "I was not the only one of the girls who thought that, you know." A faint smile flickered in her eyes at her memory. "I often think it would be nice to go back. I haven't been to Harrogate since your grandparents died. Greg and I were married there and we had the reception in my parents' garden. I remember it as a day of sunshine and friendship."

"Was it nice being married?" Grace asked, realising that this was the first time her mother had talked about her time in Harrogate.

"For me it was a blissful day, like it is for most women. Only one small thing spoiled it. You see, your father was from a poor family and he really resented the wealth of your grandparents. Daddy had secured him a job teaching theology in a school where Mummy was a governor. We all thought he would have loved it, but the fact that he hadn't got the post on his own merit just added to his resentment. We moved into a school house and..." She stopped talking and turned her gaze to her daughter.

"Yes, mother, what are you saying?" Grace said, trying to get her to continue.

As though coming to a decision, Elsa sighed and then said, "Well, after the wedding, everything came as a shock to me. Giving up the freedom of living with my parents where - if I'm honest - I was a spoiled brat with all my needs cared for. That was the hardest thing for me to get used to. Gregor would come in tired from teaching and would expect me to have everything ready for him. Before we married, he had seemed to be so uncomplicated. I soon found out how wrong my judgment was. When we were alone in our own house, I saw that the Greg I had known was a different person."

"Like he is now, you mean?"

"No, he has become worse. Every year, he seems to grow more distant. Every year, he seems to be more convinced that God is the only important part of his and everyone's life."

"And that includes you and me, doesn't it?" Grace said. Her mother nodded,

"We'd been married for two years before Greg exploded one day with my father. He accused that gentle sweet man of condescension and arrogance. Can you imagine that? My dear father who had never had an arrogant thought in his life? Greg subjected him to a tirade of abuse. Daddy just did not know what to say, he was devastated. All he had tried to do was to make things work for the two of us. Daddy had always been very good with words, but he sat like a fish, opening and closing his mouth with only empty bubbles coming out."

"Mother, that's awful! Poor grandfather! He was always the kindest man. How did it all end, did father apologise?"

"I don't think he has apologised ever. No, he never attempted in any way to say he was sorry. It may just have been coincidence but daddy never seemed to be the same afterwards. He had thought he was doing what was best for us, but from the way Greg reacted, he realised that he had got it all wrong and seemed to doubt his own judgment," she sighed, "it was not long after that that Greg was offered this living in Loriston and we left Harrogate. We never returned, except for short visits which I made on my own. When daddy and mummy wanted to see me, and you, of course, we would usually meet halfway in a little house that had been owned by one of your great aunties."

"From the photographs in your album, you seemed to have had a large circle of friends. Didn't you want to go back to see them again?"

"It would have been difficult," she said. "Your father didn't like the town and he said he never wanted me to see the place again. His attitude turned our friends against us." She shrugged her shoulders, "So I haven't been back to see them."

"Did something happen there, then? Something that you did that he didn't like. He was quite mysterious this afternoon. I thought for a moment he was going to tell me what he was feeling. It would have been the first time he had ever revealed anything of himself to me, but I was wrong; that would have meant his treating me as a grown woman."

Her mother turned her head away and remained quiet before saying, "I heard the argument with your father."

Grace started to speak but her mother interrupted, "I know how difficult it has been for you living in this house. I've wanted to speak to you many times but, somehow, he was always around."

"It's more than that," Grace said, "Even when he's out on his visits, his presence is still in the house. Wherever I turn, he seems to be watching me from every corner."

Her mother nodded in understanding,

"I know what you mean. He has always had that power. I sometimes feel that he has the ability to glide noiselessly into this place. I know how destructive it has been for you, living here with him. He has very strong opinions on every subject and especially on you and the way he wants you to behave." She had been looking at the window through a small gap in the curtains but slowly turned back to Grace,

"I have wanted to talk to you many times, but somehow he has prevented me, even when he is away. I know how wrong it is that he still thinks of you as a child, with a child's need for discipline; he cannot accept that you are now a young woman with a woman's feelings and emotions."

"That's just it, mother; I have never been able to talk to him. Even when I was little; and it is even worse now that I am grown up. If I try to tell him about the way I feel, he gets angry, just as he, you heard what he was like today, shouting me down. He just wants me to be quiet, never express my views and behave like a good little girl. I'm sure he wants me to take holy orders or something, that's why he tries to make this house seem like a monastery," she sighed, "I don't think I can take it anymore."

"I know, I've watched you become a woman and want freedom to be yourself. I've held my tongue for so long that I expect you will probably find it hard to understand but, believe me, dear, I do know the frustrations you feel."

Grace looked surprised, "How can you say that? You've always supported him completely and agreed with everything he says."

"Do you think I want to be that way?" her mother said, her voice rising with irritation. "How do you think I feel? I am a woman too, you know. I have feelings as well but I have to be a wife to him. That's my lot. Some days when I seem quite well, I get up and try to move around the house but, even if he is in the village, I sense he is looking at me with that frown and I come back to this room because that is where he wants me to be."

"There are things about him which you don't know, mother. He rushed off to his meeting and left the drawer to his desk opened," she said with a slight lie.

"Grace!" her mother cried, her mouth falling open, "You didn't look inside, did you?"

"I know I shouldn't have but, something inside me made me." She screwed up her eyes. When she opened them, she said, "He is despicable. How could you have lived with him so long? He must have a depraved mind."

"Depraved? What…what do you mean?"

"I think you know what I mean. You must have seen those things in his drawer; pictures, writing and implements. I thought I had seen everything in Paris, but never anything like that."

"No, Grace, I swear to you that I have no idea what he keeps there. I've never even been inside his study. He has forbidden me to go in there, even with O'Brien."

"But didn't you ever wonder what he was doing in there?"

Unable to answer, her mother turned her face away and looked at the blank wall facing her.

"You do know, then, do you?"

"No, I do not, but I have had my suspicions. He even locks the door, you see."

"Well, that's the end for me, mother. It is going to be different from now. I have tried to be loyal to him but I can't do it anymore. The argument was the last straw. I know now that whatever I do I will not satisfy him and I am not bothered about that any more. I was always worried that I would not be able to please him and would make him angry with me. But, although I was terribly upset when we were arguing this afternoon, even when he was shouting, I realised that I didn't care. What I had dreaded had happened and I am not afraid anymore. His ranting also showed me that I am as strong as he is." She stopped and took her mother's hand, "But that's enough about me. You have a life as well; you must get out. I'll help you. We'll practise together. We'll start by walking together around the house. Then, when you feel up to it, we'll go into the garden." Grace gave her mother a smile of encouragement. "And when you are strong enough, you can come with me into the country where we can dance together. I've never told anyone before, but there is a tree on the downs where I dance. It is my tree; no one else knows about it. It's a stunted tree, thin and poorly formed. It seems to be lonely, a long way away from the other trees. I know how it must feel and, when I dance around it, it becomes a different tree, almost mystical, almost magical. We give each other strength."

"Grace, don't let your father hear you talking like that. He will say that the tree is possessed by the devil and it will corrupt you."

"No, it's not possessed by anything, it has its own soul and it's a soul that I can feel. I can sense it making me happy, making me forget him and this house and the corners he inhabits every moment of the day and night."

"Grace," she squeezed her daughter's hand, "I would love to come to see your tree some day."

"Can you dance?"

"Not now, but when I was young, after we had played tennis, we would dance in the clubhouse. There was always music there. Sometimes there was a trio. Sometimes my young man, the one I was going out with at the time, would play the piano, or there was always an old gramophone, one of those with a big horn." She smiled to herself. "Those days were happy. After the year of hardship the country had gone through, there seemed to be a future for the world to look forward to. You won't know about your grandparents when they were younger, Grace," she reached out, took her daughter's hand and held it against her breast, "but your grandmother and grandfather were lovely people; so nice that they left me unprepared for the real world. I thought everyone was like them." She turned, picked up a mirror from the dressing table and brushed her hair back with her hand, "I look a mess, don't I?"

"No, mother, you don't, you are still beautiful. You were beautiful when I was a little girl. I was always so proud that everyone would look at you when you took me to school, and you are still just as lovely." She took her mother's hair in her hand and said, "Let me wash your hair and brush it for you; that will help you see yourself as you were."

"He may come back. He'd be furious to see us together like this."

"He won't be back till late this evening. I saw an invitation to a meeting from the Bishop on his desk, and he's driven off in the car with it." She took her mother's hand. "Come to the bathroom and I'll help you. We'll make you look like you used to."

"No, Grace. Gregor doesn't like me to use make up."

"He won't even notice. I've seen him; he never looks at you when he comes to your room supposedly to see you. He's always either looking away or pretending to read his papers." Grace stood up and held out her arms, "Come with me."

"No, Grace, I must rest. I need my rest. His doctor has said so."

"No, no, no. You rest too much. I want you to help you get your life back. I want to wash your hair and see you as you used to be." she said, putting her arms around her mother and laying her head on her shoulder. She gave her a gentle pull to encourage her out of the bed.

Slowly, her mother placed her legs on the floor and stood up unsteadily. Then by holding on to her daughter, she was able to follow her into the bathroom.

When her mother's hair had been washed and dried, Grace brushed it out and applied make up to her face.

"There," she said, "Now you look beautiful, just like you used to." She kissed her mother on the forehead and, sitting down on the floor in front of her, Grace rested her head on her mother's legs. In the first sign of affection that Grace could remember, she felt her mother's hand stroking her hair, "You are a lovely girl, Grace,"

For several minutes, they sat without saying anything and then, her mother broke the silence, "Grace, I have to say something to you."

"Yes, what is it?" Grace asked, raising her head to look at her mother.

"I think this house is wrong for you. You are ready to leave and find another life for yourself." Grace, resting her chin on her mother's knee, looked up at her as she continued, "We've never spoken like this before. You know, for all these years, I have wanted to have a talk like this with you, but whenever I suggested it, he insisted that you be taught to behave in the way he sees fit." She sighed, "I know my life is passing me by, but I have memories. I would love to get out there, play tennis like I used to, meet people, and be a person again."

"But why don't you?"

"Why? Because I can't, why do you imagine I lie in the bed here every day, hating what I've become?"

Grace looked puzzled, "Because you are suffering from your nerves; isn't that why? Wouldn't you be doing things in the house and be out meeting people otherwise?"

"That is it partly, of course."

"But the illness - isn't it that that keeps you in this house? It's a real illness?"

"Oh, it's real all right. I get so tired and shaky and I feel so depressed." She smoothed down her clothes with her hands. "Certainly, the symptoms I get are real. And it's got a name, I can't recall what it is but your father has told me; something like nervous lassitude. Yes, I think that's what he said the doctor called it. I take the tablets and I rest as his doctor has told him I should."

"Mother, how can you accept that? Only one doctor? He could be wrong; they do make mistakes," she said with horror. "I think you must see another doctor."

Her mother turned to her, and then started nervously smoothing the bedclothes. "What else?" Grace asked, "What else keeps you in this room? Why does he want that? It must be awful for you, alone here in this room all day?"

"He thinks...," she hesitated. "He thinks...," she stopped. "He does not trust me, Grace," she said still looking at her daughter. "He always wants me to stay in the house."

"I want to tell you something that I'm afraid may disappoint you. But I have to, it may help you to understand, at least partly, why he is like he is, and..." Her voice drifted away. "You may also see me differently." Her voice was so quiet that Grace wasn't sure she had heard her mother correctly.

"What can you mean, mother?" She knelt up to see her mother's face and was saddened to see anguish in it. "Have you done something which father would think was sinful?"

"I was foolish at one time and, yes, he does have a reason for wanting me to stay in the house," she said, looking straight at Grace. "He has always wanted me to be where he knows my movements."

"I don't understand, mother. Has there been someone else?"

She leaned forward and stroked her daughter's hair and then continued in almost a whisper, "Yes, there was someone else."

"Another man?"

"Yes," she said, still in a whisper. "Yes, another man."

"Before you met father or after?"

"It's too painful to talk about." She started to smooth her clothes again and turned her head away to look out through the small gap in the curtains at the window. But, even as she looked away, Grace could see that she was overcome with the intensity of her feeling.

"I must tell you, though," she said with determination, "It has remained a secret which I have never told anyone." She picked up a handkerchief and touched it to her eyes. As she turned back to look at her daughter, she smiled suddenly at the memory she could not restrain. "Grace, he was a lovely man; the sort of man who would have been a good father to you."

"Mother," she said, open-mouthed, "tell me what you mean by that? What are you saying, mother?" She got up and sat beside her mother. "I must know what you mean. Tell me, are you saying he was my father?"

"You see, Grace..." For many minutes she stared ahead and again lifted the handkerchief and dabbed her eyes. "You see, Grace, I... I... don't know."

"You must know, mother. You must see it will mean so much to me. Is there no way of knowing?"

"No, there is no way." She shook her head. "It is as important to me as I know it is important to you, but no, we will never know."

"Do I look like him?"

"I can tell you that whenever I see you laughing, I am back in Harrogate, in the spring-time where I met him," she said, smiling distantly. "I may just be behaving like the silly girl I was then, and I see it just because I want you to look like him. We didn't meet many times and I have no photographs. It will sound silly of me, but I didn't even find out his full name. It just didn't seem to matter. I only know his first name."

"Tell me what it was."

"It was...," she stopped, as though even saying his name was difficult for her, "His name was Raphael."

"Raphael? I like that name. Is it English?"

"No, Italian - although he was actually Greek. He was christened Raphaello after the artist, but in England he called himself Raphael. He told me was a writer and had come to Harrogate to do some research on Yorkshire, because his book was to be based in the countryside around there." She smiled at the memory. "We met one sunny spring afternoon while I sat alone on a park bench. Gregor was away and Raphael came and sat beside me, quite close, so close that at first I felt uncomfortable. But as soon as we started talking, I began to relax. Like many

Continentals, he was very direct and said that he had been watching me as I walked into the park."

"Didn't that sound as though he was just trying to make a pass at you?"

"No, it sounded nice, and anyway I had forgotten what it was like to have someone attractive make a pass at me. I was flattered; you see, your father never paid me compliments like that."

"I have wondered many times why ever you married him."

"I wonder myself now but there were many reasons. I'll tell you." She frowned with the effort as she tried to remember what her husband had looked like, and then nodded, "Yes, he was very handsome. So good-looking that most of the girls in the tennis club fell for him. And, to me, he seemed very intelligent. He used to talk to me for hours, about philosophy and religion. I didn't understand a lot of it but I loved it when he spoke. He was nice and, in those days, it seemed to me then that he was very thoughtful. Every week, he would bring me a book or something to read about God and Christianity and he would always take the trouble to explain anything I didn't understand. He would talk about his time in Oxford, when he did his degree. I'd never even considered going to university so I loved his stories about all that he had done there. It seemed that he had led such a different, glamorous life there. I never thought I was bright enough to go to university."

Grace laid her head down on her mother's lap and, in a muffled voice, asked. "Didn't he seem hard to you then?"

"Not to me. If he was, I never noticed it." She pushed her fingers through her daughter's hair. "What I felt for him seemed to me to be love. It wasn't until after we were married and I moved into the house that I saw his inflexibility. He was only a lay preacher then, but he was very keen on regular prayers. Going to church and meals and visitors; all had to happen at fixed times." She smiled to herself. "When I met Raphael, Gregor had gone away to a conference in London and I was alone in the house for a week while he was staying on to visit cathedrals and churches with colleagues. At first I loved the peace, but then I began to feel very lonely. Funny isn't it, I longed to be away from his restrictions but when I was, I didn't know what to do with myself."

"Until you met Raphael, you mean?"

Elsa nodded. "Yes; until I met Raphael. And he brought new language and fun into my life at a time when I needed fun more than anything. Raphael always made me laugh so much. He brought everything to life. He gave personalities even to the birds as they went through their courtship rituals. One of the male pigeons was always left out when other stronger birds won the wings of the female pigeons. Raphael gave him the name Rupert and made him seem almost human. He was so clever with words that he composed an entire poem about the bird in the few minutes while Rupert strutted in front of us."

"Why didn't you leave father and marry Raphael?"

"I probably would have, but...,"

"Why do you say 'but'?"

"He was an honest man."

"Oh, you mean he was married, mother?"

Elsa nodded, "Yes, he told me that he was married but that the marriage was unhappy. He would have left her but - well divorce was not possible in Greece where everything is dominated by religion."

Grace turned her head, looked up at the ceiling and said, "Mother, how sad for you."

"I had cooked a cake in the morning before we met and I just wanted him to continue talking to me, so I asked him to come to the house for tea. He told me about his difficulties with his wife almost as soon as we met. In fact, while we were still eating the cake, which I had made to celebrate my period of freedom from Gregor. It always seemed to me that it was fate. You see I had no reason to bake a cake. It was just me in the house and no one would have visited without Gregor being there. It must have been fate that made me cook it, so that I would have an excuse to invite him to share it with me." Grace had never before heard her mother sound so happy.

"I would like to meet a man like your Raphael, mother; someone creative, someone who could write life for me."

"Well, it was his words that charmed me. I had always loved listening to people talk, even when I was little and daddy would tell me of his travels. It's funny, Raphael was not especially nice to look at but his language, particularly with his Greek accent, just filled my mind. As we walked back from the park, words poured out of him; poetry, prose and music and it went on through the afternoon and into the evening. And, when the night came, he just did not leave. Somehow it didn't seem necessary for him to go back to his hotel. We stayed together for three days, right up until he had to return to his home in Greece." She stopped and became silent before saying, "are you shocked, Grace?"

"I'm not shocked, mother. I know you've always told me to take care, and I have, but it makes me pleased to know that you had such a happy experience." She took her mother's hand and kissed it.

"It is a man's mind that interests me and I don't think I would have been able to resist someone like your Raphael. Did you not try to contact him again after he left?"

"I never did, Grace. I never did. Although I was suffused with happiness, I also felt so ashamed of myself afterwards. His love is still with me, even today. And every day, his words are still with me. He never wrote them down but I can remember them almost word for word. We used to say them together and I can still hear his voice saying them as though he were speaking now." She became quiet as though listening in her mind to Raphael's poetry and then said,

"'There was a wilderness where I was lost.

With greying sky and distant drum

That haunted me with empty words

Repeated like that beat of drum

But then you came to take me away

To take my soul from night away'

It is not a great poem but they just poured out of his mouth, almost whenever he spoke. Many more, many more are still here in my head and will be till I die. Grace, I hope you have a love like that; a love where body and mind meet. It was the most incredible experience and my life would be poorer without it, but I am still surprised at what I did. Nothing like that had ever happened in my life before or, for that matter, since." She let her gaze roam around the room. Pursing her lips, she continued, "When Gregor came back, I was still in that intensely happy mood but, at the same time, I was almost unable to talk to him because of the shame I was feeling. I was afraid that if I looked at him, he would see it in my eyes or even hear it in my voice."

"And he found out, didn't he? I suppose that was what was behind what he was shouting at me today."

"Yes, he found out within a few days. Raphael left me a book of poetry and he had written a message on the flyleaf. It said 'The memory that will live with me forever, Raphael'. I locked the book in my bureau drawer. But Gregor must have suspected what had happened. Perhaps he saw that I was happier than I had been, or perhaps one of the ladies he used to visit as part of his mission work had told him that I had been seen with a man, but, somehow, he found the key and got into the drawer while I was out shopping."

"Shopping? Can you remember even what you were doing?"

"That was all I ever did, apart from going to church on Sundays. He didn't even like me seeing my parents."

"What happened when he found the book?"

"When I got home, he was waiting at the door. He pulled me into his study, struck me with the book and knocked me into a chair. Then pulled me to my knees by twisting my arm behind me, and made me watch while he burned the book in the fireplace." She shuddered at the memory. "Whatever small regard I had had for him, died that day."

"What a dreadful thing to do! Like a sadistic need to destroy your happiness. He seems to be fond of burning books; he tried to do it today with a book I was reading. "

"He sees books as symbols. The Bible is the only completely good book, he says. Most of the others he sees as malevolent creations. He would have seen my poetry book from Raphael as a sign of my love for someone else. When he burned it, the flames blazed up and I felt a searing heat burning into me. At that moment, that book was a symbol for me, a symbol of my love for Raphael; it almost felt as though he was burning us both. I screamed and tried to drag him away from the fireplace but a woman's strength is not enough when a man is determined. The book was left just as ashes, but he couldn't burn my memories. You can destroy objects but, as long as I live, my memories will be indestructible"

"You must have thought of leaving him after that."

"Oh, I did, but the conventions were all against it. Women did not leave their husbands; it would have been too much of a disgrace for the family."

"But, if you'd left the country to follow Raphael, you could both have lived somewhere else. He was a writer, they can work anywhere. There must have been a way you could have contacted him."

Elsa thought for a moment and then turned to the cabinet beside her bed, took out a bible with a thick wooden cover. She pressed the back cover in two places at once and it opened in two. Inside were two letters. She passed one to Grace.

"He did write twice, addressed to a friend's house - that is his last letter."

Grace read the letter. "He is obviously disappointed that you had not replied to his first letter, so you could have contacted him at the address here. It's in London – why didn't you?"

"That is the address of his publisher. He did not write the first letter until he had stopped travelling about three months after he left England."

"Yes - I don't understand what difference that makes."

"By then, I knew I was expecting you."

"Yes..."

"I just wanted you to be born into the home of the man I had married."

"But you told me that Raphael might have been my father."

"It sounds stupid, I know but I've wondered many times why I stayed. Maybe someone like Sigmund Freud could sort me out. I wanted to go but somehow it seemed to me that Raphael had come into my life for a reason and when he had left, it was all over."

"Fate, you mean? He had been sent to give you only a short time of intense happiness?"

"That would explain it. I felt that doors had opened and, when he left, they had closed, never to open again." Elsa shrugged. "Guilt, I suppose."

"But did you never try to contact the publisher's address."

Elsa nodded, "I did, many years later but the publisher did not exist then. He was dead. I was told that he and his staff had been travelling in the R101 airship which crashed in France in 1930. I have regretted not trying to contact him earlier, many times but, perhaps it was God's will." She dabbed at her eyes. "So I stayed and have remained ever since, trying to find some residue of affection in spite of having stopped loving your father from the moment he burned my book. He knew that it would hurt me more than if he had tried to beat me with his fists. The physical pain of violence does not last, but mental anguish remains."

"I tried to love him, mother, but after the way he treated me today, and after what I saw in that drawer and what you have just told me, I know I never could."

She stopped and took her mother's hand. "I'm sorry to say this but you are right; I can't live here much longer. I think I shall go mad if I do." She paused for thought. "But how can I get away? I tried once before but I had no money and there was no work I could do in Paris to earn any."

"I've never told you before, and even Gregor doesn't know, but your grandparents left you some money. Quite a lot actually, so you will be able to look after yourself. You can't get at it yet but I have some in an account that Gregor does not know about either. So you can go whenever you are ready."

"Mother, that's marvellous, how ever did you prevent him from knowing about it."

"I had to, otherwise he would have got his hands on it, and he always has plenty of things to spend his money on."

"You've been very clever, mother, thank you!" She gave her mother a hug. "I have already decided that I must find somewhere else to live, but I cannot leave you, especially after today. This is the first time we have talked like this ever before."

"Don't worry about me. I think the things you have said have given me a way to live with him and, if I can't, I will find a way out." She yawned and sighed.

"Are you tired, mother?"

"I took my tablets to settle my nerves when I heard you arguing with your father. They always make me feel like this."

"I'll leave you to sleep, then. I want to go for a bike ride. It'll help me get rid of my anger against 'him'."

Her mother lay down on the bed and held Grace's hand, gradually loosening her grip as Grace got up to leave the room, heading for the kitchen.

In the kitchen, she gulped down a glass of water before cycling along the lane to the telephone box to make a call.

"Carlton," she said into the phone, "I must see you."

"You mean you are ready for me?"

"No I do not mean that." She almost shouted in her exasperation. "I just want to talk to you again. Can I see you?"

"Not right away. I have to get a contract finished and posted to a customer, but I could be down at the river in about an hour. Wait for me near the ford."

Carlton, wearing a business suit and tie, arrived on his bike, looking flustered.

Grace gave him a perfunctory kiss on the cheek, and said, "I need to find someone." She took a brown paper covered package from under her arm took out the painting of Edward and held it up in front of him.

"Who the hell is that? I've never seen anyone like that around here. Where did you get it from?"

"I suppose, in a way, I stole it."

"You stole it?" His mouth fell open. "I've never stolen anything and I didn't think you had it in you to steal - Belari's daughter!" Carlton exclaimed. "Perhaps this is your first protest." He smiled at her. "Can I be your second protest?"

"No, you cannot. Just listen to me for a minute, will you? He lives in Paris. I don't know how I know, but I'm sure of it. How can I get there and find him?"

"How should I know? I've never even been there. You'll have to try someone else. Are you telling me that you've just seen this painting and that's all you know about this man, who looks more like a boy to me, and you want to go an a foolish chase looking for him?"

Grace nodded sheepishly.

"Well, I think the idea is ridiculous. You'd better find some other stupid chump. You must know someone."

"No, Carlton, "she said, "I don't know anyone else who can help me. You're my only real friend and my only hope. Please, Carlton." She took his hand and gave it a kiss. "What about the sister you told me about."

"Dusty? She knows Paris pretty well. Got a lot of contacts there; often goes there on business. She buys things from a dealer. Montmartre, I think, or somewhere like that - you know - one of those arty places. We don't get on very well. She's so much older; she'd left home when she was sixteen, before I was old enough to get to know her. She lives in what I think is a pretty revolting way down there in Hastings. I don't like speaking to her much because she's always seemed irritated whenever I see her. She'd probably be more interested if I was talking about business deals." He shrugged. "Or men more likely."

"Men?"

"Yes, men, there's a whole string of 'em. As a widow left well off, she's a bit of a honey pot; must be the money because she doesn't seem to be much of a looker to me." Pensively, he shook his head. "A very odd life she has. And Hastings is a strange place, too. Seems to me they're always drunk or on drugs there. Not your scene at all, Miss Belari."

"You don't know what my scene is though, do you?" Grace pouted. "You might imagine you know me, but I am not the sweet innocent you think. Paris taught me a lot about things that might surprise even you with your university life."

"Well why don't you try showing me? I can always learn new tricks."

"Get back to Dusty. I would like to go to see her, Carlton. I've been told that Hastings is beautiful in places and I'd love to see the sea, but I don't really care what it is like, I just need to get away from here. Could you arrange things for me to go there?"

"I might, if you make it worth my while," he grinned.

"Carlton!" she shouted. "Cut it out, I'm just not feeling in the mood for your crude remarks."

"Ok, sorry. I didn't mean to upset you." He got off his bike, laid it down on the grass and went to sit on a wall nearby. After a few moments, Grace did the same, settling down beside him. "Dusty ought to be able to help, Grace. She'll probably have a room she can let you have. She has a lot of property there and she lets out rooms and flats."

Grace gave Carlton a peck on the cheek.

"You're nice when you do that, Grace."

"Do you think she will like me?"

"Who can say? Sometimes I wonder if she likes anyone. She's got lots of so-called friends but they're all out for what they can get and I've never seen anyone she's close to."

"You said she was married, though. Wasn't she close to her husband?"

"I doubt it; he was an older man; George Sompting, his name was. He had a pot of money. At the time she got married, I thought she seemed fond of him. But I guess it was just show because it ended in divorce a few years later. The divorce settlement got

64

her started in business. And, not long after the divorce, he drowned in an accident that happened at one of her parties. After his death, it was found he hadn't changed his will and she got the lot. Part of the money went to buy the art gallery, which was just about to collapse so she got it very cheaply. That's what started her interest in paintings, Mum says."

"Paintings?" Grace said with interest. "Of course, she will have heard of Artemus Ruane, won't she? "

"Artemus Ruane, the mad painter? I think she knew him when he lived in the Loriston area, but I may be wrong. I don't think she would have been a bit interested in art in those days. He was just one of her eccentrics; she seems to want to surround herself with weirdos."

"Did you ever meet him?"

"Mum talked about him but I don't think I ever met him. I might have done but I would have been too young to remember. Don't forget, Dusty's much older than me - I was the result of one of the attempts my mother made to patch up the marriage with my father." He grinned. "It seemed to work, so I suppose I was useful; they stayed together right up until he disappeared out of our lives for good. Pretty tempestuous marriage, though. He always seemed to me to be either in a sulk or a rage, except when he was being funny. He had such a sense of humour there were mealtimes when we did nothing but laugh. I suppose he was only happy like that when he had another woman in tow. There were dozens of them, mother says."

"Poor Carlton, you must have been so unhappy."

"Not really, it just seemed to me that that was what family life was like. It's given to all of us to accept our situations, we wouldn't be able to survive if we didn't and kids adapt, don't they. It wasn't till I went to university and stayed with friends that I realised there were families who didn't always fight. It did me good in a way, made me keen to get out of the house, that's why I still go to church, I got into the habit of going there to think and it helped me a lot. "

"Well, I never adapted to my life, and the church never provided me with any peace," Grace said. "Living in the rectory has always been purgatory for me, and what has made it worse is the knowledge that my mother has never been happy since she married my father."

It was beginning to become cool so Grace pulled her coat closer round her shoulders. "You say your mother talked about Artemus the artist. What did she think of him?"

"She did mention him occasionally. Bit of a lad with the ladies, apparently - caused a scandal; almost pulled the village apart when he got the school teacher into the family way."

"That rings a bell, I seem to remember hearing something about that. Didn't she lose her job?"

"Mm – think so."

"I wonder," Grace frowned. "He painted the picture of Edward. Could that have been her son?"

"May have been, for all I know. I heard Mother say she had a son. You'll have to ask Dusty if you meet her, she'd know."

"Carlton. I must go to see her. Can you sort something out?"

"Ok, if you insist on going through with your stupid idea. I'll write to her."

"Can't you phone her? I can't wait much longer..."

"Oh, ok, I will, but only for you; wouldn't do it for anyone else. I'll go with you to Hastings? We could share the same room and get to know each other better? "

"Carlton, I don't want to share a room with you or anyone else. I've said already, you're the best friend I have, but it will remain like that. We can only be friends. Can you understand?"

"I didn't mean we would sleep together, Grace, dear," he said with a feigned voice. "Just hold hands and look out of the window at the sea, that's all."

"No, you can stay with your sister and I'll take a room nearby."

"When you're cruel it makes you even more attractive," he grinned.

She ignored his comment, "Just friends, nothing more, but it would be nice if you came too because I wouldn't know anyone there. Will you be able to get away from the office for a while?"

"Yes, I've got some holiday to come and it's quiet in the office at this time of the year. We could have some time together."

"Thank you, Carlton, I'd like that, but it's got to be on my terms, remember." She put her hand on his shoulder. "Do you understand?"

"Of course, but it's quite an irony, isn't it?"

"What do you mean, 'an irony'?"

"Well, you want to leave home because your father wants you to behave like a nun but you want it to work in reverse – I have to behave like a monk and abide by vows of chastity," Carlton said, with a feigned grimace.

Grace, seeing the humour, smiled. "Are you happy with that then?"

"I'm not sure about the vows of chastity. I can certainly behave like a monk. Monks had a lot of freedom. I wouldn't have minded being like Rasputin. He seemed to have had a charmed life and had many lovers; even managed it with the Tsarina. If I behaved like him, I'd probably meet someone I liked better than you"

"Oh, don't be such a romantic, Carlton. You're being silly again."

"You don't know me, Grace. I bet I could teach you things you've never even heard of. You seem to think I behaved like a celibate when I was away at University, don't you?"

"I don't want to know about that, just keep those thoughts to yourself," Grace said primly.

Carlton made a face in mock imitation of her attitude. "What will you do for money? I've got some if you need it."

"Thank you, Carlton, that's very sweet of you, but Mother tells me I was left quite a lot by my grandmother. I can't get at it yet but mother has some which my grandmother left her too. She's got it hidden away in the house and she'd lend me some. She told me I should take it. She and my grandparents lived in Harrogate. Grandmother was a lovely woman; she always had a smile whenever I saw her. I still miss her. So much of what I have came from her. She bought me my horse and she paid for my education at St. Catherine's. She often fell out with father when she wanted to do things for me; he disagreed with her about everything where I was concerned. He would never have liked her leaving me money, I know. It's invested in a trust or something which father cannot touch. A lawyer deals with it all. I don't even think father knows much about it or how much it is."

"Do you know?"

"No," she shrugged. "A lot, that's all I know; probably find out if I really needed to."

"I would, I'd really want to know."

"Yes, I imagine you would. But then, money is more important to you, isn't it?"

"It would be to you if you'd ever been without it. You've never been close to being bankrupt, have you?"

"Why, have you?"

"When my father walked out on us, he took a lot of the money and all the know-how. Mother and I had to start learning quickly. We had customers screaming at us and we had suppliers wanting to be paid. If it hadn't been for some money which Dusty lent us, we'd have been in the workhouse straight away."

"Carlton, I never knew that."

"No one did. Mother's a very proud woman. She always let people think she told him to go and that the business was buoyant. But it was a very different story when we closed at night and we went through the books together."

"How do you manage now?"

"We had one of those lucky breaks. Mother was well in with Congletons, she'd met Madeline Congleton through the church, used to spend a lot of time together. One day, mother burst into tears when they were having tea together. The next day, Congletons gave us an advance order for five years and paid for it there and then. It was only that which kept us going."

"And Dusty?"

"Dusty? We paid her back. As I said, mother's a proud woman; she wouldn't want to be indebted to

69

her. They don't get on well, you know." He stood up. "Anyway, I've got to get back to the office. I'll speak to Dusty and sort things out." He took out his diary from his jacket pocket and thumbed through the pages. "If I can get Dusty to agree to it, I could take you down on Sunday, I can have some time off. We'll leave in the evening, when your father is in church. It's a long way, but overnight the roads will be quiet and we should make good time."

CHAPTER SIX

On the following Sunday evening when her father was at evening service, Grace went into her mother's room. Tearfully, she put her arms around her mother who was also verging on tears.

"I'm going soon, mother. Carlton will collect me in his car and take me to where I am going." Grace took an envelope from her handbag. "I'll contact you, mother. I don't want anyone to know where I am going, but if you have to get in touch, there's a 'phone number in this envelope, and you can get a message to me."

Grace and her mother held each other in silent embrace until a car was heard on the drive outside. Quietly, Grace stood up and said,

"Goodbye, mother."

Slowly, their hands separated until only the tips of their fingers touched.

"Be happy, Grace."

In the car, Grace was strangely quiet and Carlton took the opportunity to put his hand over Grace's hands, folded on her lap in front of her.

"I went to church this morning and prayed for you," he said to change her mood, "sad to be leaving?"

Grace looked out of the window at the passing scenery and said, "I've lived with my mother all these years without her ever showing me any real affection. It's only now that I am leaving that I realise how much we could have meant to each other, if it hadn't been for 'him'." Grace sighed quietly, "Every girl needs a mother and I never had one all the time I was growing up...until now. We've finally got to know each other and I've left her behind in that house, with that man."

"You ought to be glad to be leaving everything behind you and starting a new life."

"But how could I be so cruel; leaving her, now that we have finally found each other?"

Carlton took his hand off the steering wheel, squeezed her shoulder and said, "Don't be sad, Grace. There are always going to be times when we have to do things we don't like doing, but sometimes it's the only choice."

"For me, you mean?" Grace turned her head in enquiry.

"For your mother, I mean."

"But what about her life, that's what I'm asking myself? Haven't I been very selfish in leaving her alone with that man?"

"That looney, you mean." He stared ahead at the road as he steered the car round a series of bends. "You could have spent the rest of your life there and then two lives would have been wasted. Your leaving home means that you can start again, you might even find that leaving your father's church and going to a new one will make a difference."

"It will be a long time before I feel I need another church; father's was enough for me. But aren't I just being selfish? How can I be happy knowing that mother is still with him, almost a prisoner?"

"The philosophy lecturer in University used to say that there are no black and white situations where only one decision is possible. He was very fond of John Stuart Mill's Utilitarianism and always said we should go for the greatest good for the greatest number. In this case, the choice you are making means you, your mother and I will be better off and only your father will be unhappy. There's something else that I haven't told you yet- your mother phoned me and said that she was really pleased you were at last going to be free of your father."

"She did? When was that?"

"The same day you told her you were going away with me." He turned his head slightly to Grace, taking his eyes off the road for a moment. "She had put two and two together and I think she thought we were eloping together."

"You told her we weren't, didn't you?"

"No."

Grace sat up straight, "But why didn't you?"

"One thing you never give me credit for, Grace, is that I'm quite a good catch." He squeezed her shoulder again with his free hand, "Your mother thinks I am right for you."

"Well, I don't think you're right for me. You're a friend, a very good friend, but that is all," Grace said firmly. "But I am so glad you've told me that she's happy about the way it's turned out." She leaned over to kiss Carlton on his ear.

"If that's the effect it has on you, I'll say it again and again and again," Carlton said, laughing. "When you touch me it's like a jolt of electricity."

"As long as it stops there and goes no farther, that's all right," she replied and kissed him again on his ear. "I'm quite flattered, thank you, Carlton."

"I'm planning to drive through the night, Grace, so if you want to sleep, I've put a blanket and a pillow in the back."

Carlton pulled the car off the road and settled Grace down on the back seat before driving on. After a while, he began to feel weary himself, so he pulled the car into a lane and climbed in the back with the sleeping Grace. He put his arms round her, kissed her quietly and they fell asleep together.

An hour later, he was awake and feeling refreshed enough to begin driving again. He kept glancing in the mirror to check that Grace was comfortable as he drove. After a few more hours, he noticed the slowly brightening dawn lightening the trees at the side of the road. A fox suddenly appeared in the road on front of him. Carlton swerved violently to avoid it and Grace woke up with a start. She sat up, moved into the seat beside Carlton and put her arm around his shoulder. Keeping his eyes on the road, Carlton leaned his cheek against her arm. She kissed the top of his head, and said. "You are so kind, Carlton."

"Better than that Edward, d'you mean? At least I've got blood and not paint flowing in my veins. That's the first sign of real affection you've shown me," Carlton said.

"A friend's kiss, that's all," she said, patting his cheek in mock reprimand.

"Oh, and there I was getting all excited."

"Carlton!" Grace suddenly exclaimed. "Look there!" She pointed into the distance. "Now I'm excited too. I can see the sea ahead of us. Isn't it incredible? This is just the place where a new life will start for me. A real life that we were so far away from in Loriston. Your sister's place looks over the sea, doesn't it? Can we go to see her straight away? I'd love to see the dawn rising over the sea."

"I'm afraid not. It's only eight thirty and if I know my sister, on a Sunday like this, she won't get up till late in the morning." He looked at the milometer, "We've made very good time, that's the benefit in travelling through the night. "We're even earlier than I thought. Dusty'll take her breakfast on the terrace with her Sunday newspapers and her view over the sea. If we call on her too early, we would receive one of her hostile receptions. She's very good at those."

"What can we do then?"

"I've got some food in the back of the car; we'll go on to the beach and have breakfast. There's a flask of coffee as well which will probably still be warm."

After a few miles, he was able to park on the beach road. The sun was rising, casting long shadows of the two figures across the shingle as they settled down on a blanket from Carlton's car. They ate in silence, drank coffee from the flask and watched the sea coming in.

"The sea is advancing on us," Carlton said.

"Like a new life rolling in," replied Grace, standing up and kicking off her shoes. Carlton did the same and, with his arm round her shoulder, they tripped to the water's edge. From a house nearby a gramophone was playing dance music.

As the sea washed in over their feet, they danced together to the music. As they danced, they pulled close together and Carlton caressed Grace. On the sea wall, a couple of older women, their shopping bags in their hands, stopped and stared at the couple. Carlton, seeing them, waved a greeting over Grace's shoulder.

"Can I have the next dance?" one of them called, slightly embarrassed, Carlton and Grace walked off, smiling at each other.

When the music had finished, Carlton stood back and said, "Grace, you don't want to go ahead with this crazy search for that canvas Edward, do you?"

Grace looked up in surprise, screwing her eyes against the sun shining off the sea.

"Isn't that why you brought me here?"

"I brought you here to get you away from your father. Now that we're here together, away from him, I thought you might feel differently about us."

"Carlton, I'm grown up enough to know that this thing with Edward is silly but it's there, inside me, and I can't change it." She kissed him softly on his chin. "I do feel differently about you, of course. I wouldn't be a woman if I didn't. But Edward dominates my mind. Can you understand that? You will always be the best friend I have ever had, but this thing with Edward is different."

In the nearby house, someone had put on some more music. This time, it was a slow waltz. It seemed so exactly to suit her mood that Grace said, "I wonder if whoever lives in the house over there has selected the music deliberately?"

They came together again and danced right to the end of the music, before falling to their knees in the beach. Tired by their dancing and the long journey through the night, they lay back on the blanket and fell asleep in each other's arms. Two hours later, they were awakened by the noisy hooting of a bus.

Carlton looked at his watch. "We'd better get along to see Dusty; I expect she will have finished her breakfast by now. I'll telephone her from the box over there," Carlton said, getting sleepily to his feet and walking off.

On his return, he said, "She's awake, had her breakfast and probably read all of the paper that she ever reads – just the gossip columns - so she's ready for us."

Grace was sitting with her hands round her legs and her head on her knees, looking at the sea.

"I'm almost sorry to be leaving this spot. This is more like where God really is. If my father could bring this into his church, I'd go there willingly."

"Didn't I tell you you needed a God? My religion is the only thing that has kept me sane at times."

As they knocked on the front door of Dusty's mock Tudor house, they could hear noisy music coming from inside. When Dusty came to the door, she was quite a surprise to Grace. She was large, dressed in blowsy clothes and weighed down with silver bangles and necklaces.

She almost had to shout over the music as she welcomed them in.

"Yes?" she said enquiringly, obviously still waking up from a nap. "Oh, it's you, Carlton, and this must be Grace." She stepped out, embraced Grace and stood back at arm's length looking at her. "You told me she was attractive, Carlton but she's more than that with that lovely, long hair. Come on in." She led them down the corridor and called over her shoulder. "You'll find me untidy I'm afraid, but you won't mind that, will you?"

She pushed open the door at the end of the passage and held it for them to pass through into the lounge. Dusty threw several items of clothing, an empty bottle and a couple of books from the chairs onto the floor and indicated that they should sit down on the leather sofa. Grace, feeling uncomfortable in the company of this unusual woman, sat on the edge of the settee and folded her hands in her lap.

Dusty threw things out of her way onto another armchair, carefully eased herself down and said, "I know you'll think I'm in a mess." She threw her arms out in a melodramatic manner to take in the room. "I must apologise for the muddle. I'll get round to tidying it all up soon. I've got a woman who comes in but I'm sure she is untidier than me, and a greater boozer. Cheap, I'll grant you, but what I save on wages I lose in alcohol. God, she drinks like a fish! I reckon she could drink me under the table." She turned to look at the open door of the drinks cabinet. "I've just had my morning G. & T. I limit myself to just the one before lunch, but if you want one, I'll join you just to keep you company."

"I'd prefer coffee," Grace said and Carlton, strangely quiet, nodded that he would also like a coffee.

"Now you've said that, I think I need some too," said Dusty, putting her hand on her forehead. "Rather a heavy night last night, I'm afraid. One of my usual weekend parties, y'know. You've been to one haven't you, Carlton?" Carlton, with a look of disgust on his face, swung his head slowly from side to side. "Only difference was, last night's was a bit wild."

Grace, attempting to bring Carlton into the conversation, looked across at him, surprised to see that he was grimacing.

"Why, what happened?" Grace asked, trying to stop Dusty from seeing the way Carlton was behaving.

"Oh, they all had too much to drink. Not that that's surprising, but this time it was even worse. It was a hot night, you know. Gerald is a literary agent friend of mine - one of those big men, y'know, the sort who makes haystacks feel inferior – and he has a thirst to go with his size. One of his authors had won a literary prize and to show his appreciation to Gerald, he'd given him a crate of whisky. Well, Gerald's a generous man so he insisted on giving everyone here a bottle all to themselves."

"A bottle each, all to themselves! But it's practically poisonous in that quantity isn't it?" Grace asked, "I don't think I've ever tasted it; to me the smell is too unpleasant."

"Stay that way. Vile stuff. And what it does to women couldn't be printed. I'm not easily shocked but I was amazed at the behaviour of some of them, especially those who had always pretended to be ladies."

"Oh," Grace said, apprehensively, wondering what she was about to hear.

Before replying, Dusty looked over at Grace and with raised eyebrows said, "You're the daughter of that pretentious prig Belari aren't you?" and laughing, she added, "Reminds me a bit of you, Carlton."

Carlton ignored her.

"Better to say I _was_ his daughter; I'm free of him now."

"Thank God for that, I wouldn't wish him on my worst enemy, he's such a pompous oaf. I just wondered what his effect will have been on you."

"When I say 'free', that's just what I mean - mentally as well as physically, I never mean to see him again."

"Strong words!" Dusty said, raising her eyebrows. "I hope you mean it; I wouldn't want you to be... well... shocked," she looked over her reading glasses to see how Grace had responded before continuing, "for now, I'll just say that it started with nude bathing and went on from there."

Carlton spoke for the first time, "Really, Dusty, if you must have these sordid parties, you should take more care to keep quiet about them. Even at the party you had when I was here, there was so much noise the neighbours practically lynched you."

"Oh, that doesn't happen any more. Oh, no, no, that's all in the past. I found a way to keep them quiet," she said with a sneaky smile. "I invite them all. And you'd be amazed at how broad-minded they can be. You know, I used to see them at garden parties and such like and they looked as though their dresses were made entirely from respectability fabric. But you find out that respectability is only as deep as the fabric."

"You'll remember Mrs. Downington, Carlton, she lives at the top of the road in that big house; had us over for hymn singing or something like it one evening. A pillar of society, you would have said; that is, if you want your society to be dull and predictable. She was one of those I always thought was a lady. How wrong can you be?" She winked at Carlton knowing how it would provoke him. "I now know what the 'Down' in her name means. She's a beautiful woman, who can blame her with her husband away in the Middle East? It's only to be expected that she would have desires. He's probably got his own harem over there anyway. As I said, beautiful dressed - and even more lovely undressed! The sort of figure I had before the alcohol got to work on my body. One of the men called her a 'rattlesnake'. That was just before he chased her into the sea!"

"Dusty, I wish you wouldn't always talk like that," Carlton said, causing Grace to glance at him with a look of incredulity on her face. "You make it sound as though the only thing in your life is depravity."

Dusty saw Grace looking in wonder at Carlton, and said, "Don't mind him; he's just jealous, dear. Nothing exciting happens in Loriston, does it? I expect,

Grace, that's why, like me you wanted to get away from the place." She grinned, "No, I'm wrong. I did once see the paper boy's dog chasing the headmistress's little bitch terrier once - never caught her, though. Should be grateful, I suppose, a public display of sex would have shocked the town's twitching curtains."

Carlton turned his head away and looked out of the window.

"Anyhow," he said, turning back and trying to change the subject, "you said you had a room Grace could have."

"I do," replied Dusty, turning to Grace. "It's getting very stuffy in here, my dear. Let's make a move and get a change of air. I'll put the kettle on and we'll have coffee when we get back. Come on, Grace, and bring your case with you. You stay there Carlton, and think pure thoughts! The newspaper is here if you want to read about the world outside Loriston." She threw over the newspaper, which thudded heavily against Carlton's stomach.

Grace followed her out of the room. At the top of the stairs, Dusty turned and said quietly. "We don't get on awfully well, your Carlton and me. We're so different, I wonder if we had different fathers. I know daddy spread himself around but mummy always seemed above that sort of thing. Carlton's more like her and even worse, he's dominated by his religious morality."

"I don't think you may know everything about him. He talks about living a loose life in university." Grace spoke quietly so that Carlton would not hear her as they stood on the landing.

"Talk, my dear, just talk – I invited a few young things round when he came to my do. Quite busty

81

creatures and probably amenable if you follow me," she smiled, "Carlton stayed quiet - never even spoke to them."

She carried along the landing and turned into a large room with an even better view of the sea than from the lounge. Grace saw with a gasp of delight that it had a double bed in which looked straight out over the sea.

"Oh!" Grace exclaimed as she saw the view with the morning sun streaming in, "This is like heaven. I've spent most of my life in the rectory, where every corner has a dark presence. We were surrounded by glowering vegetation which hid any views."

"Good, I'm glad you like it. I had looked out a room over the road where I have a house I've just converted. But, now that I've met you and can see that you're not like the normal fuddy-duddy young Loriston girls Carlton seems to prefer, I'm sure this will be better for you."

"Has he brought girl friends here?"

"God, no, he wouldn't want them to meet me. I met them at the family home in Loriston. Most of them were apprentice missionaries, I shouldn't wonder. He's always gone for that type – sanctimonious – someone he could take to church with him."

Grace was staring out of the window, "I've never seen anything like this, the view is just beautiful."

Dusty was sitting on the bed, Grace went over to sit beside her and together they looked over the sea to a yacht in the distance, Dusty said, "I'm sorry if it seems I treat Carlton badly. I don't mean any harm, I just tease him and I'm sure it's good for him. He's so inhibited, comes from being a devout churchman but I haven't had much success with him, he always reacts in that hoity-toity way."

"Probably because he thinks you don't like him, you know."

"Don't like him? Of course I like him, he's my brother. But he does need to free his ideas up a bit, don't you think?"

Grace laughed, "I don't see him quite like that."

Now it was Dusty's turn to laugh. "Oh, I see," she said, "You and Carlton are ..."

"No we're not," Grace interrupted, "Funny what you say about his girl friends, he keeps saying I should go to church while I am here." She walked back to the window, "he does try it on a bit with me, though?"

"And you don't respond when he tries it on?"

"I think he's nice, but not in that way. He's just not right for me."

"Sad for him; I can see that he's crazy about you."

"Yes, he gets very tiresome and I wish he wouldn't."

"You're like me; you never want anything that comes too easily."

"I've never thought of it like that. No, I don't think that's the reason; there is just something about him which doesn't excite me at all."

"If you ask me, I'd say that it's his sanctimonious nature; comes from spending too much time in prayer – probably got a lot in common with your father, y'know," she said only partly joking. "He's always been very critical of me and the fun time I have, we're almost at two extremes, him with his God and me with my friends and my fondness for alcohol and men. As I said, sometime wonder if our mother spread herself around as well as our father."

Grace, unable to think of a reply, remained silent, looking out at the view.

"Young, attractive girl like you, there must be someone else..." Dusty asked.

Grace took a while to speak as she turned back to dusty and sat against the window sill, "Well... there is, but..."

"But he doesn't love you, is that it? The old story - love unrequited is twice as desirable."

"It's not even as simple as that. There is someone else. But... well, it's not easy to explain."

"Shouldn't be difficult. Someone you met in Loriston? Someone you met on holiday? A married man, or just someone not available? What else is there, unless he's a ghost or something?"

"Not a ghost, Dusty. But you are not too far off."

"Not a ghost! I should hope not," Dusty said, frowning. "I'm sorry dear but I'm completely lost."

Grace stood up, walked to the window and stood looking at the view.

"You're an artist, Dusty - you paint portraits, Carlton says?

Dusty nodded, "I do paint, not often these days but, when I do, even I can see that it is pretty good, although I say so myself. Why, what's the connection?"

"Do you ever get attached to the people you paint?" Grace asked, turning to look intently at the sea outside the window.

"Well, yes, I suppose I do; I do have a passionate nature. I think all people with an artistic temperament are that way. Sometimes I get quite emotional about them." She frowned, "But I still don't get it. What are you saying?"

"I have a painting of a young man, I brought it with me." She turned back to Dusty, framed by the light from the window, which made her hair glow. "As soon as I saw it, he lived for me; he was real, not just a painting," She pursed her lips, "he has dominated my thoughts ever since I saw his portrait."

"Mm," Dusty grunted, and shook her head, "I've heard of it happening but I would never have thought it of you – you're not the type I wouldn't have said," still shaking her head, she said. "Have you seen him - do you know that this fellow even exists?"

"I don't. I haven't any proof, if that's what you mean, but, sometimes you just know these things. That's the way it is with me. I just know him and know the sort of person he is."

"Do you know the name of this amazing man, or even where he lives?"

"I don't really know anything for sure if I'm honest with myself," Grace shrugged. "The only thing I do know about him is that he probably lives in France and that his name is Edward. I think about him all the time. Whenever I sleep, I dream, and whenever I dream, I dream about him," she shrugged her shoulders, perhaps I'm going crazy Carlton says I am."

"Go and get the painting for me. I must see this young man."

Carlton was slumped in the chair asleep as Grace picked up her bag and took it upstairs. She took out the painting and passed it over to Dusty who stood up and took it to the window. After staring at it intently for a few seconds, she said, "He certainly is gorgeous... though a bit pale and unhealthy looking for my taste. But love is love; nothing can stop its madness."

"So you do think I'm mad, like Carlton does."

"Only as mad as any woman who is in love with a man. Whether in a painting, or wonderful and naked in your bedroom, it's just the same chemistry, whoever it is and whatever the situation." She held up the painting to look at it again. "No, I don't think you are crazy at all..." Her eyes scanned round the room as though sub-consciously checking that no one was listening. Then she looked askance at Grace and, with a thoughtful smile, said, "You see me sitting here, a fat middle-aged, disillusioned frump, but I wasn't always like this. I told you I have a passionate nature. Well, when I was young, I was a 'heedless romantic' as they say." She nodded to herself as her memory took her back to her youth. "And what you are going through, happened to me when I was about your age."

"A painting, you mean?"

"Not a painting, no but I fell in love vicariously."

"Your husband?" Grace asked.

"No, Grace, not my husband, certainly not him. He looked like a bull mastiff even in the early days when I first met him, it was his personality which attracted me, not his looks. It was a long time before I met George that my passion, the sort that you have, was kindled. It so overtook me that I have never experienced a feeling like it, either before or since, certainly not with George." She smiled at the memory. "With me it was a film actor." She stood up, went to her room which was across the corridor, opened a drawer in the dressing table and took out an envelope which she passed to Grace. "I was given the photograph of him by a friend. It's in that envelope. Open it, it will say something about me that I still keep it, but every time I take it out of the envelope, even now after so many years, I get a thrill."

Grace opened the envelope and looked at the image, wondering what to say when Dusty continued.

"You'll see in the photograph that he is an incredibly handsome man, you'll know what I mean about the emotional states we women get in. I did them all; I was weak at the knees, I couldn't eat – worried my mother stiff – I just sat staring at things, anything, it didn't matter what it was because I never saw them. I would go to bed and the nights would pass, but I couldn't sleep."

She turned to look at Grace, framed in silhouette against the strong light from the window. "So, yes, don't feel silly; I know just how you feel. Love is supposed to be a time of happiness. For me it was almost the reverse, for me it was like an illness."

"That's exactly how I am, Dusty. Tell me more. What happened, did you meet him?" Grace said, sitting on the floor in front of her.

"Well, no, that's just it, I didn't meet him." She pondered for a few moments before continuing, "Can you take disappointment, Grace?"

"Why do you ask?"

"Because that was what happened to me, and it may well happen to you. The friend told me that the man in that picture had seen me and wanted to meet me, but my girlhood dreams ended in disappointment. My friend wasn't the friend I had thought she was. She was motivated by jealousy, because a man whom we had both met, and she fancied, preferred me to her." She grinned. "I know that may sound strange as you look at me now, but I really was a looker. I'll show you my album when we get some time together. People like I was create envy as well as admiring glances. And my friend was cruel and I never suspected it for a minute. She knew me well and just wanted to hurt me for being attractive when she was not. When she saw the effect that the picture had on me, she told me inflated stories about the man you see there. When

87

she told me he had asked to see me..." Dusty leaned over and pointed at the image. "Well, wouldn't you want to meet him? When she saw how I obsessed I had become, stupid ninny that I was, she told me she had only given me the picture as a joke." She shrugged, "Some joke, eh!"

Grace looked down at the photograph again. "I know what you are saying, Dusty. He's incredibly good-looking. What do you mean that she had given you it as a joke?"

"She'd given me a photograph of a man who no longer existed. Beautiful, but dead, very dead - he'd been killed in a plane crash many years before. My friend told me she thought I'd see the funny side but I was too far-gone for that. There was no humour in it for me. I wasn't just disappointed; I was distraught." She placed her hands over Grace's and said, "Why do you think I am I telling you this, Grace? Because, dear girl, it may turn out that your man Edward is not real and only exists in the imagination of the artist."

"That had occurred to me, but it won't happen, I just know he is real. The artist who painted him was his father, you see. I think that Edward was his love child. He lived in Loriston. Carlton's mother told him a lot about this painter." Grace stopped and suddenly laughed, "Of course, how stupid of me; she's your mother as well and you would have known him ... Artemus Ruane."

"Artemus? Yes, of course I knew him," Dusty said, moving with difficulty. Something in the tone of her voice when she spoke the name of Artemus, made Grace wonder – could Dusty have been one of his 'women'?

"Come on down to the lounge. We'll have coffee and keep Carlton company. I imagine he's lonely by now. He'll certainly be pining for you." As they walked from the room, she added, "Don't worry yourself about forgetting I'm Carlton's sister. I know we are very different, if not I'd probably have shot myself." A grin spread over her face as she turned and faced Grace at the top of the stairs. "Someone at one of my evenings asked me if I was his mother. I would certainly have been a young mother at fifteen so I wasn't particularly flattered by that question. That's the difference in our ages fifteen years."

Carlton was stretched out in the same position, sound asleep with his legs spread out in front of him. He woke up with bleary eyes as Dusty said, "He does look sweet like that, doesn't he?"

Grace nodded. "Yes, he does," she replied, and then to Carlton, "Sorry to wake you, you must be tired out after that long drive with no sleep."

Carlton, who was still waking, yawned, stretched and looked at them distantly.

"Well," Dusty said, when they were seated in the lounge drinking her particular blend of strong coffee, "this ought to perk you up, Carlton, my lad." She smiled at him over the rim of the cup. Then, turning to Grace said, "Tell me more about this Edward."

At the name 'Edward', Carlton grimaced, got up and went out on the terrace to drink alone in the morning sun.

"The reason I am interested, you see, is that I knew Artemus quite well. When I say quite well, I don't suppose I've spent long in his company for more than..." she shrugged, "about six times, I suppose. But he's that sort of man. You don't need much of his time to become enchanted by him."

"Do you still see him?" Grace asked. "Do you know where he is now?"

"Oh, I've no idea. I've completely lost touch with him. I don't suppose I've seen him for nearly, I don't know, perhaps ten years, maybe longer. But he's just one of those men you never forget; a man who would engage you not just with his eyes and his voice but with his visions too."

"You mean the way he paints?" Grace asked.

"Mm," Dusty nodded, "a bit more than that. The way he paints is certainly visionary but his visions are also in his thoughts. He leaves you with a different view of things. He's that sort of man, if you see what I mean, a sort of visionary, at least he was when I knew him."

"Yes, I understand, but I was wondering if you know someone who can help me find where he is."

"Oh, I don't know. He left England a long while ago. I expect you know about that, though. He loved the countryside around Loriston and used to go back with his son and an older French woman, a sort of carer, I think. I handled some of his paintings not too long ago. A couple of them he must have done on one of his visits back to his old house because I recognised some of the details. But, apart from knowing that he is somewhere in France, I've no idea of his whereabouts."

"But you are sure he is in France are you?" Grace asked, her eyes lighting up at the thought.

"Well, as sure as you can be about anything where he is concerned. The last I heard about him was a long while ago. Since then I tried to contact the gallery where I saw his paintings, but it has closed down. It was run by a drug-crazed Romanian who had no idea of business ethics, so I'm not really surprised. Of course, there's always a chance Artemus may have returned to England, but I don't think so because he loved the atmosphere and the light in France. And it was also where his mistress came from - you know he got her in trouble, didn't you? They had a son".

"Edward?" Grace asked.

"Yes, Edward, his son?" Dusty said. "Well, he must be grown up by now but I've never met him, and I don't know where he lives either. It was very sad that his mother died in childbirth, so the story goes. He may be in France with Artemus. He's probably been there most of the time, since Artemus took him there when he was little more than a baby. They spent some time in Paris, I know. He used to sell his paintings in the gallery there, the one that has closed down, I mean."

"Do you at least have the address of the gallery?"

"I don't think I've got it - probably threw it out when they closed."

"I do so much want to meet him. Is there any way you can find the address of the gallery, that would be a start?" Grace asked.

"Not going to be easy. Depends how much you want to meet him," she teased.

"It means more to me than anything else," Grace said.

"I can see that, dear. Well, if you're really serious, the best and probably the only way, is to go to Paris and make some enquiries. You might meet someone who knows. Artemus did have a lot of friends, you know, people who bought his work, some hangers-on and some students that he used to teach. Quite a circle, I'm told. "

"I'll do anything, go anywhere to find him," Grace said," but I'll need somewhere to stay. Where do you stay when you're over there?"

"I only go to Paris to look at paintings for my gallery. The Ruane paintings I bought sold very well, incidentally. They were unbelievably beautiful. So there is probably another gallery there selling them." Dusty said. "Where do I stay? Well, it used to be in a hotel near that gallery where he sold his paintings. When I go, I sometimes stay in that same hotel, sometimes with friends or, more often, with one particular friend."

Carlton, who had been feigning reading the paper, called in from the terrace. "Grace, this whole thing is stupid. Give it up and be sensible about it."

"It's not stupid, Carlton." Dusty called back. "You're sounding like a jealous bear. If you know one thing about this Grace, it is that if she wants something she will find a way to get it, and nothing you can say will change that. I can see that and it's time you did." She turned back to Grace. "If you want, I can give you an address of the girlfriend I stay with. She has a spare room in her apartment and I expect she would be happy to put you up. Her place is fairly central."

"That's nice of you but..." Grace hesitated. "what is she like?"

"What is she like?" Dusty paused, thinking. "Intriguing, I suppose is the best description. Wait a minute, you probably know her, she lived with an aunt in Loriston for a while, learning English, I seem to recall. That's where I first met her."

"Do you mean that French girl who came to the school? I was very small but people talked a lot about her?" Grace paused to think. "Yes, I remember, Melanie something, wasn't it. She is a friend of yours?" she asked, and when Dusty nodded, continued, "Yes, she used to come to my father's church. I think she was in the seniors at school when I was in the infants. I didn't have very much contact with her, but I've always been sorry I didn't keep in touch when she returned to France." She smiled to herself. "She used to give me chocolates which she had sent to her from France. Yes, I remember her being really nice."

"Nice is not the word I would use, but she is certainly interesting. I'll look out her address and drop her a line." Dusty turned to the pile of books beside her, pushed some out of the away so that they fell to the floor with a bang, and took out a book of addresses. Before opening it, she said, "You are a lucky thing, you know. I'd loved to have seen inside that house of Artemus's again. Were there any more paintings?"

"Yes, one of them on the wall was incredible – a mythical painting like I've never seen before, animals and people all mixed-up. I love Greek mythology, it seemed like a scene from that time. It's hard to describe the effect it had. There were quite a few other paintings, too. I didn't touch them so I suppose they are still there."

A loud cry from Carlton out on the terrace interrupted them as he rushed in. Grace put the painting in her bag, just before Carlton burst into the room. "Dusty, there is a freak in your garden."

Dusty laughed "No, he's not a freak. He might look a bit odd but he's just the gardener. Sometimes he drops in without telling me."

"Do you mean?" Carlton spoke slowly and deliberately. "Your gardener wears a pink tutu and angel's wings on his back?"

"Mr. Gilbert? 'Ole Henry', they call him round here; he's pretty eccentric but I can't imagine him in anything but old, smelly tweeds." Suddenly, she laughed as a thought struck her. "Ah, no, that's not the gardener, that must be Gerald. Particularly hard night last night, as I said. We missed him, thought he had gone home; we were all too drunk to notice him going, you see. He must have fallen asleep in the potting shed." She stood up and walked over to the window and onto the terrace with Grace following her. Outside, at the bottom of the garden, a large, overweight man stumbled around wearing a pair of angel's wings.

"Oh it is Gerald, how nice! I missed him last night. I was pretty far gone myself but I did worry a bit where he had got to." She waved and called out, "Hey, Gerald." Gerald waved back but seemed confused. Dusty turned round to explain to Grace and Carlton. "He's my beau at the moment. I hoped he'd taken a taxi home, but he must have fallen asleep in the Summer house." As she spoke, the winged man dreamily waved before ambling down the garden and out of the gate. "Oh good, he's going to walk home. I'm glad he's not driving; he won't be in a fit state. Dear man, he's always such fun to have around. His wings stand up remarkably well, don't you think, after all the swimming and the night he's had? The pink tutu looks a bit grubby, though, even from this distance. He'll be going home to freshen up and then on to the office, he never stops working, partying and working is all he does. Married for a while but his wife left him for an accountant, solid, reliable and dull, can you believe that? How she could give up an exciting man like Gerald I don't know. A literary man who lives amongst authors and books, he'll be on the 'phone to his writers as soon as he returns, that is if he doesn't fall asleep when he gets there. He'll still be pretty loaded, even now."

"He looks hideous", complained Carlton, "with all that fat and hair. Why on earth do you mix with such people, Dusty?"

"Now, Carlton... you must meet people fully clothed before you make judgments about them.

When he's clean, he has immense charm, if you know what I mean?" she winks at Grace, "and dressed, he looks fantastic. I don't suppose there's another literary agent who looks so good. In my experience, they're puddeny sort of people but I don't meet many of course."

Grace laughed. "It's hard to imagine him with a suit on, but he does look as though he could be very amusing."

"You should learn from this girl, Carlton. She is much broader-minded than you. You always were stuffy, even as a boy."

Carlton rolled his eyes and shook his head. "I'm not stuffy at all, Dusty - you'd be surprised if you knew more about me. But there are limits. I draw the line at obscenity."

With mock haughtiness, Dusty said, "It may seem like obscenity to narrow-minded God worshipping people like you, Carlton, but to us it's just enjoying the pleasures God gave us. I notice Grace here isn't at all shocked."

"I'm glad you two get on so well together," Carlton muttered sarcastically to himself, as Grace and Dusty stood side-by-side in front of the window.

That evening, while Grace and Carlton were sitting at the table, Dusty served them a meal. In the distance, the sun was setting over the rim of the sea. "I like the sound of the people you seem to mix with, Dusty." Grace said, taking the plate that was offered her. "Can I meet them sometime?"

"Of course you can, they'd love you I'm sure. Remind them of their own youth, I shouldn't wonder. I haven't got a soirée planned for a few weeks. I think, if you came, you'd be the star of the show." She passed over a plate of steaming vegetables and Grace and

Carlton helped themselves. "I'm so glad you came. I must admit, when Carlton first rang I was tempted to refuse. Knowing what your father was like, I was afraid you would have been far too narrow-minded for me. Even when I decided to take a chance, I was going to give you the spare room over the road," She got up to fetch a bottle of wine from the kitchen, "but now that I've got to know you better, I can see I had the wrong idea about you. I hope you'll join in the fun and come to some of our dos," she called through the kitchen window, which she used as a serving hatch.

"That's if associating with sex-crazed weirdos in pink tutus and angel wings is your idea of fun, you mean," Carlton interrupted.

"I know what you are thinking and that's quite enough for now, Mr. Green-eyes. You brought Grace here, after all. You should be happy to see her enjoy herself."

Shaking his head, Carlton looked down blankly at his food and started eating in silence.

"Anyway, Grace, I'll introduce you to some of my friends. You should meet Jim, the singer from the bar by the prom. He's into Greek mysticism; I suspect you'd like him." Dusty sat down at the table in front of her piled-high plate. "And I know you'd get on really well with Estella…"

At the mention of Estella, Carlton stood up aggressively. "Oh come on, don't tell me you're going to expose Grace to middle-aged whores."

"If you find my plans objectionable, you're perfectly welcome to leave the table and eat on your own, if you prefer," replied Dusty, looking sternly at Carlton's standing figure, "and anyway, Estella is a burlesque dancer, not a whore." Dismissively, she turned her back on Carlton to address Grace again.

"It's no concern of mine what she does. She looks fantastic for her age and her dancing is so exciting. Carlton told me you love dancing, Grace, so you'll find lots to talk about with her."

"I've been inspired by Isadora Duncan and the free way she danced."

"That's good, Estella is very experimental - I think she was also inspired by Isadora Duncan."

"I'd love to meet her, she sounds fun. Where does she dance?"

"Oh, not here in Hastings - far too stuffy for her. Well, maybe occasionally in one or two men's clubs, but mostly in London night clubs." Turning to Carlton, who had resumed his seat and was eating quietly, she said provocatively, "We'll have to wait till she's stopped succumbing to carnal lusts, of course."

At her words, Carlton, shook his head and sighed. "God, she's blubbery and revolting. I can't imagine any man wanting to see her dancing, let alone naked."

"Not any more, dear brother - she's lost weight since you saw her last and it's made her much more appealing. She still has that covering of puppy fat that many men like, though. I know Gerald fancies her - all the better for it, I say." Grace could see that Dusty was obviously enjoying the discomfiture of her brother. "I know that she feels the same about Gerald, too; nothing wrong with the occasional fling, gives us all a boost. I'm pretty sure though that Estella's heart is far across the Atlantic with her man. I've never seen her do anything more than occasional petting."

Carlton threw down his fork and looked at Dusty, aghast. "Ugh, Dusty, don't try to make her sound like a free-loving saint. She sounds like just another one of your loose women."

For a few seconds, Dusty's expression tightened with annoyance. Then she relaxed, leaning back casually in her chair and smiling at the effect she had had. "Carlton, as per usual, you're being a very stuffy boy. I was tempted to say young man but I think you still have some growing up to do."

Carlton shot to his feet and glared at Dusty. "You're always trying to make me sound like a child. All I can say is good luck to you and your darling Gerald. I hope he's every bit as warped and twisted as you are. I'm sure you could spend a very happy life together grovelling in dirt." Then he turned his anger on Grace, "And I hope you find all this obscenity amusing. As far as I'm concerned, I like my entertainment more subtle." He stomped off, leaving his dinner unfinished.

Dusty rolled her eyes and gently sipped from her teacup. "Family dinners; they do bring out the worst in people, don't they? You choose your friends but there's nothing you can do about your family, is there? I suppose I really should be used to him and his narrow church obsessions by now, but..." She shrugged and looked over the table at Grace. "Sorry, my dear, that was largely my fault. I can't stand priggishness and he just irritated me."

Grace looked down at her plate, feeling some responsibility for having brought them both together again. "I didn't know he was like that," she said, "maybe I should go to him and smooth things over? I've never seen him so upset before."

Dusty leaned over and put her hand on Grace's arm. "Don't even think about doing that. He'll be all right. All I can say is, thank god you haven't got anything going with him. I can see he's smitten with you. It's made him even more insufferably narrow-minded than he used to be. But, then, I've never seen him in love before."

"I'm afraid that's partly my fault. I told him I couldn't ever love him, but he just won't believe me. He's such a kind boy, but that's all he is for me. I always thought he was nice until tonight."

Seeing Dusty ploughing unconcernedly into her food, she resumed eating. Then, looking up, she said, "Sometimes I wonder, Dusty, is there ever anything like real love, the sort you read about? I hear of so many unhappy marriages that I begin to wonder if it's only an illusion that men and women can get along together. I've gone through my life without ever coming close to being in love; that is until I saw Edward's painting."

Dusty put down her fork and looked out meditatively onto the ocean. "You and I both, Grace. I've never been more than infatuated with a living man; even Gerald I know is only a passing phase for me." She pushed her plate away and put her elbows on the table. "I know I should have loved my husband but I never did. The thing between us – well, if I'm honest with you it was just one of those enforced affairs. I thought I was pregnant, you see. It turned out it was just one of those phantom things. I put it down to the only real pleasure George and I shared which was his cooking. I must have some allergy to the spicy food he kept cooking for me. I put on weight and had dreadful wind. We lived in this little flat with thin walls so I couldn't let myself go. It all built up inside me and I was convinced I was expecting." She shrugged her shoulders. "We did that 'marry in haste, repent at leisure' thing. Poor Georgie, I still miss him a bit - but not much I must admit. The only real thing we had going was eating, and he really was a fantastic cook. We had that in common, that and my phantom pregnancy. Not much of a basis, is it, but I have to say he did have rather more substance than your Edward." She noticed that there was still food left in the dishes. She pulled her plate back and started eating again. Then as a thought suddenly struck her, she stopped with her laden fork part way to her mouth. "What you've just said, Grace, is quite profound. Thinking back, the only time I was 'head over heels', as they say, was with my actor in the photograph. Perhaps, all we have is that illusion you just talked about. And when, after the honeymoon period, reality descends, relationships just break apart or, if they don't break apart, they trundle along without excitement. I suppose with some people, it can take many years but often it is much shorter. Sometimes it doesn't even last to the morning after the wedding. Estella was like that once."

"Once?" Grace asked.

"Yes, once. She makes a habit of getting married. I think it's five husbands so far." She looked away. "No, it's six, counting the Brazilian tango teacher, Ingres. He was brilliant at the dance, she says, and Estella was just bowled over. When he flung her backwards so that her head nearly touched the ground, she told me she felt that this was a real man; perfect control but with a simmering violence in him. She always had a weakness for that type. During the wedding celebrations, she and Ingres entertained the guests with their version of the tango. It was so erotic that, when they finished, the wedding party applauded for what must have been five minutes. By that time, Estella was so wild, that she dragged Ingres from the room and up to bed." She pondered.

"And...?" Grace asked with a smile. "Go on, Dusty."

"Sorry, I was back at her wedding, I went to Brazil to send her off, you see. I was just remembering the tango they did. I've seen her dance it since then at one of the clubs here, and it certainly is the most exciting thing I've seen anyone do in Hastings. As I said, she dragged Ingres up to bed and what happened? The so-and-so fell asleep. Yes – sound asleep, unmovable. Estella told me she looked down at that sweaty, snoring mass of flesh and just got up, dressed, went to her car and left. Never saw him again."

"But they were married. She couldn't just walk out."

"Well, she did, and it turned out that he made a habit of marrying his dance partners and never bothering to divorce them."

"What about…?"

"Sex, you mean?" Dusty interrupted. "Estella met one of his other wives in a bar in Rio. Apparently they were both on the dance floor doing the tango and recognised each other because they both performed a movement peculiar to Ingres. They swapped notes on him and his prowess, or rather lack of it. Apart from the eroticism of his dancing, everything else was a disappointment. Turned out he poured everything he had into his art and at that he was a genius. But in everything else he was impotent."

"Impotent?"

"Yes, impotent. Why do you look surprised?" Dusty asked.

"No, I wasn't looking surprised; I was just recalling the time I lived with a sculptor in Paris for a short time."

"Good for you," Dusty said. "What happened? Did he bed well?"

101

Grace laughed. "I thought it was me, and maybe it was; I was very naive. I'd never even touched a man before."

"And?"

"You used the word."

"What, impotent?"

Grace nodded. "Yeah," she said, deliberately using a word she had never used before. "Dead from the neck down. He was certainly an amazing sculptor but, although I suppose I should have noticed, it somehow never occurred to me that all his figures were of men."

"Well hung men, I assume."

Grace nodded. "I left when, for the third time in a row, I came home late from working as a waitress and caught him in bed with another man."

Dusty pursed her lips, nodding her understanding. "There are many like that in the art world. I've grown to expect it." She put her hand on Grace's shoulder and squeezed affectionately. "My poor old thing, it must have been pretty rotten for you."

"It wasn't just that. There was his anger. When he lost his temper, he would hit out. I started out loving him, at least I thought it was love, but pretty soon I couldn't stand him touching me. Then I couldn't be near him and I rapidly reached a stage where I felt sick at the thought of being in the same room with him. It was because of that and when I found the third man in his bed that I left."

Dusty carried on eating while looking at the sun setting over the sea and colouring the clouds pink. Grace saw that she was looking away because there were tears welling in her eyes. When she had recovered her composure, she said, still looking out of the window, "It often seems to me that our illusions are more important than reality. If you've got a good dream, it can carry you through this pretty bloody awful life. This sunset is probably the closest we come to heaven, Grace."

Grace tried to find words of comfort for Dusty but, when none came, she just smiled in sympathy as Dusty turned back to her. Dusty smiled and in their smiles the two very different women found common ground. Grace, grateful to have found a woman to whom she could talk about her dreams and her fears and Dusty, seeing in Grace the daughter she had never had.

They finished eating and Dusty said. "I'm beginning to feel a bit tiddly. I think I've finished most of two bottles of wine and you're still on your first glass."

Grace nodded. "I don't drink much, but I can tell that this is a good wine," she said, holding her glass up to the light and admiring its colour.

"Gerald imports it from a vineyard in France, where he has a share in the ownership."

"What about Gerald? Do you not have love for him?"

"Lord no, he's fun for a while but I couldn't take living with him. I'd find him palling after a very short time." She drained her fifth glass of wine. "When I think about it, I know I probably couldn't take any man for very long. It may seem sad - it does to me anyhow - but this is probably my destiny. Grow old and spread my waistline in this house." She put down her glass and rotated it in here stubby fingers. "But I could have had a much worse prison than this, couldn't I?" She turned back and pointed to the receding sunset. "Every night there is a different one. An art form, painting itself in different colours each time I look. I couldn't want more than that. Now, you've probably had a long day with not much sleep last night so you're probably ready to turn in. I know I am, and I suspect Carlton is up there with his head under the pillow, trying to drown out the memory of my contrary manners."

Grace laughed and got up to take the dinner things into the kitchen, but Dusty restrained her.

"Leave them for Geraldine; she'll do them in the morning before her first stolen G. & T., which usually comes before she makes breakfast. I complain about her but she's not a bad old girl."

Grace put down the things and went gratefully up to bed. She did not draw the curtains as she changed into her nightgown so that she was able to see the sky outside, which was black and starry, with the full moon casting silver streaks of light over the sea. Behind her, she heard a tread as Carlton passed the bedroom door, and stopped outside. "Good night," he called, from behind the closed door.

Grace went to the door and opened it slightly.

"You don't have to be distant with me, Carlton, I'm really sorry that you saw things the way you did. I hope you've got over your irritation with us," she said, leaning her face against the door surround.

"I was just upset with her vulgarity, not with you, Grace. She seems to lack the basics of common decency. She used to go to church and you would have thought that that would have given her a moral basis. I'm not sure it's the right thing to do, leaving you with her; I don't want you to be like her."

"Carlton, you are not my keeper, I'm quite able to look after myself. I don't want to be a prig."

"D'you mean I am then?" he asked aggressively.

"Dusty thinks you are," Grace said, "but, no, I don't think you are but I can see that you need to bend a little."

"If by that you mean follow her lead that I will never do."

Grace smiled at him. "I don't want to change your behaviour, you must live your own life."

Carlton softened a little and said, "We mustn't forget the risks if you stay here. Her parties can get pretty wild. Her husband ended up dead, remember. How do we know you won't be her second party fatality?" He grinned ironically at Grace and it was obvious he had fully recovered his composure.

"I won't be. I can look after myself; I've been in even more wild situations than this in Paris. And I already I begin to feel that I can trust Dusty."

"But you've never seemed to trust me. I wonder if you like my crazy sister better than you do me. Me, who you've known most of your life, while you've only just met her."

"Stop jumping to conclusions, Carlton. I never said I prefer her company to yours. I think she is great fun and that's what I like about her. That's all. Of course I prefer to be with you."

"It's just all so unreal here. I'm sure she's gone off her head. She doesn't have a man to give her any stability. George used to control her a bit." Grace noticed that he was carrying his pyjamas under his arm. "Anyway, with the driving, I didn't sleep much last night. I seem to be in a dream now so I must get into bed. Can I stay with you, here?" he said walking into the room.

"Carlton, I am so grateful for what you have done, you've shown me a way out of a miserable life. I will never forget your kindness and we will always be good friends. But I've said this many times – it's no more than that," she said, firmly.

"Something happened when you went into that artist's house. Until you saw things in there, we were getting on well. You always were unusual, Grace, different from any other girl I have known, but I like that and we would have been good together. That day when you went to that stupid artist's house seems to have tipped you over the edge and now you're different. I even wonder if it was that place that was haunted and some spirit had got in to you. That stupid Edward thing has changed you, made you sort of crazy. I don't think I know you any more, Grace." He began to walk out of the room and called over his shoulder, "I may not be here in the morning." Then he was gone, slamming his bedroom door noisily.

Grace put out the light and leaned her head against the wall. She listened to his footsteps going along the landing to the bathroom and wondered what to do about him. The full moon shone through the window as she stood up and turned off the light. In the distance, a dog howled mournfully, seeming to echo her own feelings. Although the evening was warm, she pulled her dressing gown more tightly around her. After a few moments, she went to her case and took out the painting of Edward, holding it up to the light from the full moon so that she could see it more clearly. Her sadness about Carlton overcame her and she wiped her eyes with the back of her hand. She looked at the painting of Edward, propped it up against a chair and knelt down in front of it.

Quietly, she said to his image, "Carlton thinks I'm crazy. I know he's not right, but even if he is, I'd sooner be crazy with you, Edward than sane with anyone else." She held the painting against her breast, lay down on the bed on her back and fell asleep.

The next morning she found that Carlton was still there and seemed to have come to terms with the situation. Later in the day, Dusty suggested that they walk on the beach. Carlton refused, saying he had some reading to do.

The day was beautiful and Grace walked barefoot beside a slightly tipsy Dusty as the sun was heating the sand almost to the point of discomfort. As they got close to the pier, they began to hear music from a group playing on the beach. Grace's pace quickened in time with the beat of the jazz band. She and Dusty started to sing, Grace in time with the music, Dusty's voice quavering and confused. Grace became excited with the rhythm and started dancing, slowly at first. As she drew closer to the players, they responded to her enthusiasm and increased the tempo. Soon, Grace's movements became a wild dance of joy and celebration, kicking up flurries of sand and swirling so that her skirts flew out horizontally. Several passers-by noticed her and, impressed, started to clap in time with the music. Just a few others were slightly shocked by her boundless free spirit. When the piece came to an end, she paused for breath, looking up at the sky thoroughly exhausted by her exertions. As she did so, a round of applause came from behind her. She turned to find the group of people had grown and were shouting their appreciation. Slightly embarrassed, she waved her thanks to them. Dusty, impressed, put her arms around her and gave her a kiss on the cheek.

"They love you, Grace. You're an amazing dancer; better in some ways than Estella. You must meet her soon. She could get you work as a dancer if you wanted," she laughed.

Grace cast her eye across the sea as she tried to collect herself, attempting to slow her heartbeat.

Casually, she walked over to the edge of the beach. Dusty followed and waited behind Grace who was silent for a time, then began to shiver.

"What's wrong? How can you be cold? I would have thought you'd be boiling hot after that dance." She put her hand on Grace's forehead. "You're not sickening for a fever, are you, you seem pretty warm to me?"

I'm not cold. I just realised... something." Her mood had changed and she shook her head as though trying to clear it. "No..., it's stupid. Forget it," she said to herself.

"Are you all right, Grace? Is anything worrying you? If there is, you can tell me," Dusty said, putting her arm across her shoulder.

"I'm just excited. I get like this when I dance; it takes me away from ... wherever I am." She stepped to the edge of the sea and let the water lap over her feet. She stared intently at the water as if tempted to jump in and swim across to another world. The two of them were quiet while they meditated. Then she turned abruptly away and began to head back across the beach. Dusty followed her in silence, a thoughtful look on her face. Then she smiled to herself as if an inspired thought had struck her. She caught up with Grace and laid a hand on her shoulder to give her support.

"I understand, Grace, I get like that sometimes. So excited I find it hard to stay still. Life sometimes just spills over, doesn't it?"

Grace, staring vacantly ahead, seemed completely unaware of Dusty's words but after a few moments, she recovered sufficiently to say, "It certainly does with me. Something takes over and I ... lose control." She laid her head on Dusty's shoulder.

"Carlton reckons I'm going crazy. Do you think I am, Dusty, I do sometimes feel as though I may be? I just get overcome and even forget who I am. I did just then when I was dancing. It's as though there is a spirit inside me controlling what I do."

"Alcohol does that for me! But you don't drink much, do you?" She stopped walking and said, "Tell me, Grace, you're not on anything like drugs, are you?"

Grace shook her head.

"Then you're lucky that you don't need those things. There's another world which some of us are able to enter. Drugs and alcohol can remove the inhibiting effect of those stupid conventions which get in the way of enjoyment. But some people - and I think you're one of them - have it within them to enter that state of unreality without such aids. If I were superstitious, I'd think Isadora Duncan had been reborn in you." They were walking along the sea front and passing the inevitable rows of eating places, serving chips in various forms – with fish, with peas, with sausages. "I'm hungry, Grace, let's eat now and we'll have an early night tonight."

They ate out in a small restaurant where Dusty was known and the waiters fussed around her flirtatiously. Dusty had a few more drinks and was so far gone that she wasn't able to notice that Grace was still in her own world, living in the present but thinking on that elevated plane which the exhilaration of the dance took her into. When they had finished their meal and returned to the house, it seemed that the walk had cleared Dusty's head, but both of them were confused; one with alcohol and the other with the excitement of dance. The 'phone rang for Dusty and Grace went up to her room to read a book called 'The

Power of Human Thought' that she had found on Dusty's shelves.

Grace was reading on the bed, occasionally looking at the view of the sunset over the sea and was beginning to drift off when there was a knock on her door. "Come in," she said sleepily.

The door opened and Dusty entered with a look of pleasure on her face. She seemed to have sobered up and sat down on the bed beside Grace.

"You were talking about wanting to go to Paris, Grace. You know I told you I go there on business to pick up paintings for my gallery; that was how I bought some by Artemus on one visit. When I'm there, I drop in on Melanie and stay with her. I spoke to her on the 'phone just now." She said haltingly. "Something I think you'll like, Grace." Grace raised herself on her elbows and looked up in anticipation.

"I'm going to book a train for the weekend."

Grace turned to look at Dusty in confusion. "What do you mean 'train'? Where too, you are not sending me back home, are you? I couldn't bear that."

"No, not home, ninny, I mean to Paris." Grace continued to look bemused. "Your boat train to France so you can look for Artemus and Edward. I told you about Melanie, who lives in Paris. That was her I was speaking to on the 'phone, in case you heard me talking. I've arranged for you to stay with her in her flat near the centre of the city. She'll put you up while you track down your Edward." She gestured towards the painting, propped against the wall.

Grace was motionless, unable to speak for several seconds. When she finally found her voice, she said. "But... Dusty that's marvellous." Her face broke into a broad smile of pleasure, "thank you. I can pay you, my mother has given me enough money, you know."

"No you don't, this is my treat, It'll be perfect for you; Mel has a lovely flat close to the centre. A fairly nice part of the city. In a way wish I were coming with you."

"Dusty, why don't you. It would be lovely to be there with you."

"I'd like to but my assistant at the gallery is away travelling from today and I have to be there to run the place." She put her hand on Grace's shoulder and squeezed. "You'll like Melanie; she has lived a full life, if you know what I mean but if she takes to someone, she has a heart of gold. I'll drive you to the station on Saturday, and then it's over to you."

Grace looked at Dusty, then at the portrait, then at Dusty again, trying to take in what Dusty had done for her. Finally, she said. "But what did Melanie say? I want to be sure we will get on with each other."

"She will _love_ you. Not a chaste woman as I said, but that just makes her more human."

"But will she understand about why I will be there?"

"Not only understand, she's excited about it. Well, I didn't give her all the details; I just told her you are looking for a man. You can fill in the gaps when you meet her. She will want to show you round Paris. Have you been there recently? "

"Not since I lived there with that artist for a few months.

"Living with an artist, does Belari know about that?"

"I never told him but I went back to Loriston after it all went wrong and, because father is such a suspicious man, I expect he will have wondered, or maybe even found out somehow."

"You know, I can't get over you being his daughter. You're so human and he always seemed like a machine powered only by religion."

"That was why I left home. I had to get away from him. Living with him around was bad enough when I was young but, after Paris, going back to the house was like Hell, except that it was colder. As cold as charity."

"Cold as charity!" Dusty exclaimed. "Yes, I know what you mean. I went to see your father once when I had a problem. What did he do? He read me pages from the Bible, the sort of thing Carlton does to try to show me the errors I am making. When I left your father I was more confused than I had been before. There was no contact with a fellow human being, no interest in my difficulties. His answers to life's difficulties were all contained within the black covers of the Bible."

Grace nodded. "That's exactly why I had to get away. You want to talk? Then read the Bible. You have a problem with puberty? Here is the Good Book. You don't feel loved? You have God's love and can ask for no more." Grace got up, looked around her room, then at the view through the window. In the distance, a liner was sailing by, black smoke coming from its funnels. Seeing the smoke from the ship sailing away from England, Grace felt a momentary interruption in her mood of elation. "You've made me so welcome, Dusty. I've grown to really like it here with you," she said, looking down at the painting, her excitement lighting up her face. "I've got to find the man in the painting. But I don't want to leave you. Sounds stupid doesn't it?"

"Well, you can always come back. I've loved having you here. You've made me realise that what

112

this house needs is youth. I have too many friends who have lived the best part of their lives and have become complacent, bored and sometimes even suicidal."

"But you seem to be happy with them."

"Happy?" she said, looking up at the ceiling. "What does happy mean?" She stood up and went to stand beside Grace, looking out of the window. "When I was your age, Grace I was like you, I wanted that all-consuming love to overtake me." She slipped her hand through Grace's arm. "That's what we all want, isn't it? But I looked around me at the friends I share my life with, and I can see that they too were looking for that same Holy Grail, and found only an imperfect human to share their lives with. It takes many of us till the end of our days to finally accept the imperfectability of man. We can try to change ourselves but, in the end, it all comes down to the fact that we are driven, as that philosopher, Hobbes, said, by a need to avoid pain and gain pleasure for ourselves. That often means hurting those whom we share our lives with, and not just hurting – sometimes it grows into destroying. That would have happened to me with George, and perhaps George's death was the result of the desire to destroy which exists in me."

"George? But surely, that was just an accident wasn't it?" Grace interrupted, trying to bring the conversation back to normality. "You can't blame yourself for that."

"But I can," Dusty replied. "And I do." Grace turned her head and looked quizzically at Dusty. "It was I who arranged the dinner party with a few friends for his birthday. It was a token gesture to show him that I still cared for him. I knew he had been unhappy since we had separated and then divorced. With his looks, you see, – he really was an ugly man, the sort no other woman would want in her room – he was incapable of finding another partner. Well, what I mean is, except for those he would have to pay, I know there were many of those, but that was no substitute for the kind of selfless love that we all want."

"But how can you blame yourself for wanting to give him a happy party?" Grace asked.

"He had been trying to give up alcohol – not very successfully I might add – but I knew that he was depressed about passing his fortieth, I got in his favourite brandy, gave him a few before the other guests arrived, opened champagne to start the meal off and served his favourite claret while we ate."

"It sounds as though you did all you could for him."

"Too much, dear; I never thought...," she stopped, overcome by her memory. "You see, he loved this house as much as I do now. I know it tore him apart when he had to leave, after having made it over to me as part of the divorce settlement. I knew how much he loved swimming off the beach here, so I practically forced him to go in."

"You can't blame yourself for that, can you? Surely, you would have done it just for him, wouldn't you?"

"You see, he was absolutely sizzled and I was pretty far gone, as were his friends and, before he stripped off, they were all saying how cold the sea was, so I gave him another whisky, to 'keep you warm, George.'" We all gathered on the beach to cheer him on. I thought he would just go in as a gesture, swim round and get straight out. But no, he just kept on swimming, for so long that, in the dark, we lost sight of him." Her voice faltered. "And he never came back; we got a boat and went out looking for him but there was no sign; his body was washed up on the beach miles from here, three weeks later."

"Suicide?" Grace asked.

"Perhaps, perhaps not. Dear God, I wish I knew, if only I knew."

"Whatever it was, you can't feel responsibility."

"That's how I tried to rationalise it at the time, and I still do. At the inquest, they asked a lot of awkward questions but, well, the best they could do was to return a verdict of death by misadventure."

"That was right, wasn't it? I mean, nobody pushed him in."

"But guilt won't go away by rationalisation. It remains and invades quiet moments. Its ally is insomnia, which interrupts those dark nights when sleep won't bring forgetfulness. Alcohol is my support. I hate the stuff. Hate what it does to me. It has destroyed my looks and has made me become the same blubbery creature that Carlton sees in Estella."

"Surely, it's all a matter of our own self-image, isn't it? You see yourself as blubbery and middle aged but I don't see that. I see a warm person who wants to give to those around her, but has not yet found out how to do it without clothing generosity with cynicism." She stopped in realisation that she was just a guest, and therefore should not exceed the convention of speaking only pleasantries. "Am I wrong to be saying this, Dusty?"

"No, you're not wrong, Grace. No one has ever said that I am a warm person before – thank you for that; but do go on talking, it takes my mind away from George."

"It seems to me that we all feel that our lives should be peaceful and rewarding. But the reality is always different; it never gets there. There is always a chasm between us and the nirvana we think we should be able to find." Unsure if what she was saying was making any sense, she glanced at Dusty for reassurance and saw that she was nodding in agreement. "Carlton looks for his fulfilment in his God and thinks I would find mine the same way. He makes it obvious that I am being stupid about Edward, but what he doesn't see is that it is my attempt to jump that chasm. Edward is my dream; sometimes I suspect that is all it is. No," she shrugged, "it is more than that - I am convinced, without any doubt, that I shall only find myself when I find him. My father has his God who he says answers all our needs, but it is that complacency – the unthinking conviction of his and Carlton's - which I cannot accept. I have Edward as my religious quest. I know that if I were to say that to my father, he would simply ridicule me. That would be his defence."

"Defence?"

"Yes, defence; you see I know him better than he does himself. I see that because he cannot face reality, he places God on his banner which he then waves in front of anyone he thinks may see through what he thinks of as his impregnable strength."

"I think I know what you are hinting at; I too need some sort of quest as much as you do. Unfortunately, I haven't yet found my Edward, and I suspect I never will. For me, alcohol dulls the disillusionment that comes from seeing what you call a 'chasm' between me and contentment. Do you know, since you've been with me in this house, I have seen that there is an emptiness in all that I am doing here; these wild parties – the booze – the lewdness and all the rest. I want to find my 'Edward' and I know I won't find him with things as they are."

Grace embraced her. "Can't you come over to France later; I shall really miss you, Dusty. I've grown to love our talks together. And I am so happy in my room here with this wonderful view."

"Of course, I can cancel the train if you'd rather not go." Dusty said with a teasing grin.

"Now you're tempting me," Grace laughed with her, "but I really am grateful to you for organising all this for me. Thank you so much, Dusty." She gave her a hug to show her gratitude.

"What I will miss most is your youth, your gaiety, your dreams of Edward and now, your dancing. Never forget your dreams, Grace. When they go, as mine have, existence becomes just that - 'existence'." She pursed her lips to suppress her feelings and said, as she stood up, "I think we should both get some sleep."

"That is, if I can sleep," Grace replied. "I feel so excited. Thank you once again, Dusty."

CHAPTER SEVEN

The following morning, Grace went in to Carlton's room to tell him the news.

Carlton was standing by his bed, putting things in his suitcase. His expression was blank as Grace joined him, and he would not look up to greet her.

"Are you okay, Carlton?" she asked, kneeling on the bed to look into his face.

"No, I'm not. I'm pretty bored, actually. You seem to spend all your time with my ugly sister. So I've decided I'm going home."

"Oh... Carlton, I am sorry, but you didn't seem to want to be with Dusty and me when we went for a walk. You'd got that management book you're reading and you just said that was what you wanted to do."

"Grace, how can you be so insensitive? I came here to be with you, not to spend my time reading a boring book."

"Well you should have come with us."

"To be with you, not with her, that was why I came. Seeing you two together just makes me see how little I have in common with her. If I'm honest, I have to admit I can't take much more of her."

"Oh, Carlton," Grace replied, trying to pull him down to sit beside her, "I am thoughtless, and after you have been so kind to me." She took his hand and gave it a kiss, pouted her lips and said in a girlish voice. "Can you forgive me?"

He did not respond for a while, then he nodded reluctantly and said "Ok."

"You should have come with us yesterday; we had such a lovely time on the beach."

"Dancing, yes I know."

Astonished, she said, "How did you guess?"

"I was walking nearby and saw you."

"Why didn't you join in?"

Carlton sat down on the bed beside her. "Not for me, was it?"

"Carlton, don't be so stick-in-the-mud, you should have joined in with the dancing, not just watch me from a distance. Come on, let's unpack your clothes," she said, opening his case. "Oh, you've only got a few things in here; you must have just started when you heard me coming here." She began to empty the few clothes out, putting them in the drawers. "I was hoping you'd stay until the weekend," she said, as she turned back to pick up the remaining items. "You see... I'm going to France, and it would be nice if you could see me off." Carlton looked surprised and stared at Grace curiously.

"You're going to France?" he frowned, "you never told me - and why this weekend?"

Grace stopped putting away the clothes and walked over to him. Carlton looked away, and then laughed quietly to himself in self-mockery. "Don't go away, Grace, and come back to Loriston with me. I'll find somewhere you can live, away from your father, and you can forget all this stupidity. You'll soon recover from this Edward nonsense, and we'll be happy together."

"I don't want to 'recover' as you say."

"Ok. I shouldn't have said 'recover'"

"Well, you said it, and you've made if plain that you think I am crazy to be trying to find Edward."

"I didn't mean it like that."

Grace caressed his hand and said, "You know why I came here. And you will know that I'm going to do what I have to do and go to France to track Edward down." She put her hand under his chin and pulled his head up to look at her. "And Dusty has very kindly bought me a ticket and arranged for me to stay with a friend of hers." She tousled his hair "I have to go, you know that, don't you?"

Carlton looked at Grace, blinked several times and then smiled in amusement. "This is a joke, right? You're just trying to irritate me like Dusty does, aren't you?"

Grace shook her head. "I'm not, it's all booked".

"Oh yes? How do you think that makes me feel... pleased? Do think I should be pleased that you prefer a painting to me?" He turned away in annoyance. She placed her hands on his shoulders and turned him to face her.

"Carlton, I've told you before, it's real to me and I can't change it – it dominates me. I was afraid you'd react this way. Please try to see, I need to do this." She hugged him tightly but his response was half-hearted, unsure what to make of a situation which was new to him.

"If you ever do meet this 'paint boy', and you find out what a useless fantasy he is, come back to me. You're the only woman in my life and I shall always feel the same about you, no matter what happens."

"Carlton, Carlton," she said, burying her face in his shoulder. "You make it so hard for me. I'll keep in touch with you; I'll write and tell you everything."

"Ok, Grace. I'll stay till Saturday. I have to go back then, to do the books for Monday." He held her away to look at her. "Sorry if I seem to find it difficult to understand, but that's just the way I am. I like the real world, not a flummery."

CHAPTER EIGHT

On the following Saturday, Carlton drove Grace and Dusty to the ferry in Dusty's car. Dusty arranged for a porter to take Grace's cases to her cabin and Grace remained with Carlton. He kissed her peremptorily as she prepared to leave him.

"Grace, keep in touch and take care of yourself. Write whenever you can."

"Whenever I think of you, you'll be wearing shining armour, Sir Carlton."

"What, as the Black Knight?" he joked.

She smiled in affection, hugged him one last time and kissed him on the cheek as Dusty returned from her mission.

"Better go now, Grace, boat's preparing to leave." She gave Grace a long, affectionate embrace. "You go with my best wishes. I shall really miss you."

Grace ran towards the boat, turned back quickly to wave them one last farewell and then boarded, as Dusty called out, "Give my love to Melanie."

After what seemed an interminable journey, first across the choppy sea and then the transfer to the train, Grace finally reached the outskirts of Paris. The train pulled into the station just as dusk was falling. The platform was alive with Parisians. As Grace looked out of the carriage window, she particularly noticed their stylish clothing. She stood up and tried to make her own clothes a little more presentable, but still felt very shabby in comparison.

As she stepped out of the carriage, struggling with her bags, an elegant, well-dressed, attractive young woman who had been waiting at the platform walked up to her.

"Are you Grace Belari?" she asked with a smile. She spoke in good English with only a slight French accent.

"Yes, and you must be Melanie. But how did you recognise me?"

"Dusty rang me with the seat number she had booked for you, so it wasn't difficult. You did step down from the carriage she said you'd be in. And anyway, we've already met, haven't we? When I stayed in Loriston with my English aunt – you still look familiar, even though we have both grown up since then."

"Yes, I always meant to write to you to thank you for your kindness."

"Kindness?"

"Yes, you helped me out several times when I was in difficulties."

"Did I? It was a long while ago." She frowned, trying to remember. "I hope your journey wasn't too tiring. I always arrive worn out when I travel too far."

Grace smiled. "I think it helped that I slept most of the way," she said, as a man who had been standing behind Melanie stepped forward and took her bags.

"Welcome to Paris, Grace," Melanie said. "This is my driver; he'll take your bags."

"You have a driver?"

"This is Pascal," Melanie replied by way of introduction. Pascal bowed and without stopping, collected Grace's bags onto a trolley and walked off.

Grace followed Melanie along the crowded platform as they picked their way through towards the station exit.

Melanie talked to Grace throughout the car journey, telling her the names of the roads and major buildings. When they arrived at the apartment block, Pascal preceded them with the cases put them in the flat and then left without a word.

Grace gasped in delight as she followed Pascal into Melanie's flat. "This is a wonderful place!" she declared, eyes shining with excitement as she glanced around the apartment. "You seem to have everything, including a nice view; and it's so tidy. I'm afraid I'm not very good at putting things away."

"I'm not either, Grace. There is a woman who comes in to clean up every day."

Grace looked around the walls. "I like your paintings. Do you mind if I take a closer look at them? "Grace asked. Melanie waved her hand in their direction, pleased at Grace's interest.

"Isn't that a Braque?" Grace asked, feeling sure that she was looking at an original.

"I believe it is, but I honestly don't know anything about paintings."

"I don't suppose you have any by Artemus Ruane?" she called over her shoulder.

"No such luck, Dusty has told me about your interest in him."

Melanie took Grace's coat and carried it into the dressing room alongside the lounge.

"So, since we last met, you've lived all those years in Loriston?" She held Grace at arms length to look at her. "You've changed, but I do remember you as a little girl, and now you are a very pretty young woman. I last remember seeing you at your home with

Reverend Belari when I came to visit. You still live there, do you?"

"Not any more!"

Melanie picked up a bottle of mineral water from the table and poured it into glasses for them both. She remained silent as she drank and then said, "I did know; Dusty told me that you'd left home and she said that you weren't planning to go back. From what I remember of the rectory, I can understand how you must have felt, but it can't have been easy for you, leaving the place. I remember it was a beautiful house."

"Leaving was not too difficult really. Being away has been a great relief for me."

"Even before I stayed in Loriston at my aunt's, my leaving home had happened. And I've never been back. The relief I felt when I finally got away was like finding an oasis in the desert," she said, and stood up. "Now, before we talk too much, I'll show you to your room." She led Grace into a large bedroom with a double bed. "Just make yourself comfortable. There's a bathroom through that door," she said, going outside and pointing, "and I have arranged a meal for us in the dining room."

"Thank you. This is all marvellous. But…"

"Yes, is there something wrong?"

"Nothing wrong, but..." Grace paused awkwardly, searching for the right words, "Dusty didn't mention how I should settle my debts with you, Melanie."

"Call me Mel when we are together. You don't have to worry about paying, there will be no debts. You are a friend of Dusty's and that's all there is to worry about." She smiled to give Grace reassurance. "When you've changed into something more comfortable, come to the dining room and we'll eat together." She closed the door.

Grace looked around and, although feeling a little self-conscious in the impressive bedroom, still collapsed on the bed in relief.

She was so excited that she got up almost immediately, looked through the window, and saw that the flat looked out onto a busy Paris street, alive with pedestrians and traffic. The muffled sounds of cars and horns penetrated the otherwise quiet flat. She turned from the window, sat down on the bed, started opening her cases and took out the portrait of Edward and sat there just gazing at it. After a while, she got up and changed her clothes, but still felt under-dressed when she remembered how Melanie looked. After examining her plain clothes in the long mirror and straightening her hem, she opened the door and went to the dining room.

Over the meal of cold meats and salad, the two women talked for several hours. Late in the evening, Mel said, "I am always late up, help yourself to things in the morning

In spite of having slept on the journey, Grace went to bed early that evening and drifted off quickly. She woke to bright sunlight streaming through her window, put a dressing gown on, went to the kitchen and poured herself some juice and croissants and sat down at the breakfast bar. Before long, Mel came in bleary eyed. She shuffled over to the icebox, got herself some juice and said, "You'll see that the flat has a balcony, Grace. In the summer, when it's too hot to sleep in the flat, we'll get out on to the balcony with our s blankets and soak in the traffic noise, the shouting, occasional fights and the smell of food from the restaurant beneath."

Grace said, "I love the place already. It's pretty much like heaven for me, Mel. This part of Paris might not be the most elegant but it's got life and it's got purpose; everything I missed out on in Loriston. You can't imagine how empty, dull and pointless my life was there." They took their drinks onto the balcony, and sat on the steps outside the door.

"Oh, I certainly can imagine," Mel said emphatically. "My parents were just like yours sound, completely without feeling. In fact, mine were worse, I think. Those long winter nights and Sundays were the most awful. We just sat and said nothing. I often used to wonder about them; how they could possibly have had sex together to produce me and my sister. There seemed to be no physical or mental contact but, somehow, they must have done it, otherwise I wouldn't be here, would I? I don't recall them ever laughing or even smiling. All the time I lived there, I had an empty, leaden feeling in my stomach. You know how dull lead can look. Over there, look." Mel pointed to the flashing on the roof of the next apartment. "That was me, dark and heavy. I never sparkled, I never shone, and I just remained inanimate like that lead. You may not have liked Loriston but it was a paradise in comparison with Larondelle. Thank God I had a spinster aunt in the place who was well enough off to pay for me to stay with her so I could get away from my family." As she spoke, she stood up, went to the edge of the balcony and stretched her arms to the sky. "Now I am free from them," she shouted, "and living in this ugly, lovely city. I don't yet know who I am, but I don't mind." She turned to Grace. "I am so much nearer to myself now than when I lived in that empty place I grew up in." She came and sat on the step beside Grace. "Why did you take so long to leave Loriston and your parents? Your father must have been very difficult to live with?"

"I wonder why myself. Now that I am away from them, I constantly wonder," she thought for a moment, "I suppose it was just that I felt I had a duty to them. They made me the person I am. Not intentionally of course, they didn't have any understanding of what they were doing or of what sort of person I was, but at least they did it, and I guess I feel some sort of gratitude and indebtedness to them..." she stopped in mid sentence, "no, not *the* ,I mean, to my mother."

"Gratitude? Just for being yourself?" Mel looked puzzled. "Tell me something, Grace..." She hesitated as though unsure of how to proceed, and then finally asked, "Does that mean that you like yourself, I mean really like the person you are?"

"Shouldn't I? What are you saying? Do you think there is something strange about me, about the way I am?"

"No, no, I didn't mean what you're thinking. I don't mean that I find you strange. No, not at all. We've only been together for a short while, but already you seem like a close friend. No, I'm just surprised that you seem to be content with yourself."

"I don't think I'm perfect; don't think that for a moment. But I wouldn't be anyone else. I want to be me." She looked at the young woman beside her. "Aren't you happy with yourself then, Mel?"

Melanie breathed out and looked away with a sigh. "Well, there are things I haven't told you yet and, no..." she hesitated, putting her fingers to her lips before she spoke, Grace saw the brilliant red lipstick Mel wore had transferred to her fingers, absent-mindedly, Mel wiped them clean on her dark dressing gown. "No, I am not happy with myself; not at all."

"But why not? You're a really kind and lovely person. You've already made me feel as though I almost belong here with you."

Melanie frowned and was obviously finding it difficult to speak, so Grace spoke to fill the silence. "You have a career. You have somewhere to live. And you must have a well-paid job to afford all this. Isn't that enough, at least for now?" Grace asked, putting her arms on Mel's shoulders.

Melanie still said nothing for a time but finally, standing up and taking in the flat as if seeing it for the first time, she said, "Look around you, Grace. Look at this room, at the furniture, at the ornaments and the paintings. If you look into the drinks cabinet, you will see that it is full. Would it surprise you when I tell you that I drink very little alcohol and that I particularly dislike the smell on a man's breath?"

"What are you saying, Mel? What does this all mean?" asked Grace in bewilderment.

Mel said nothing but just stared blankly at the room. Slowly, she turned so that the two girls were facing each other and Grace saw that she was on the verge of tears. It was some time before Mel could speak. When she did, her words were halting. "Think back to when I was at your school. Did you see how the other girls laughed at me because I was so slow at learning? It was the same at school in France, even my family made fun of me - another reason why I left home. I'm well aware that I am not very bright but one of the things I do have is my looks. I did notice when I reached puberty, boys began to treat me differently. The way they looked at me much more admiringly made me feel more confident. It was a feeling I had never had before. Being wanted made me feel strong. I knew that that was what I needed and that it might help to take me out of the pointless, awful life I had always had." She turned her face away from Grace and let her eyes wander round the room. "What do you think a girl who possesses little intelligence but knows she is attractive to men could do in Paris, Grace?"

"You mean...?"

"Yes, that's what I mean. I am kept in this flat by a wealthy man. His name is Ricard. He's away in Africa with his 'wife' – he'll be there for another month, which is why I can be free and happy for the time being and enjoy having you here. For another month, I am my own woman; I can do what I like, without him breathing down my neck. And while I am free, I want us to enjoy ourselves. I want to show you Paris. Show you the parks and the shops and take you to clubs to hear jazz, Paris is the European centre for that music and it sets me on fire. I want this to be the happy time which we both need."

"Will you be so unhappy when he returns, then?" Grace asked. "Surely, he must have some nice qualities, he seems to look after you very well," she said, looking around.

"Nice qualities? Sometimes I pray the plane he is flying around in will crash into the jungle which he always tells me he finds so wild and thrilling. When he says he finds me as wild and thrilling as his jungle, I feel physically ill." She got up and walked into the lounge. Grace followed her as she moved her raised arms around the flat. "All this could be just what I need, but it's nothing more than a trap. It feels like a prison holding me like a rabbit in a snare. You see, there is nothing else for me out there," she said, pointing out through the window. "That's why I want us both to enjoy ourselves while I still have a little more freedom for the next few weeks."

Grace sat down on the chaise-longue and pulled Mel down beside her. She put her arms around her and kissed the tears from her eyes. When Mel had calmed down a little, Grace fetched a blanket to cover them and they lay there in silence.

After a while, Mel fell asleep and Grace herself drifted off, day-dreaming about Edward. She imagined she saw him walking towards her through a long, dimly-lit corridor. At the far end, a bright light shone behind him so that she saw only his silhouette, but he was still recognisable to her. He seemed to be walking in slow motion down the corridor, taking an endless time to reach her. When he eventually came close to her, the light changed and she could see him more clearly; not as he was in the painting, but older and even more beautiful. As she looked at him, the light faded and she was awakened by the clattering of breakfast cups as Melanie, who must have woken up before her, had started preparing food for them. Grace looked around the room at the effect of the sunlight, scattering shadows and bringing the day outside to noisy life.

She called out to Melanie, "When I was at home, my mother found sunlight depressed her because it just emphasised all that she was missing in her life. But just come and look here. Have you noticed the effect it creates in this room? It just glows."

Melanie came out of the kitchen as Grace was sitting up. She went to sit beside the younger girl and laid her head on her breast. Her voice when she spoke was muffled.

"Grace, for the first time in years, I feel really happy. Let's try to make it last. Whatever happens later, we will have this time to remember."

In silence, they held each other close for a few moments before making their way into the kitchen where the meal was almost ready.

Later, as they ate, Grace said, "Try not to think only about that man's return. Try to think beyond that. I am sure there will be a way out for you, let's work on it together."

"But how can we? To do anything we need money. Living in this city is so expensive." Mel said. "Are you thinking we should go somewhere else?"

"I wasn't thinking anything, just that I'm sure there will be something we can do to get you out of this trap you are in. I couldn't have suggested leaving Paris anyway just yet, Mel. I've come to Paris for a reason and I can't leave until I'm finished."

"A man, Dusty said you were looking for a man," Mel said, with slight disappointment in her voice. "Who is he? Have I met him?"

"You won't have met him; at least I don't think so," she picked up her coffee and watched the steam rise from it. "This will sound strange, I know, but... I haven't met him either."

"What?" Mel frowned. "That sounds mysterious, Grace, does he have a hold over you?"

"No, it's nothing like that. He doesn't know me and I don't suppose he will ever have heard of me, but that doesn't stop him having a hold on me." She looked through the window. "Not a hold over my body, you understand, but over my soul."

Mel looked surprised. "What! You mean an evil spirit of some sort?"

"No, certainly not evil, more a benign spirit; at least I hope so."

"I'm completely lost, Grace. You've never met him and yet he holds your soul. Do you owe him money?" Suddenly, she put her hand over her mouth. "Is he like Ricard, who pays for all this?" She waved her hand around the room.

"No, he is not. I know it sounds silly. Sometimes even I have difficulty in coming to terms with it myself, so I'm not sure that anyone else will understand. You see, I love this man, but I have only ever seen a painting of him."

Melanie's mouth fell open. "How can you have you fallen in love with just a painting?"

"I know it's difficult to understand. It's not the painting itself, it's the person it portrays."

"You're dead right, Grace, - it is difficult to understand - but, if you tell me more, perhaps I'll begin to understand. What else do you know about him?"

"I know nothing about him. I just think he's the most beautiful creature I have ever seen, and just looking at his image was enough to capture me. I have come to Paris just to look for him."

"In a big city like this, a man can easily get lost. I meet people who live here and never see them again. Why Paris; are you sure he lives here?"

"I can't be sure; I just think he's living in Paris. But even if he is not, I think this city will help me find him. I know that his father, the artist who did the painting, is living somewhere in France and he sells his paintings in Paris."

Grace told Mel how she had found the painting. Mel listened interestedly and said, "I remember about that house; that was where Artemus Ruane lived whenever he was in England. I used to see him when he came to the shop next door to where my auntie lived. All we kids used to love him. He had the habit of buying sweets, coming out of the shop and throwing them into the air for us to catch. He had such a memorable face. You couldn't forget him; he looked as though he was a character from the Bible, sort of like Moses. There was also a strangeness about him. Some of the younger kids were frightened of him, but there was something else as well... a sort of mysticism. You know the sort - you wouldn't have been surprised if he could perform miracles. And, you know, there was something astonishing that happened once. A girl named Jeanie had an illness which the doctors could not diagnose. Her mother took her out into the street one day as Artemus was passing by. When Artemus saw her, he touched her forehead and then very slowly made the sign of the cross. Within a week, the girl was able to come out to play with us. We all thought that was amazing."

"She might have got better anyway, of course," Grace said.

"Oh yes, I know, but we were all convinced that it was his magic."

Grace pondered. "That's funny, you know, because when I went into his house for the first time, it all felt pretty creepy to me. I expected to be frightened but I just felt a sense of complete peace. It was almost like going into a church... " She stopped in mid-sentence and smiled as a thought struck her. "Not my father's church, of course. Perhaps it would be better to say like being in the presence of a saint."

Mel smiled. "I did once go to his house; my aunt wanted to buy a painting for me, just a small one for me to take back to France. There was nothing there, but I did feel very much at home. You like to dream, don't you, Grace; even though he was definitely different from anyone else I have ever met, I would never have called him a saint."

"Perhaps not a saint, but the way he painted was a miracle. I've never experienced anything which moved me so much as his painting of Edward Alleyne." Grace said.

"Edward Alleyne!" Mel said. "Was that the name of the man in the painting?"

"Yes... yes, it was. Do you know him?"

"No, I don't know him, but, when I stayed with my aunt, I remember her telling me that there was a teacher called Miss Alleyne in the school? My aunt had known her well, they were quite good friends. There was a very pretty woman in a framed photo on the sideboard; I used to look at it a lot. When I asked who it was, my aunt told me it was the teacher, Miss Alleyne, and that she had had to leave Loriston School suddenly. I'm sure her name was Alleyne, hold on... yes, I remember now, her name was Zelda Alleyne."

"Zelda!" Grace almost shouted the name. "That was the name on one of the paintings in the deserted house. "'Zelda. The only love' the artist had written on the back of it. How can I find out more about Zelda Alleyne?"

"I have no idea but, with such an unusual name, the Edward in your painting must surely be her son." She stopped suddenly as a thought struck her. "She was French, like me, and I seem to remember that the girls in the school told me she had died giving birth to him. Artemus would disappear for long periods and go France to the place where Zelda had lived."

"Oh, really!" Grace cried excitedly. "Where was that? Do tell me!"

"I've no idea, I'm afraid, nobody ever told me that."

"Your aunt would surely know; is she still alive?"

"No, she became senile and died in a nursing home."

135

"Oh, how sad to die like that." Grace stopped. "If only she'd been alive we could have asked her where Zelda had lived in France. That would have made things simple for me. Artemus quite probably left England to go to France to be where her memory was. His house had obviously not been lived in for many years. I've never seen so many spiders' webs; fortunately I'm not scared of them."

"Did you take the painting of Edward?" Mel asked.

For answer, Grace got up and went to the bedroom. She took the painting out of her case and came back, holding the portrait of Edward in front of her.

"Mon dieu, Grace, that man is beautiful, just beautiful." She stood up, took the painting from Grace and held it at arm's length in front of her. "I can see why you are hooked on him. Yes, he does look like what I remember of Zelda in the photograph my aunt had. She was lovely. I can see why you are crazy about him. He's gorgeous." She laughed impishly at Grace. "Wish I'd seen him first."

"Hard luck, Mel, you can't have him," Grace joked. "But you can see why I'm trying to find him. How can I do it, though? I just have to find him somehow; that's the only reason why I came to Paris."

"And I thought you just came to stay with me?" Mel laughed.

"Of course, but I've found you," Grace laughed with Mel. "I still have to find Edward."

"Well now, let me have a think," Mel said, pursing her lips, I'll go and make another coffee, that'll get me thinking." When she returned and had refilled their cups, she said, "Yes, there is one thing we could do. Ricard has a man who works for him; a sort of private detective. He's English by the way. He visits me to see if there is anything I need."

"That's very thoughtful of Ricard, isn't it? He must have some good qualities after all."

"Ricard is not thoughtful unless it's about himself. No, the reason he wants the man to contact me is that he wants to check on my movements. To make sure I am here, waiting for him," Mel said, screwing her face up. "But the man himself, his name is Alec, is very different from Ricard. He and I talk together and I see him often. I know he dislikes Ricard as much as I do. I'm sure I could ask him to look for Edward for you."

"Would he do it?"

"He'll do it for me."

"What about the cost?"

"Don't worry about the cost. He won't charge if he does it for me."

Something about the way Mel spoke made Grace wonder about her relationship with Alec. "Wouldn't Ricard mind if he found out? I don't want you to do anything which is going to put you at risk, Mel," Grace said, suddenly feeling worried for her new friend. "Please don't do anything you might come to regret."

"Don't worry, Grace, Ricard will never know about this, trust me. I know what I'm doing."

"Do you? Are you sure? You seem to be chained by Ricard to this life you are leading." When Mel made no reply, she asked, "What is there between you and Alec, Mel? Is he more than just a friend?" Again Mel did not reply.

"Sorry, Mel, that was presumptuous. I've no right to ask questions like that."

"No, you and I are friends and you're right to ask. Don't worry about it."

Grace remained silent, looking at Mel and continued eating her breakfast. When she had finished, she started to clear the things away and take them into the kitchen but stopped at the doorway and said, "Mel, what is it like... to give your body to a man like Ricard; someone you don't even like?"

"I..." Mel frowned, obviously taken aback by the question. "Are you a virgin, Grace?"

"Well, you know Loriston," Grace replied. "You know the type of people who live there. I could have found someone amongst the soldiers in the camp nearby, or even among the few young men remaining in the town; but not someone to love, not a spirit one could connect with mentally and physically. I never wanted just a physical relationship." She drained the rest of her coffee before starting to gather up the breakfast things. "Yes, I am a virgin," she confirmed, looking down. "Even though I've lived with a man in Paris, which would be enough for most people to think we were sexually involved, but..." she shrugged. "well, he got his pleasures from men. I did try, but I got no response from him." She picked up the tray, walked over to the sink and continued, "I'm not sorry, Mel. It might sound like a sad admission at my age, but I'm not sorry that I'm still a virgin."

"It's funny how we've become friends," Mel responded. "We're so different. You hardly knew me when I lived at Loriston. In those days, the age difference was very important to us. If we'd been closer, you would know that my feelings towards men always dominated me. Even from the age of thirteen, I was what is coyly called 'intimate' with men." She looked up to see what effect her words had had on Grace and, seeing no response, continued. "You ask what it is like to give your body to a man." She looked around the room, trying to think of the right words to express her feelings. "It can be the nearest thing to heaven, or the closest thing to hell. With Ricard, it is a hell to be endured and nothing more."

"And Alec?" Grace asked

"Alec is a heavenly man."

"But is he 'your man'?" Grace asked, hoping that she could see a future for Mel without Ricard.

"Ricard has several girls around Paris. Alec has to look after them all when Ricard is away."

"Does that mean…?"

"I don't know what it means." Mel tried to smile. "I think he likes me more than any of the other girls. But I don't know." She stood up to refill their coffee cups. "Alec is so kind, you see."

"To you alone, or to the others as well?"

"I only see him alone so I don't know what he is like with the others," she replied. "But that's my worry, isn't it. Shall I speak to him about Edward?"

Grace debated with herself before saying, "I don't know. I'm doubtful about the whole business of getting this Alec to find him. It seems to me that you could wind up in trouble if it's not done very carefully."

"Alec is a professional and I know he would be careful; he always is, no matter what he does."

"I just had an idea; I don't know why I didn't think of it before." She banged her head with her fist. "Why don't I make a start by looking in the telephone directory?"

"Sounds like a good idea!" Mel turned to a cabinet, got out the directory and looked under the 'A's. She shook her head and said, "There's not an Edward Alleyne here, I'm afraid." As she spoke, she skimmed quickly down the pages of the directory and said regretfully, "Nor is there an Artemus Ruane either. I can't think of any other way to trace him except to ask Alec."

"All right, thanks Mel, for being so helpful. I would like Alec to try for me, if you would ask him."

"He's taking me to dinner tonight, because it's his birthday. I'll speak to him then."

Later on in the early evening, there was a knock on the door and Melanie leapt up to open it. It was Alec, dressed in an immaculately-cut suit and carrying a large bouquet of flowers which almost concealed him.

"Alec, how lovely! Yellow roses! How did you know I'd be wearing yellow?" she said teasingly, holding the flowers against her yellow dress. She kissed him and pulled him into the room.

"Alec, this is Grace, who has come over from England to stay with me." Grace was still in her dressing gown and her hair was unkempt, in contrast to Alec, who was immaculate in his suit. Melanie indicated the chair opposite where Grace was sitting.

"I'm just going to put these in a vase," she said, as she walked out into the kitchen.

There was an awkward silence as Grace sat facing Alec, waiting for him to speak. At first, Alec just stared straight ahead, avoiding eye contact with Grace, but he finally turned his head to address her. "What's a nice English girl like you doing in this tough city, then?"

"I've never thought of it as being tough. I find it beautiful."

"It may seem like that on the surface, but it's not like that if you dig deeper. It's when you need to make a living here that you see the other side of things. The corruption is here in plenty. It's just hidden by good manners and fashionable clothes."

"Is that why you wear a nice suit like that?" she asked, smiling at Alec and trying to bring a little humour into the situation. She was hoping he would laugh with her but he just stared coldly at her with obvious displeasure.

"How long have you been in Paris?"

"Only two days. Why do you ask?"

"Laughing at the way people dress does not go down well here. It may take you a while to realise that but I assure you, you will."

"I'm sorry; I didn't think what I was saying."

"This is a city where clothes matter. You can slop around England in your old clothes and eating the tasteless food they serve there and no one cares, but here in France, appearances matter. So don't say ridiculous things. I dress in a certain way because it's necessary."

Grace looked in amazement at Alec's face trying to see if he was serious. Realising that he was, she fell silent, looked away and said nothing else. When Melanie returned with the flowers arranged in a large vase and put them down on a low table in front of them, she noticed that the atmosphere was cold.

"I think I'll leave you two to talk," Grace said, standing up and going to her bedroom.

"See you later then, Grace. We'll be off soon," Melanie called after her and sat down close to Alec on the settee. When Grace had shut her bedroom door, Melanie knelt on the floor in front of Alec.

"I hope you teach her some manners while she's here," he said stuffily.

"Why? What did she say to you?"

"She just got up my nose with a stupid remark about my suit. I can't take rude and arrogant little girls, especially priggish English ones."

"The last thing she would be is intentionally rude. She wouldn't have meant it, I'm sure." Melanie put her head on Alec's knee, and looked up at him. "I'm so glad you're here, Alec."

"So am I. This place without Ricard is like a sanctuary. Things are going badly wrong for me lately."

"Why, what has been happening?"

"It's too complicated to go into. Ricard says we're not making enough money. He's been sending messages to everyone saying we have to make another twenty per cent. Typically for him, he doesn't say how." He shook his head despairingly. "God, if I had half his money I'd..."

"You'd what?"

Alec gripped her hand.

"You want to know what I'd do? I'd take you to the town in England where I've managed to buy a house with money put away from what Ricard pays me; a quiet little place, full of nice people."

"Would you now? And suppose I didn't want to come?"

"I know you'd jump at the chance. You could start that smart dress shop you've always wanted... and I'd get away from all this gambling and dealing with perverts and druggies."

"What do you mean? I though you liked Paris."

"I just can't take much more of the bloody people I have to do business with. They have an odour about them and when I shake their hands they are

142

dirty, always dirty. They leave an unpleasant smell on my hands."

"Alec, I've never seen you like this before. Tell me what's changed?"

Alec stared blankly straight ahead.

"Oh, nothing new, I suppose. It's just been building up for some time, and I've reached my limit."

Mel stroked his hand lightly and said, "Can't you tell me? Surely there must be a way we can sort things out?"

Alec shook his head. "Some things can't be helped just by talking."

Melanie got up from the floor and sat on the chair arm beside him. She pulled his head down against her thigh and stroked his hair.

"Alec, whatever has happened, you can tell me about it, surely?"

When Alec replied, his voice was muffled and quavering. "I don't know. I suppose I've just run out of energy. I was taken in by Ricard's offer of a job and I was a fool to do it. I always thought Stepney was a tough place to grow up in; there was a lot of crime but it was just petty in comparison with what I see here. Getting to university was a revelation for me. I should have stayed there, but I don't know, I just got bored with lecturing on the same subject." He sat up and rested his chin on cupped hands. "Paris has two faces. People see the tourist places, the chic-looking women, the food, Montmartre, the Folies Bergère, the glitter and they think it is all like that. That's what annoyed me about your little friend. It all seems so romantic. It's all glitz on the surface and suspicion and hatred beneath. I want to get back to something that is real. Find a way to leave this place with you and get away from Ricard."

"That's exactly what I'd like to do, but he'd find us, no matter where. I probably know him better than you. He has his spies everywhere." Melanie shuddered and screwed up her eyes in desperation. "He terrifies me, Alec. When he comes near me, it feels as though worms are crawling over my body."

"Well, he's a long way away, so he can't crawl over you now. It's just the two of us." Suddenly Alec raised his head and smiled. "So let's enjoy what we have." He stood up and pulled Melanie towards him, guiding her towards the bedroom.

CHAPTER NINE

The next day, Melanie and Grace dined out at a smart and busy Parisian restaurant.

Grace was subdued and pensive, in contrast to Mel, who was constantly laughing at the slightest provocation. They ordered drinks, and as they sipped them, looking round the dining room at the other diners, Mel babbled on about clothes, and the way everyone was dressed; constantly telling Grace about a fashion show where the two girls had waxed lyrical about the dresses on display, before suddenly noticing that Grace was saying nothing.

"Grace, are you okay? I've just thought, you're very quiet while I've been doing all the talking. You've been quiet all morning. Is there anything wrong?"

"No, I'm all right," she replied, but Mel could see that something was wrong and reached out to touch Grace's hand.

"Come on, tell me. What is it? Aren't you happy here with me?"

Grace gazed out of the window at the rooflines of Paris and the Seine before she spoke.

"Just something saddened me. That's all." She turned and gazed into Mel's eyes. "I don't really want to talk about it."

"But you must. If we're friends we should share everything, good and bad."

Grace nodded slowly, took a long drink from her cocktail and in a lowered voice so that only Mel could hear, said, "While I was making breakfast this morning, I had to go to my bedroom."

"Yes?" Mel said. "And...?"

"I walked past the bathroom. You'd left the door open a little and I was going to call out some funny remark to you, so I looked in."

Mel's face clouded. "You saw what I was doing?"

Grace nodded. "Yes."

Mel, with her elbows on the table, lowered her head, covered her eyes with her hands and remained silent. When eventually she looked up, she reached into her handbag, took out a handkerchief and wiped her eyes. Now it was Grace's turn to cover Mel's hands with hers, in an effort to comfort her. "Tell me about it, Mel," she said.

"It's all part of this bloody Ricard situation," Mel answered.

"How do you mean?"

"You haven't met him, and I hope to God you never have the misfortune to do so. He is odious, insidious and always has to be in control. He is like a Svengali to his girls and each one of us is his Trilby." Mel sighed as she returned the handkerchief to her handbag. "The difference is just that Svengali used hypnosis to subjugate Trilby, who became his mistress. Ricard uses cocaine. He supplies it free to all his girls. That's how he ensnares us."

"Why do you take the stuff? If you refused it, he would lose control."

"I wish I could; if only I could!" She held up a hand dramatically. "I would give this hand to be free. Sometimes I think that might be a way out; to have an accident or an illness so that I would have to spend time in hospital and be without drugs. That might just be a way out. Ricard is strangely vulnerable in some ways. If any of his girls are ill, he drops them totally.

146

Never wants to see them again; or even hear about them."

"Strange man."

"Oh, he's strange all right, but, more than that, he is evil. You wouldn't believe how vile he is. When ever I see him, it always surprises me that slime doesn't drip constantly from his hands."

The two girls sat in silence for a while then Grace, wanting to change the subject, said, "Is Alec always like he was with me when I first met him?"

"Like what?"

"He was irritable when you were out of the room. I thought he was dressed well so I paid him a compliment, and he started lecturing me on how to behave."

Mel was eating and her hand stopped halfway to her mouth.

"You have to see the situation he is in. Can you imagine it? He is a very educated man, but he's doing a job which could be done by a village idiot with muscles. What's more, he is working for Ricard and Alec has to do all of Ricard's dirty work. He finds it degrading."

"I understand now when you said he hates Ricard as much as you do."

Mel nodded and Grace continued, "So what is there between you and Alec? I get the impression…"

Mel looked at Grace sternly and addressed her seriously. "What is Alec to me? Alec has been the start and finish of my life. He has brought me the only real pleasure I have had since knowing Ricard." She sighed. "I want to tell you something else, Grace. I have slept with many men and I can tell you there has never been a heaven like there is with Alec. He is not the man you saw last night. He is gentle to me and so

147

unsure of himself. He needs me and I need him; together we make a team."

"In what way, a team? What is he like?"

"In bed, do you mean? He is very tender and loving."

"No, no, I didn't mean that. I meant how do you work together as a team?"

Mel took a glove from her bag and put her right hand in it and held up her gloved hand. "Just like that," she said. "A hand in a glove, that's how close we are."

They soon finished the meal and the waiter brought tea for them. They remained silent while he filled their cups, then Grace asked," Why did he get involved in this work then? There must surely be lots of other things a man like him could do."

"You won't understand, but it's not quite as simple as that. Once Ricard employs you, he owns you and he never lets go. No matter where Alec went, Ricard would find him. Ricard would kill Alec if he knew what he talks to me about, he is that evil."

"Are you serious?" Grace asked in astonishment. "Do you really mean... he would kill him?"

"That's exactly what I mean. I just thank God Ricard is away for another three weeks. But when he returns, so will the agony."

"That's terrible! Is there nothing either of you can do?

"To him, we are no more than a page in a bank balance. If the page ceases to record a return, he simply tears it out. That's what he is like. He'd do that to me and he'd do it to Alec"

Grace looked aghast. "I know these things can happen but it just seems so unreal. There must be something you can do, surely."

"The easy solution would be that Ricard would die. Every night I pray that the following day, he will die flying his plane in Africa."

"And if that doesn't happen?"

Mel lowered her voice and looked around at the other diners. There were only a few and they were sitting in another part of the restaurant, at tables some way away from them. "He could also die in an accident when he returns to Paris."

"That would be unlikely though, wouldn't it?"

"Alec has friends, you know."

"You mean...?" Grace's mouth fell open in horror.

Mel saw the effect her words had had. "I guess you are as shocked as I am at what I've grown into. That's what I meant when I said I had been coarsened by this life." Mel picked up her fork and allowed it to swing slowly back and forth between her fingers. "Like this fork, Alec and I could swing one way or the other. We are on the edge. Ricard has made many enemies. He feels secure surrounded by his heavies but there is a price for everything. The more his wealth grows, the more vulnerable he becomes."

Grace was at a loss for something to say but suddenly she began to feel the terror which Mel was experiencing and how desperation forces desperate measures. "Mel, you must get away."

"Where to? Do you mean Loriston?" Melanie shuddered. "I think I'd sooner die here."

"I didn't mean Loriston. I never want to go back there to live either, but there must be other places. I just can't see why Alec should be controlled by Ricard in this way. You told me he is an intelligent man, with a degree in philosophy, and he had once worked as a lecturer, and..."

"And you think he could go back to that? " Melanie shook her head. "No, he earned a pittance and lived in a box room. No, it just wouldn't work. We have both been there and I could never do it again." She stood up. "Come on, I need to get away, I find it depressing to even think about all this." She shrugged.

As they were leaving, Grace said. "What about the bill? We haven't paid the bill."

"Don't worry, we don't have to, this is one of the restaurants Ricard's boys 'protect'. We never have to pay here."

The head waiter saw them get up, rushed over with their coats and fawned over them as they left.

"He seemed a nice man," Grace said, when they were outside and walking towards a taxi rank.

"I find it nauseating," Mel replied. "It's completely artificial, you know. I once went there with Ricard and they all toadied to him and I thought, like you, that they were very nice, until I happened to be in a cubicle in the ladies room when two of the waitresses came in. You should have heard the foul language they were using about Ricard and me. They called me his 'whore'."

"How disgusting! Did you tell Ricard?"

"No fear. He would have got them sacked or beaten up."

CHAPTER TEN

In a dark and narrow backstreet in the city, deserted apart from an occasional couple passing through on their late-night liaisons, Melanie and Alec emerged from one of the clubs, arms linked. They walked past nightclubs and seedy bars and, a few blocks down, Alec pulled Mel into a dark corner and kissed her.

"Why can't it always be like this?" Mel sighed

"It will be, one day. I've been working on some ideas for us."

"Tell me."

"Too early yet. I'll tell you when something positive happens."

Alec hailed a taxi and took Mel's hand as they were driven through darkened streets.

Mel, sensing that the mood was right, said, "Alec... Grace came to this country to meet a man called Edward Alleyne."

"Yes, I remember you told me. Has it anything to do with me?"

"Well, what I was wondering was, could you try to find out where he is living, or maybe just something about him. We think he moved to Paris with his father maybe 10 or more years ago."

Alec remained silent for a moment and then said, "Why should I?"

"It's a bit difficult to understand Alec, but Grace has fallen in love with this Edward Alleyne."

"So, should I be surprised? If she's in love with him, why doesn't she contact him herself?"

"Well, this is even harder to understand; you see... she's never actually met him."

"Never met him? But that's ridiculous to fall for a man she's never met. I said she seemed a silly girl. How can she know what he's like?"

"She doesn't." Mel said. "You have to know her to understand. She is an unusual girl but she has a way of convincing herself and also convincing me. Edward is an image in a painting."

"Well, so am I. I had my portrait painted by Antoinette Germaine. I gave it to my mother for her birthday."

"No, you don't understand. She has never met Edward. She has only seen him in a painting."

"Mel you're not making sense – in love with a painting? She must be crazy! How can you expect me to help a stupid girl like that? She needs to go to a psychiatrist. I can tell her a good one if she wants."

"That's not what she needs, and I hope you never say that to her. I know you've only met her once and you didn't get on, but... I've come to know Grace well, and she is probably the best woman friend I have ever had. She is a very deep person. Quite unlike anyone I've ever met. Somehow..." she shrugged, "she has connected with Edward and, for the sake of her sanity, she must meet him. I don't ask you to do much for me, do I? I'd just like you to do this. Please," she pleaded

"I'm sorry, but it still seems crazy to me," Alec replied.

Melanie grasped both his hands in hers, kissed them and put her head on his shoulder.

"Even if it is crazy, you could help. She is convinced he lives here, either in Paris or somewhere in France. Could you just try to find out where he lives? Please, for Grace's sake and for me."

Alec said nothing as he went through options in his head, then he said, "There's something different about you, Melanie... I don't know what it is, but something about you has definitely changed. You seem more at ease, more positive. If that's down to your little girl friend then she must be good for you." He looked out of the window as the taxi swerved to avoid a drunken pedestrian. "OK, Mel, for your sake, I'll try to find the fellow in this painting. Edward Alleyne, you say? Get me as much detail as you can, and I'll make some enquiries."

"That's all we know, except for the painting and that his father is a painter, Artemus Ruane." Melanie leaned over and kissed him again. "Alec, you are so wonderful."

"Better than your silly girl friend, do you mean?"

"She's not silly," Mel pouted, as she ran her hand up and down his leg.

CHAPTER ELEVEN

Grace and Mel were reading in the lounge of Mel's flat. The curtains were drawn and the lights were on, casting a halo around their heads. With a sigh, Mel stood up and said, "You seem to be quite happy to sit here reading, Grace, but I'm getting bored, I need to do something. I want to go out and do some living."

Grace, absorbed in her book, looked up from it reluctantly.

"Sorry, Mel, I'd just got to an interesting bit," she said. "What would you like to do?"

"Well, I'm not sure if you'd like it, but there's a club in the square round the corner. It's noisy and dirty, and sometimes the people there are not very pleasant. But the music is great and I just love the atmosphere."

"Let's go then," Grace replied, closing her book and stretching her arms to the ceiling. "But what sort of clothes should I wear?"

"Are you sure you want to come?" Mel looked surprised. "Have you ever been to a sleazy dive before?"

"I don't know. I often went to a sort of bar with my sculptor friend the first time I was in Paris. There was a jazz group who played there. Nobody ever danced. It'll be my first time to the sort of club you're talking about. Tell me more about it."

"It can be rough. Sometimes there are fights. I've only ever been there with Alec before, and he has always kept the sort of men who go there away from me. But I just feel like a bit of excitement. Do you still want to come?"

"Why not? I've left my childhood behind in Loriston. I want to do what grown-up women do; I'd love to come with you."

Mel sat motionless and Grace asked again, "What shall I wear?"

"Well, that is a small problem which we'll have to sort out," Mel said, standing up. "I'm not sure you'll have anything which will do, from what I've seen you wear so far. Let's have a look in your wardrobe, anyway. They went into Grace's room and opened the door of her wardrobe. Mel started to take out the clothes, one by one. As she looked at each one, she screwed up her face and put them on the bed.

Grace picked them up in turn, making comments as she did so.

"Mel, this one is lovely. My aunt in America sent it for my last birthday."

"Yes, nice enough if you're going to a birthday party but you need something, well..., something sexier, an outfit that shows off the fantastic bosom you have. Wish I'd been blessed like that, I'd be a lot more successful with a figure like yours. You need something to show off your cleavage and make the men's eyes light up."

"Well, what about this?" Grace picked up a yellow dress but again Mel shook her head. She searched through the wardrobe and pulled out a short-skirted dress. Grace stripped down to her underwear and put on the dress. Again Mel shook her head.

"Haven't you got anything more revealing?"

"Mel, I don't really want to have men looking at me because of my breasts," she screwed her face up.

"I want a man to be interested in me, someone I can talk to."

Mel laughed. "If you want to talk you'd be better off in the public library. In this club, the only way you can talk when the music is playing is by shouting. Even then, you only hear one word in five." She reached into the wardrobe again. "Try this one on, it looks a bit better. I like the colour - not that it really matters much. The light inside is so bad, I reckon you could go in naked and no one would notice the colour," she laughed again.

Grace undressed and put on the dress. "No," Mel said. "It just does nothing for your figure." She pondered for a moment. "I know, I think I've got something. Come in to my room. Ricard sent me an outfit from Chanel. It was obviously a bit of wishful thinking because it's far too big for me in the bust and just makes me look droopy." She reached into her wardrobe, pushing coat hangers aside until with a sigh of satisfaction, she said. "Look, here it is. This'll look great on you. The bright red colour will be just right, and it ought to fit nicely." She brought out a slinky dress and held it up to Grace.

Grace took it and danced around the room, holding it against herself and admiring her image in the mirror. "I've never worn anything like this! D'you think I can get away with it? It's very low cut"

"Only one way to find out. Try it on."

Grace slipped into the outfit and pirouetted around in front of Mel. "That looks absolutely stunning on you!" Mel exclaimed.

Grace smiled and nodded her head in agreement, as she admired herself in the mirror and then started to dance with Mel, dodging in between the furniture.

"I thought you said you hadn't danced before."

"I meant I've never been to a night club dance, but I've danced on my own many times."

"Well, at least you won't be a complete amateur. Now we've got some clothes for you, you can help me choose mine."

Grace liked every one of the outfits Mel tried on and chose one which blended with the colour Mel had chosen for her.

It was still very early in the evening and the club was silent and almost empty as the two girls walked in. They stood by the bar for a while just looking around. In the dim light, they could just make out a small group over in one corner.

"Not much life in here, yet." Mel said. "It always seems dead until the music starts."

As though on cue, spotlights went on at the far end of the hall and a band began playing with a pounding, heavy beat. As soon as it began, Grace began to follow the rhythm, with her hands at first and then with her whole body. As the beat became wilder, she said to Mel. "Come on, let's dance!"

"Not yet, thanks," replied Mel. "I'll wait until a few more people come in. I'd feel pretty silly with that lot watching." She nodded her head in the direction of the few men sitting near the band and ogling the girls.

"I must dance. I can't stand still while that music is playing," Grace said excitedly.

"No, no, just wait a bit." Mel put a restraining hand on Grace's arm to hold her back but she couldn't stop her. Grace, overcome with the emphatic beat of the music, danced out onto the floor. As her body moved in time to the music, Mel and the barman watched in amazement and began to clap their hands, partly to the rhythm and partly in

157

appreciation of her dancing. Grace had never felt so wild before and enjoyed the appreciation of her audience. She increased the tempo of her dancing, entering the trance-like state which music always seemed to inspire in her. More people came into the club and a group assembled around Grace, watching her dance and applauding her. As she danced, the band played louder and more people got up, following Grace's lead. When the music ended, Grace bowed her head in exhaustion and then walked over to Mel, who had herself been dancing with a man and was just leaving him.

Seeing Grace, the man said to her, "That was fantastic. Whatever you are on, I'd like some of it."

When they were alone once more, Mel said to Grace, "Are you all right? You've gone pale."

Grace, overcome by her exertions and still in a state of euphoria, allowed herself to be guided by Mel through a swing door into a quieter room behind the bar. She leaned on Mel's arm until they were seated at a small table and had ordered drinks. As she drank, Grace returned to reality and began to look around the room.

"That music went straight into me, Mel," she said in an odd voice. "It was wilder than any other music I've heard before."

"If I didn't know you had never taken drugs, I would have assumed, like that fellow I danced with, that you were "on" something," Mel replied, smiling quizzically. "I would never have imagined that a girl from Loriston could dance like that." She looked over her glass as she drank. "You're a surprising woman, you know, Grace."

Grace smiled weakly, still under the spell of the music. "Why do you say that?"

"We've been together for only a short time and every day I see you differently. You're nothing like I would expect a priest's daughter to be, especially one being brought up by that Reverend Belari."

"We never know ourselves completely - how can we expect to know other people? I'm no more unusual than anyone else."

"Oh, yes you are. I'm very sensitive; I can sense that there's something ethereal about you. The way you can just abandon your inhibitions is amazing, for someone brought up in a rectory."

"Why?"

"Well, I'd only met you a few times when I came to your house in Loriston and you and your parents always seemed very 'proper'. I don't mind telling you that when I met you at the station, with your box pleats and little girl look, I thought I had made a dreadful mistake in inviting you to stay with me."

Grace laughed nervously, partly to cover her disappointment at what her friend was saying and partly because she found Mel's comments amusing. When she had met Mel, she had felt an immediate liking for her and had felt that the feeling was mutual.

"Why do you say that?" she asked.

"You seemed so… well… conventional… if I'm honest, I thought you'd be boring. You seemed so well brought-up."

"Can't I be well brought-up but still able to enjoy myself?"

"I'm not explaining myself very well, am I? Let me start again," Mel said, for a moment wishing she'd never started the conversation. "You see, since I have lived in Paris, I've grown away from the sort of life you lived back home. Living here is, for me, so different from anything I knew before, and it has changed me."

"It's even more so for me, you know."

"Yes, I saw that as soon as you got here," Mel said. "When I first arrived in Paris, I was like you, except that I had nowhere to live. I was still like a child. I loved meeting new people and thought everyone would be simple like they were back home...and like they were in Loriston." She took a drink from the glass in front of her. "The best thing I could find to live was a room in a sort of doss-house, which was so small that the only thing I could do there was sleep. Pretty soon, the charm of being in Paris disappeared and I felt desperately lonely. I seemed to spend a lot of time in tears, got down about the unfairness I saw in this city where there were people incredibly rich and dreadful poverty. As it happened, the doss-house room was good for me, because it meant I got out of it as soon as I could. I spent much of the day walking the streets. Without knowing it, I walked past Ricard's office. He must have seen me many times and finally sent one of his men out to invite me to go for a drink.

So that's how I met Ricard. You know that he changed my life completely in many ways. He introduced me to a set of people with pots of money and what seemed like glamorous lives. For those first few weeks, he seemed so exotic with his perfectly tailored clothes and expensive motorcars. It wasn't long before he moved me into this apartment, and it was then that I realised what a swine he really was. I soon found that he never gave anything without wanting something in return, and with interest on top." She shrugged her shoulders and looked to be so close to tears that Grace squeezed her hand in sympathy. Mel took a few moments to regain her composure before saying, "I just had to change and... well... all the things that have happened to me have coarsened me. What's more, I've even started to like what I've become. Things don't worry me so much, I can cope, I can survive in this hostile place."

"And you didn't think I could; me with my rectory upbringing. You must have been very worried, thinking I'd get in your way."

"Did you think that?" Mel looked surprised. "To be honest - yes I did wonder when I first saw you."

"And?"

"Well, I guess it didn't take me long to see you in another light. I have seen many more sides to your character now, especially when you were dancing in there." She nodded in the direction of the dance hall. "You were different again. I've never seen dancing as free as that."

Grace stood up and, humming a song called 'Set me Free', started to dance for a few moments. "Like that, do you mean?"

"Yes, exactly - you said you have had no training, but wherever did you learn to dance like that? I've never seen anything like it. It was... well, lots of things... exciting, unique, incredible and, what's more, although I am a woman, it was erotic even for me. I expect every man in the room was aroused. How can you get so rhythmic? I need a male partner to psyche me up just to get on the dance floor, but there you were dancing on your own perfectly happily. Where the Hell does it come from?"

"Where does it come from?" Grace raised her eyebrows. "I've no idea. It's just in me, I suppose."

"But, even if you didn't have proper training, you must have had some lessons to be able to dance like that."

"No, I've never been trained; my father would never have allowed that. He always told me dancing was a sin. Tonight is the only time I've ever danced in a club with other dancers watching."

"I don't see how you can possibly dance like that then, I certainly couldn't do it. Did you see someone and copy them? You seemed almost – well... possessed."

Her remark made Grace go quiet and a look of anxiety passed across her face.

Mel noticed and asked. "Did I say something wrong?"

"No, Mel, it's nothing you said. " She breathed in and out quickly. "I just wonder myself where it comes from. When I am dancing, it feels so strange, I am completely taken over and it is almost as though I'm looking at someone else doing it."

"Are you happy when you dance?" Mel asked

"Completely."

"Then why worry? It doesn't matter even if your inspiration comes from the jungle."

"You sound like my father."

"God, no! That's the last thing I would want to be." As she spoke, she suddenly stiffened when she looked into the dance hall. "Grace, I didn't sleep well last night and I've suddenly come over very tired. I think we'll go now, if you don't mind."

Although she wanted to dance more and, confused by Mel's sudden change of mood, Grace nodded her agreement. When they had collected their coats and were walking back home, Grace said, "What was wrong back there? I thought you were enjoying yourself."

"I was, but I saw a man come in."

"Yes?"

"A friend of Ricard's."

"Isn't he a friend of yours as well, then?"

"No, he certainly is not," she shuddered involuntarily. "Ricard expects me to sit with my hands in my lap waiting for him to return. If that man had seen me, he would have made sure that Ricard knew about it, and the story he would hear would be embellished. I would have been there, not with you, but with another man, or something like that."

"I would have told him that it was just you and me."

"I don't want you meeting Ricard. He is so evil that if he decided he didn't like you, there's no telling what would happen."

The girls turned a corner and faced a sudden gust of wind which made them clutch tightly to each other. They stayed holding each other until they reached the flat.

When they were back in the warm and had thawed out a little, Grace said, "I've been thinking about what you said back in that night club." She paused as though wondering whether or not to speak her thoughts but then continued, "Perhaps I really am possessed, Mel. What I mean is - you've seen my home in England; there was so little to do to pass the time that I spent much of my time reading. There was a library in the house, full of books which had been owned by my grandfather. I hardly knew him because he always kept himself to himself and spent much of his time reading in the library in his house in Harrogate. He must have loved books as much as I do. Almost everything he had on his shelves was interesting, even science books."

"But you didn't learn dancing from books, did you?" Mel protested.

"Not really, but you do learn a lot about yourself."

"How come?"

"Well, let's start with my name, 'Grace'. It just seemed like a name which suited me until I read grandfather's book. He must have given my mother the name because it was ringed in pencil. It comes from the 'Graces' in Greek mythology and one of those Graces inspired dancing."

"Yes, but that wouldn't have made you dance like you do."

"No, of course not, but it did start me wanting to learn more." Grace replied. "So I read a lot and, in one of grandfather's books, there was a description of ancient Greek dancing – orgies sometimes but more often as a form of curing where people with mental problems were encouraged to dance themselves out of their melancholy."

"Never heard of that," said Mel, and then, looking askance as a thought struck her, she said, "But I know that dancing can sometimes lift me out of a bad mood."

"It happened a bit like that with me," Grace replied. "I was feeling pretty miserable one day. It was after father had punished me because he saw me smiling to myself during prayers. He seemed to think you shouldn't show any pleasure when talking to God. Anyhow, I went into the library to be alone and I found a book where Dionysian dancing was described. It was a very small book and I read it through. It left such an impression on me that I wrote down notes in the margins. Just as I was putting it back on the shelves, I noticed another book about Greece. I took it out and when I opened it, I found that it had been hollowed out and inside was a book about dance. On the inside cover of this book was an inscription to my grandfather from Isadora Duncan. Just imagine that! The woman who transformed dancing in Paris over a quarter of a century ago must have known my grandfather well enough to write 'To dearest George, I'll never forget that night'. Granddad always seemed so correct and quiet that at first I was quite puzzled. There must have been a side to him that no one else saw. He must have thought so much of the book which Isadora had given him that he hid it in the bigger book so that no-one else would see it, and he could read it while he was in the library. Grandmother was very different from him; I never saw her read anything except romantic novels which she got from the lending library. Perhaps, apart from Grandfather, I was the only other person who had seen the book and read that dedication. I did find it very moving, so much so that I held the inscription close to my breast; I don't know, it somehow seemed to inspire me."

"My god, I've heard of Isadora, older people around here still talk about her and her wildness. I wonder what she meant by that inscription?"

"I've often wondered as well, of course. Isadora had so many lovers, both men and women, that grandfather could easily have been one of them. It makes it even more likely because he went to so much trouble to conceal the book. I suppose that was because he didn't want my grandmother to know about Isadora and be suspicious about anything that could have gone on between them. It might have happened when he was in Moscow on business, which is where the book was printed, obviously for a very small circulation."

"The book?" Mel asked, and then laughed. "Oh, I see. You mean it was a pornographic book?"

"No, not completely, although it contained many erotic dance scenes and there was a pen and ink drawing on the inside of the back covers which was very suggestive." Grace laughed. "In her day, Isadora was pretty wild and completely amoral."

"Grace, now you've really got me interested. Tell me more."

"About Isadora completely changing the dance scene and reviving the spirit of Greek dances, you mean? I've read a lot about her work and her tragic life. Her two children were drowned in a car which slid into a river, and she was killed in 1927 when the long scarf she wore caught in the wheel of a car and strangled her. But if there is one person I owe my sanity to, it is Isadora."

"Why is that? I don't see the connection. Tell me more."

"Well, it's a bit difficult to explain and I've never told anyone before. It's going to sound stupid, I know."

"Try me; I don't think I'll find it stupid," Mel said, encouragingly.

"I've read her story so many times that I feel I know her personally, perhaps even better than I know myself."

"Go on, Grace, tell me more."

Encouraged, Grace continued, "You're right to wonder where my dancing comes from, because that is exactly what puzzles me as well. Nobody taught me and when I am doing it, movements just seem to come without my thinking about them at all. This is hard to say but...," She allowed her voice to drop. "I get to feel that it is not really me who is dancing."

"What do you mean, of course it is you. I've seen you."

"Do you remember when we got back here after leaving the club, I said I felt that I could be possessed?" Both girls looked at each other as she spoke and Mel, in puzzlement, waited for Grace to continue. "Well, I think it is the spirit of Isadora inside me which is making me able to dance."

"God, Grace, that's creepy. What are you saying; that she is haunting your body?"

"No, not haunting, because that makes it sound malevolent and I think she has the opposite effect. I admit that I don't really know what I'm saying. All I know is that I never thought about dancing until I went into the library, picked up grandfather's book and held Isadora's message close to my breast and danced. It was always my room, an empty room, because no one else ever went in there. I never knew my father to read anything except books on religion and God until one day, when I went to dance in the empty room, I heard him behind me. He must have fallen asleep there after looking for a reference for a sermon or something. He was furious with me, he got me so upset that I never danced in that room again, but I just had to dance, so, ever since then, whenever I felt miserable, I'd go out and dance in the countryside."

Mel, meditating on what Grace had said, got up to pour them both a drink. "You don't think...?" she said passing a glass to Grace.

"What?" Grace frowned and when Mel said nothing further, repeated, "What? What are you thinking?"

"It's a way out idea but, could your grandfather have had an affair with Isadora which resulted in a baby who became your mother? You said that he was quiet and reclusive, perhaps it was guilt that made him like that."

"Hmm," Grace said pensively. "What a thought that is to take in. It's certainly never occurred to me that I could be related to Isadora; but I'd love it if it turned out that I was."

"It sounds incredible I know, but stranger things have happened," Mel said. "Of course, there's no way of finding out, unless there is another book with letters between Isadora and your grandfather in your library."

"I don't intend to ever go back, but you've got me thinking - if it should happen that I do go there, I'll go through each book and look." Grace said. "I'd love to know for certain, now you've said that."

"I bet you would," Mel said, draining her glass and getting up to pour another, but, before she did, she said. "Come on, I said I was tired back there in the club and it was true, I'm almost dropping on my feet. Let's go to bed and dream."

"About Isadora?" Grace asked with a smile, as she made her way to her own bedroom.

"And your grandfather, of course!" Mel called from the kitchen as she washed the glasses.

CHAPTER TWELVE

One morning, a few days later, Mel came into Grace's bedroom while she was still asleep. She sat down on the bed as Grace slowly woke up, opened her eyes and smiled sleepily up at her.

"I was out with Alec last night, Grace."

"Did you have a good time with him?"

"Yes! We went to that same night club where you danced. It was a different sort of evening, with cabaret, and a jazz trio. You'd have loved it."

"I would have been in the way, but perhaps we can go together another time."

"There's something else I have to tell you, as well," Mel said. "Alec has found an address, somewhere where he thinks your Edward may be living, or have lived"

Immediately, Grace sat up in bed.

"Already? How marvellous!"

"Well, he can't be sure, but he has found a place where an E. Alleyne used to live. He can give us the address."

"I must go to him. Tell me where it is and how I can get there."

"Slow down, slow down." Mel said. "It's only an address; we don't know that the E. Alleyne is your Edward."

"I'm sure it is him. It's fate; fate brought me here and fate has allowed Alec to find him." She jumped out of bed, and on her way to the bathroom called over her shoulder, "I can feel it! I am really meant to meet him!"

As Grace slipped out of her night clothes and into to the shower, Mel called to her through the open door, "Before you get too excited, one thing you must know is that the address is in a pretty tough neighbourhood."

"I don't care about that. I just want to find him. I'll go to the toughest area, however bad it is."

"It's not just tough, Grace."

"What is it then?" Grace called out, raising her voice above the noise of the shower.

"It's sort of a Mafia hangout. Drugs, and, well…" Mel finally blurted out, "more murders there than anywhere else in Paris."

"I don't care. As soon as I'm dressed, I'm going."

"Well, you're not going on your own, anyway," Mel said firmly, as Grace emerged from the bathroom in a towelling dressing gown. "You need someone like Alec to be with you. He knows the area and can make sure you come out safe."

"I'll be all right," Grace smiled. "Why are you so worried? If there is a problem, Edward will look after me, I'm convinced of it."

"Sometimes, I wonder about you, Grace. Is it just that you've never been in a difficult situation, or are you really just plain stupid? These people are criminals; they'll have knives and guns. Just get it into your head; you are not going there alone. Alec has the address and I won't let him give it to you unless he goes with you."

"Just give me the address, Mel. I'm going as soon as I've dressed."

"I don't have it. Alec has it and he is keeping it. He has said he is going to take you," Mel said, coldly. "And that's an end to it."

Grace stood in front of Mel and stared at her as though challenging her. Finally, with reluctant grimace, she said, "All right, you can both take me to the address, but I'm going in on my own. And I want to leave straight away."

"You'll have to wait until this evening. Alec has work to do until then."

"I won't wait. I'm going on my own this morning!" she screamed. "And you and your precious Alec will not be able to stop me. Give me the address," she demanded, holding out her hand.

"Stop behaving like a spoiled brat. Alec has gone to a lot of trouble looking for this Greek God that you imagine you're in love with." Mel said, sitting down and folding her arms. "When I say trouble, I mean trouble, He has spent days questioning people. It doesn't help when you call him 'my precious Alec', either. He has done this for you. God knows why, when you've treated him like a second rate pimp."

"I don't know why you say that. I never said anything like that. He's just too sensitive; it was he who was rude to me."

"You don't understand him, do you? Why should you, how could you know what life is like out there with a home where everything was provided for you? Alec came from the back streets and had to work hard for everything he has. And, what's more, he hates every minute of the life he's in, but there is no way out for him. He had nothing. No well-off family to provide for him. He had to work at anything, digging ditches, working in sewers to pay for his degree. And I mean work, in dreadful and often dangerous places. Have

171

you even noticed the odd way he holds his arm? Do you know why?" Mel's voice was rising in anger as she poured out not just her feeling for Alec but also her terror about her own situation. "I'll tell you why. He got stabbed in a fight, and not one he had started. He was trying to protect a stupid woman like you who had got herself into a mess."

Grace stood with her mouth open as Mel continued, "Do you understand what I am saying? I love that man. I certainly don't want him getting in to any more trouble, but he refuses let you go alone. I can't stop him, and I don't want to. I know he has many faults, but beneath it all he has a heart - he is the only man I could ever think of spending my life with. Do you understand that?"

Grace went over to the chair and knelt beside Mel, whom she could see was overwrought. "I am sorry Mel, I was just being selfish. It's nice of Alec to go to so much trouble, and to think of me like that. I do appreciate what he has done and I can see how you feel about him."

She burst into tears, embarrassed by her own insensitivity, and the two girls ended up in each other's arms.

That evening, the girls were waiting in the apartment, already dressed in their outdoor clothes, when a horn sounded outside. Mel looked out of the window into the dark street outside and saw Alec's Citroen.

"There he is, Grace. Come on," Mel called; and before she had buttoned up her topcoat, Grace was through the door and off down the stairs.

Alec was sitting in the passenger seat in the car beside a driver when Grace reached him. He jumped out to open the rear door and Grace got in. He smiled

172

politely at her and then turned to give Mel a kiss as she climbed in beside Grace.

As soon as Alec had got back into the front of the car, the driver noisily engaged gear and they drove off.

"Alec," Grace said, "I want to thank you for the work you have done in finding this address. It was very kind of you."

"It's nothing," he replied tersely. "We're going to find this Edward somehow."

For the rest of the short journey they remained silent as the car drove out of the area Grace knew, and into a part of the city she had never seen before. The streetlights were dim and the few people who were there walked furtively and stared suspiciously at the car. When they stopped at traffic lights, a large black man tried to force his way into the car, but failed to open the locked doors. On the other side of the street, a man exposed himself and urinated in the gutter.

Grace turned to Mel and said, "I can see what you mean now, Mel. I would have been scared on my own."

About five minutes later, Alec signalled to the driver to stop the car. He turned round to Grace and said, "Are you sure you want to go through with this silly idea, now you can see what this area is like?"

"Oh yes! I'm very sure. Why should I be otherwise?"

"Mel has already told you how dangerous the club is. It used to be just number 22 but is now called L'Appareil. I don't know why they called it that, but I do know its reputation."

"I can see it's not very pleasant, but I have no choice. I must find Edward and the danger doesn't matter to me."

"I'll tell you this, Grace," Alec said, using her Christian name for the first time. "I am known here, so you will have to go in on your own. If they see me, they will just clam up. We'll be parked close by with the engine running. If you get into any trouble, yell and we'll have the car door open for you. You'll have to get the hell in quick because we'll be driving fast as soon as you're inside."

Grace got slowly out of the car and looked carefully around her before walking off along the dimly-lit street. It seemed to her that there was someone watching her from every window. A man ran out from one of the houses and collided with her, knocking her to the ground. She regained her feet, brushed off dirt from her dress and watched him running off. She had been warned about bag snatchers so was quite anxious until she found her bag on the ground beside her with nothing lost. The street stretching out in front of her remained quiet and as she walked her footsteps echoed loudly off the dark houses as she passed. Towards the end of the street was a larger building, alive with raucous music and what seemed to her to be mocking laughter. She paused in front of the building with a racing heartbeat. Outside, leaning against the wall was a large woman dressed in florid clothes. She looked Grace up and down and said, "Oui?"

"Je cherche un homme," Grace said hesitantly.

"Yeah, don't they all? Yer English ain't ya? What sort of bloke you looking for, dearie?" the woman asked in English.

"You're from England?"

The woman laughed. "'From' is right and I'm stuck here in this hole, even though I'd give my right arm to go back."

"Why can't you?"

"Why, what's it to you?"

"No reason, I was just being polite, that's all?"

"Don't worry then. What's a nice girl like you doin' 'ere. You want a man, you say? Wouldna' thought you'd 'ave much trouble there. Still....," she shrugged, "there's no accountin' for tastes, I s'pose. Better go on in."

She stood aside, pushed open the large door and followed Grace in. Inside, slim figures were silhouetted dancing sensuously against a background of noise, music, smoke fumes and flashing lights.

"What sort of man d'you want, then?" the woman yelled above the music. "We've got 'em all 'ere. Skinny 'uns, tall 'uns, fat 'uns. They're all well 'ung, if you're looking for a good time." She nudged Grace and grinned with a toothy smile. "Or, if that's more your style, we 'ave them as you 'ave to encourage a bit, if you see what I mean? Never been to my taste but some women like to 'ave to make the runnin'. Just tell me what sort you're after and we'll 'ave 'im ready for ya. You got the money I s'pose."

"No, no. It's not like that at all. I'm not looking for a 'good time'. I'm looking for one man in particular that I think might be here."

"Yeah, I know, tall, dark, handsome and with a big wallet and well filled slacks. Tha's the only sort we 'aven't got. Nearest we got is Gaston, who never fails. Got great talent, 'e 'as." She turned and yelled to a spindly man who looked as though he had been painted by Toulouse Lautrec. "Gaston, attendez cette

175

femme." She took hold of Grace's arm "'E'll give ya a good time luv, don't you worry."

The spindly man, put his arms round Grace, kissed her and began pawing at her, pulling her skirt above her knees. Grace screamed and hit him in the face with her fist. He reacted violently, shouting abuse and knocking her to the ground with a blow to the head. Grace lay still, dazed for a moment, while the large woman shouted at the man and pushed him away. Again, he reacted violently, almost knocking her to the ground alongside Grace. At that moment, Alec suddenly appeared with a gun in his hand.

"C'est tout!" he shouted, pointing his gun at the man and pulling Grace to her feet with his other hand. The fat woman stood back, looking scared.

"Is he here?" Alec demanded.

"Who d'ya mean?" asked the fat woman.

"Alleyne," Alec replied.

"Eric Alleyne? Is that the one ya mean? No, I got rid of him. Is that who yer lookin' for? Wha's 'e done now, the useless lump of tripe? S'posed to bring me loads o' women and never brought one."

"Eric Alleyne. Not Edward?" Alec asked.

"Edward? No. 'E was def'nitely Eric. Why? Did 'e tell you 'e was Edward?"

"He didn't. What did this Eric look like?" Alec asked.

"Look like? Well, he was black, fat and ugly, about fifty, I should think. If you know 'im, why d' you ask me?"

"I don't know your man," Grace said, beginning to shake with shock. "I just know he's not the man I am looking for."

176

"Come on, then," Alec said, grabbing Grace's arm. "You've seen enough of this place for one night." He walked backwards towards the door, watching for any movement and pulling Grace along with him. Outside, the Citroen was waiting. Before getting in, Grace leaned against the car, clutching her stomach, and vomited into the gutter.

"Ugh," She said, wiping her mouth with a handkerchief which Alec had pulled from his top pocket. "That man kissed me with his mouth wide open and tried to put his tongue against mine. I smelt his breath." And she vomited again.

Mel pushed open the car door and screamed, "Come on! Get in! Quick!"

Grace forced herself into the back seat and the car roared off, leaving behind a crowd of people who had come out of the club, shouting and throwing bottles. One ricocheted off the car and another, narrowly missing the rear window, smashed to pieces on the road.

After they were a safe distance away, Alec turned to Grace and said, "I'm sorry you had to go through that. I would have taken you in myself if I'd realised it was just a matter of finding out if they knew your Edward. I shouldn't have let you go in on your own. Like I said, I know many of them. They know me and they know Ricard. They would never have tried anything like that if I had been there. Ricard could destroy them all."

Grace, slowly beginning to recover her composure looked puzzled. "What do you mean - destroy them all? Does he have that power; what sort of man is he?"

"Doesn't matter exactly what he is. You just need to know that he's a very powerful man."

"Powerful? In what way powerful?"

"Look, let's just leave it at that. There are people in very important positions in this city who owe a lot to him. He's not a man to fool around with" he said angrily.

After this outburst from Alec, no one spoke for the rest of the journey.

When they drew up outside the apartment, Alec said, "I'll leave you here. I have to go to another meeting." He kissed Mel perfunctorily, briefly shook Grace's hand and the car sped away, leaving the girls on the pavement.

Back in the apartment, Grace rushed in to the bathroom to brush her teeth, and try to wash away all traces of the residual taste of the man's mouth and of the unpleasant scene in the brothel. She then flung herself on the living-room couch, curled up in a foetal position with her head buried in her arms and began to shake violently.

Mel watched her for a few moments then sat down beside her on the couch. She held her close and gently stroked her hair.

Slowly, Grace turned to look up at Mel. "Do you think I will ever find him?" she asked. "I don't think I could go through that again. Those people were like ghouls; they would have watched that man paw me and enjoyed the spectacle. I've never seen such beastly people before and I never want to go through that again."

"That's what I tried to warn you about," Mel passed her a handkerchief, "does that mean you want to stop looking for Edward, then?"

"When I was in that hideous place, I just felt that I would have to give up. Even if he had been there, he would not have been the man I want to meet," Grace replied, sitting up and wiping her eyes, "so I suppose I should be glad, shouldn't I?"

"Well, it just shows that finding him is not going to be easy," Mel said, still holding on to Grace. To distract her, Mel said, "After that place, I think we need some coffee, don't you? Will you make it for us? And you could also make us some of that 'special menu' you did on Monday. I feel like eating at home tonight."

Suddenly active, Grace went off into the kitchen to put the kettle on and busy herself with the cooking.

While she was doing it, Mel stood in the doorway and watched. "I think we have just about enough in for that tomato dish, don't you? You must be feeling hungry after the way you were outside the club."

"Being sick, you mean? Ugh, yes and I could still do with something more to clean out my mouth. Have you got any of that Merlot wine left? I'd love some right now; alcohol is good for killing germs."

"Yes, there is another bottle, I'll go and get it."

When she returned, Mel poured a glass of wine for Grace and sat down at the kitchen table while she continued to prepare the meal. Mel's attempt at therapy was helping; Grace had stopped shivering and was beginning to return to her normal self.

"How do you feel about the search for Edward now?" Mel asked, as she leafed through a copy of Vogue, trying to make her question appear casual.

"Well, it might surprise you but I'm already feeling better and now, more than ever, I know that I need him. If he was here now, I would cook him a huge meal and we could all have a good laugh together."

"You're a true romantic, Grace," Mel sighed with a shrug of her shoulders. "I suppose I used to be like that. I always wanted meet a man who would love me just for myself - I still do!"

"Alec?"

"Well, yes, I suppose so. In his own way, Alec is certainly very attractive but I always wonder about him. Is it me he needs or just my body? You saw the way he kissed me. Afterwards, he just couldn't wait to get away. When he's like that, I wonder who he's going to."

"Why do you say that?"

Mel continued to look meditatively through her wine glass, rolling it around to diffract the light, and then said, "What is he doing now? Might he be saying the same things he says to me, but to some other woman?"

"Mel, don't you know him well enough to trust him?"

"How can I trust him? The work he does for Ricard means that he has to be dishonest - has to tell lies. That's what he gets paid for. I know he lies to me because I've found him out many times. It just seems to be in his nature."

"Maybe it's not his true nature," Grace said, "Maybe he has had to be dishonest to survive. In a different situation, he could well be the sort of man you could trust."

"Who knows, but somehow I doubt it. No, Grace, he will never be the dream man that your Edward is to you."

After the turbulence of the evening, the two girls ate the rest of the meal in silence and then went quietly off to bed.

CHAPTER THIRTEEN

A few days later, even before the girls were up and dressed, the phone rang. Mel picked it up and listened with growing excitement.

"That's marvellous, Alec!" she said. "I'll tell her straight away." She looked around for a pencil and jotted down the details. "She'll be so thrilled. We'll see you later this afternoon, you can tell us more. Thank you so much!"

She put down the 'phone and rushed into Grace's bedroom. "It's happened at last, Grace! He's done it, and I'm sure it's right this time. Alec is just going off to see one of his contacts who knows an address for an Edward Alleyne."

Grace sat up in bed, smiling with pleasure. "Does he know anything about him? What he looks like? How old he is?"

"Hold on, Grace. I know you want to know these things and I'm sure he could find them out, but we don't want him to start visiting the place himself. So far, he's just got the name via one of his contacts, but that's pretty impressive, I think." She continued, "What's more, I could go with you because Ricard has sent a message to Alec about being delayed in Africa for another week. We can only hope it's by getting a spear in his back." She laughed ironically. "But I guess you would sooner go alone."

"Mel, I hope you don't mind, but I really need to do this on my own."

"Don't worry. I understand, dear," Mel replied, in an almost maternal way.

Later that evening, Grace rushed to look out of the window when she heard the familiar sound of Alec's horn as he pulled up outside the apartment. Hoping to impress him, she had dressed herself in a fashionable outfit from Melanie's wardrobe. She opened the door expectantly, only to find Alec in a dishevelled state, with traces of blood on his face and shirt. In spite of his appearance, he seemed in good humour, and responded to Grace's outfit by commenting, "I see the French climate has had a good effect on you."

Grace laughed with him and echoed his joking mood with a quick response, "But not on you it would seem. Can we do anything to help? Your face looks a real mess." She took his arm to guide him into the apartment. "Mel is resting in her room, because we weren't expecting you till later, but I'll go and get her right away."

Just as she spoke, Mel came in to the lounge, looking bleary eyed. "Oh, Alec, whatever's happened to you?" she cried, and rushed across the room to encircle him protectively in her arms.

"I've just had to do a bit of sorting out on a client who tried to rob one of our girls - someone who was difficult to persuade."

Melanie hugged him. "Oh my God, Alec! Are you sure you're OK? You look the worse for wear."

"Well, let's put it this way; I am in much better condition than the difficult client."

"Why, what happened to him?" Melanie asked

"I'll just say he's not too well. I didn't hurt him that badly. He'll be Ok, but I don't suppose he'll be a client of ours ever again."

Melanie removed his creased jacket and said, "Let me clean you and your clothes, and then you must rest. Grace, can you get me a bowl of hot water?"

Alec, clearly still suffering slightly from shock, allowed himself to be guided to the sofa where he collapsed, his face wincing with pain. He sat there just gazing up at the ceiling through half-closed eyes and an occasional groan escaped his lips as he began to feel the effect of his many bruises. Grace came back from the kitchen with a bowl of hot water and went to sit with him while Mel helped him remove his jacket, unbuttoned his shirt and started to bathe his scars.

"Is there anything I can get you?" Grace asked.

"A double whisky would help."

Grace went to the drinks cabinet, poured a large glass of whisky and raised it to her nose. She grimaced at the unfamiliar smell and quickly passed the drink to Alec, who downed it thirstily.

"Looks to me as if another one would help even more." Grace said.

"No thanks, I only ever have one - the rules of the job," he replied with a smile. "But thanks, anyhow." He finished the dregs in the glass and gave it back to Grace.

Mel finished cleaning him up and gave him a lingering kiss on the one part of his cheek which was not bruised.

"I'll have a bit of a rest here for a while," he said with a groan.

As he lay down, his unbuttoned clothes gaped open to reveal his naked chest.

Grace looked away awkwardly, as Alec fumbled clumsily with the buttons on his shirt to cover himself. After a moment of silence he began to speak, but avoided eye contact with Grace.

"Before I forget, or before I fall asleep, a contact I have in the Lot region returned an enquiry I made last week. He says he's found out there's an artist who lives in a small town called St. Antonin."

Grace's eyes lit up and she drew her chair closer to the couch.

"And what has he told you about this artist?"

Alec looked up briefly, pleased and amused by her enthusiasm.

"Just some details about a man who is a painter who apparently has a son; but that was about as much information as I got." The way Alec spoke made it seem that he knew more. "They don't know very much about him, such as his actual address, or indeed anything much else, it seems. Apparently, he doesn't paint anymore, too old, perhaps. But at least, he's still there. I don't know if you're still interested after that fiasco in the night club?"

"Of course I'm still interested. Do tell me, what... what is this artist's name?"

Alec looked up to the ceiling, appearing to sift through his memory.

"Hmm... wait a bit now, I need to think." He cast his eyes round the room and frowned, to draw out the suspense. "Ah yes, that's it. Ruane. Yes, Artemus Ruane."

Grace leapt to her feet in amazement. "That must be him! That's Edward's father! What did you find out about Edward?"

Alec reached into his jacket pocket and fumbled with several sheets of paper, taking a brief look at each one, until he found the one he wanted. He handed it to Grace.

"Here, it is. Ruane lives in St Antonin, on the Aveyron. Nice part of the world, apparently. I've heard of it but never been there myself. My contact acquired this information from the bank manager in the village, who is what you might call 'a good friend'. He was able to pass on a little information about the father, but the strange thing is that there are almost no details of his son. He got the bank details for Ruane, but except that there is a son, nothing for him - no job, no school details, nothing. It's almost as if he's a ghost, or perhaps he's got a criminal record." He gave a wry smile. "The father certainly exists, but it's unusual, normally I get more details from this contact, but there seems to be no information about the son."

Grace quickly read the sheet of paper then gave Alec a grateful kiss and a crushing hug which made him grimace in pain.

Seeing him wince, Grace said, "Oh, I am sorry Alec. I forgot you're hurt, but you are fantastic! Thank you so much for doing this."

Leaning over, she hugged him again, rather more cautiously, and Alec responded by putting his uninjured arm carefully round her shoulder. He was clearly enjoying Grace's excitement at his latest news and, ignoring the earlier awkwardness between them, gave her a friendly kiss on the cheek. Mel returned to the room at that moment and pretended to take offence at the sight of Alec kissing Grace. "Hey, what's going on between you and my man?" she demanded, with a smile.

"Oh, Mel, he's done everything I could ask for!" Grace responded. "All the details are here." She held up the piece of paper.

"That calls for another drink, then." Mel declared, as she picked up Alec's glass.

He sat up gingerly and said, "I have already refused a second drink once, but I suppose I'm not going anywhere for a while so, perhaps I will after all. I certainly feel that I need it."

Mel poured a small whisky into the glass and held it to Alec's mouth while he drank it down gratefully.

"Alec's found the details of a man who could be Edward's father - Artemus Ruane. There can't be many artists of that name around, and even though Alec has not much detail, I know he has a son, so I am going to see Edward at last." Grace beamed with pleasure and leant over Mel to give Alec another kiss.

"Oh, Alec, you're brilliant!" Mel declared and also gave him a kiss.

"Well, don't go rushing to St. Antonin just yet. The details of the son are so vague that I'm a bit suspicious. Are you absolutely sure you want to go, Grace? You don't want another experience like the last time."

"I just have to go there as soon as I can," Grace stated firmly. "And another good thing is that it'll get me out of your hair and give you two some time together, before Ricard gets back."

"It'll certainly be safer than the first place you went. I don't know St. Antonin, but I'm told it's a lovely medieval town, not far from Albi, where Toulouse Lautrec grew up."

Mel, seeing Alec grimace as he tried to find a more comfortable position, got up from the couch and said, "My poor Alec, you must be in agony with all those bruises. Let me run the bath for you. A good soaking will make you feel better."

"No, no. I'll do it, you two stay together," Grace insisted and got up to run the bath. When it was full, she returned to find Alec undressed and in Mel's dressing gown.

Alec was obviously making the most of the attention Mel was giving him and followed her carefully into the bathroom where they fixed themselves another drink, set up some relaxing music on the gramophone, undressed and got into the bath together.

They were startled by the sound of the 'phone ringing. Grace, who was already packing her clothes in her room in readiness for her journey to St. Antonin, picked it up and listened to the voice on the other end. When she put it down, she rushed into the bathroom.

"Mel, Alec, you must get out and get dressed quickly."

"Why what's wrong? You look worried." Mel said.

"I don't know who was on the 'phone but he said Ricard is back and has heard about you and Alec, and he's on his way here."

The bathwater scattered as they jumped out, dried quickly and threw on their clothes. Alec appeared to have recovered sufficiently to be able to look after himself.

"How long before he gets here?" Alec asked

"He didn't say."

"Well, you shouldn't be here, Grace," Alec said." Finish packing and go. If he arrives before you've gone, just stay in your room."

A few minutes later, they heard a key in the lock and Ricard burst in. He was dressed entirely in black and was wearing a large hat which shielded his face and made him look even more menacing than Mel remembered.

Grace went to her room, shut the door and hurriedly finished her packing.

"Oh, Ricard, what a ... Ricard, how... how nice to see you," Mel stammered, and moved to put her arms around him. "What are you doing here so soon? I didn't think you'd be back yet."

Ricard thrust her violently aside and she fell back into a chair.

"Get out of my way, you bitch!" he shouted, and rushed straight at Alec, who struggled desperately in his grasp for a few moments. He eventually managed to break free and slipped past Ricard through the door and onto the balcony, looking for a means of escape.

Ricard quickly caught up with him and gripped fiercely him round the neck. The struggle continued until Alec lost his balance and fell back over the balcony but just managed to grab the handrail as he went over, and was able to lower himself onto the balcony below. From there, he caught hold of the drainpipe, slid down to the street and disappeared rapidly from sight.

Now Melanie rushed onto the balcony behind Ricard, with a wine bottle in her hand. "My God, what have you done? You've murdered him, you beast!" she screamed, springing forward and hitting him repeatedly with the bottle.

Ricard gripped hold of her wrist and shook her violently. "You whore! You'd cheat on me after all I've done for you? Get out of my way. I'm going after your precious boyfriend. He won't get far." He knocked the bottle from her grasp, smashing it on the floor, punched and kicked her to the ground and dashed off through the apartment and out of the still open door.

Mel was lying on the balcony, crying uncontrollably as Grace rushed from her room in response to her cries. She reached down to support Mel as she tried to get to her feet.

"Are you hurt badly, Mel?"

"No, I'll be bruised, but not too much," Mel replied. "But you must leave quickly. Ricard doesn't know you're here yet but he will be back and he'll probably bring one of his thugs with him next time."

"I can't leave you, Mel. Not when things are like this," Grace declared. She pulled Mel to her feet and sat her down in a chair.

"But you must leave, he could kill you. Nobody knows you are here. You'd wind up as just another suicide in the Seine. I can look after myself. I've been in worse situations than this."

Grace shuddered. "But what will you do?" she asked.

Mel caught her breath to calm herself. "I'll go and stay with a friend, and then try to find Alec before Ricard does. Neither of us can stay here."

"Well I've almost packed my bags already. I'll help you pack."

"Thanks, it would be a great help. We need to be out of this place as soon as we can."

Within fifteen minutes, they were ready to leave, with Mel lugging a case into which she had thrown as much as she could, including jewellery and money, and Grace carrying all her baggage. Once outside, they hailed a taxi. Mel gave the driver an address and they moved off through dismal streets, eventually pulling up outside a darkened house. The driver helped them out with their bags and Melanie rang the doorbell, which was opened almost immediately by a voluptuously clad woman.

"That was quick, Beatrice," Mel said.

"I saw you pull up with your bags and all. It seemed so strange so I came down straight away. Is there something wrong? Come in, quick. How can I help you, Madame Ricard?" she inquired in a cool voice.

"It's not Madame Ricard and it never was. That was just Ricard showing off, so you can forget all that formality now. It's just 'Mel', as it always was when I lived here. We've come to get away from Ricard. Can we come in?" Mel asked, and when Beatrice stood back, began dragging their cases through the door.

"Thank God. I'd always thought you were too nice for that pig. I thought he was on one of his Africa safaris. Is he back already, then?"

Mel nodded as the two girls made their way into the dark passageway.

"I thought he was still going to be away for a few more weeks. What brought him back? I've had lots more clients with him out of the way. And I've enjoyed the freedom from his crooks peering over my shoulder all the time," Beatrice said as she led the way into the house.

"You and me both! Somebody must have ratted on Alec. Ricard is back to bust him, and me I as well, I shouldn't wonder," Mel replied gloomily, as they walked into a dark and dingy room, pervaded by a stale smell of cooking.

They put their cases down gratefully. Without thinking, Grace wrinkled her nose up at the smell.

Beatrice, noticing her reaction, stared suspiciously at Grace for several seconds, and then said, "Who's this? She doesn't look like one of Ricard's girls."

"She's not. Grace is from England; a friend who's been staying with me."

Beatrice took Grace's hand and in a teasing tone said, "Hello, dear, you find yourself somewhere to sit, then. Yes, we'll just chuck that washing on the floor, it won't harm." She began to clear the chairs. "It's my night off. I was thinking I'll have to do some washing," she turned to Grace. "I'm Beatrice, a 'working' girl. Melanie and me used to work here together."

"OK, OK, let's not go into detail," Mel said, laughing. "I just want to know whether Grace and I can stay the night."

Beatrice frowned momentarily, then her face cleared and she said, "Well, you won't be very comfortable and it's not what you've been used to, but if you don't mind that, I can find somewhere for you." She looked around the room with her hand on her chin, thinking. "Yes, one of you can stay on the couch, and one can have a bed. You'll have to fight it out between you. It's not marvellous and certainly not as nice as up there in Ponceville, Mel."

"Ponceville?" Grace frowned.

"That's what she calls my flat," Mel grinned. "But, thank you, Beatrice, I was sure we could rely on you. We always used to get on well, Beatrice and me," she said to Grace, "which is lucky for us now."

Removing a few more bits of clutter, the girls flopped out into the chairs, which creaked under them.

"You still haven't had the chairs fixed yet then, Beatrice," Mel chuckled. I remember how the neighbours used to complain when you had clients in."

"Sod 'em, I say. They're no better than they ought to be," Beatrice grinned. "Bet you need a drink. I haven't got much in, though. The last customer had such a thirst! Don't really know why he came, all he

191

wanted to do was drink. Nice, though, and he paid well. There's no food, only leftovers."

"We've already eaten," she lied, "but a drink would do us nicely."

While Beatrice busied herself with drinks in the next room, Mel turned to face Grace to tell her about her relationship with Ricard.

"I met that creature Ricard," she began, "after I'd been here with Beatrice for a few weeks. I stayed here whenever I was 'working'". She smiled knowingly at Grace. "When I first met Ricard, it seemed like a passport to a better life." She grimaced. "The passport turned out to be to prison and I hated being tied to him. Living where I did was like being in a straightjacket. I never thought I'd say this, but," she called through the open door at the back view of her old friend, "it's really nice to be back here with you Beatrice, free to breathe,"

After a clattering of things in the kitchenette, Beatrice came in with a tray of drinks and biscuits and put them on the floor in front of them.

"You can't hate that bastard more than me. Look at me," she said, pirouetting in front of them. "I'm past my best so he tossed me out." She passed the drinks round. "But I manage. I make more than I did with his lot. He used to send me posh people and I never knew what to talk about. Different sort now, more down-to-earth, I say. You can have a cup of coffee with 'em afterwards and they tell you about their wives and families. Done me good 'as Ricard. Got one fellow – bloke with an unhappy marriage - asking if he can live with me. I'm not sure yet, but he seems all right. Got a good job driving a bus all over the country. Sometimes goes abroad even. Said he'd take me with him when there's a spare seat. What d'you think about that, me 'aving an holiday?"

"Sounds very nice, but what would you do about your work in this place, Beatrice?" Mel waved her hand round the room.

"Oh, he don't mind that. Says with his money, we'd make a tidy packet between us." She laughed showing tobacco-stained teeth. "Imagine that! Me, Beatrice Lalonde! Him and me could actually buy a place. What d'you think to that, Lady Melanie? " She grinned toothily again and turning to Grace, said, "I always called her that; she's always so smart, see? The posh clients always liked her for it." Turning back to Mel, she added, "If Charlie - that's the bus driver's name - if Charlie and me get a place, there'd always be a job for you, Mel." she laughed so loudly that it started her coughing.

"Yes, and you'd introduce me to another man like Ricard and I'd wind up hating him just as much." Mel shuddered. "A savage. He hasn't got a decent thought in his head."

"Any one who thinks like that about him is a friend of mine, Mel." She looked at Grace. "And that goes for you too, Grace."

"You're looking tired, Grace." Mel said. "Go and get to bed in the other room. I'll find somewhere to sleep here after I've had a drink with Beatrice."

Later that night, in the early hours, Mel and Beatrice were still seated at a table in the main room. Mel's make-up was heavily smudged, and she was becoming steadily drunker. At intervals, she and Beatrice laughed raucously as they recounted old times.

Grace could not get to sleep with the laughter and loud conversation from the next room and the excitement about the possibility of seeing Edward, as well as the incident with Ricard. The shabby, hard bed creaked under her every time she moved. Her thoughts revolving around Edward; images of him kept flashing into her mind, and it seemed as if he was trying to say something to her.

In the morning, after her fitful sleep, Grace was awakened by the sunlight fighting its way through a dirty skylight. Wide awake in an instant, she sat up in bed then put her feet to the ground, wondering what to do. As she tiptoed through the door into the next room, she saw Mel and Beatrice collapsed in the chairs where they had been talking the night before. Mel was looking terrible. Around her on the floor, cigarette butts, ash and empty bottles had been dropped. Grace crept past them, into the bathroom and turned on the shower. The noise woke Mel and she peered blearily through the opened door at Grace's silhouette against the shower curtain.

Grace emerged from the shower, dried herself on a used towel and returned to the lounge, still only partly dressed.

Mel was now stretched out on the sofa, eyes half-open, obviously badly hung-over. Grace stepped over her outstretched legs to get into the kitchenette, where she boiled a kettle and made coffee for herself and Mel. Beatrice was still slumped in the other chair, and looked as though she would be there for the rest of the day.

Slowly, Mel sipped from the mug. "Thanks, Grace, I needed that. God, what a night! Beatrice must have told me practically her whole life story. I didn't like to tell her that I've heard it all before. She can certainly put it away, too. I've never drunk so much Vermouth before and, the way my head is feeling, I hope I never do again. I don't even like the stuff but she found a stash in the back of a cupboard and she wouldn't let me refuse." Mel gradually shook off the effects of the drink sufficiently to remember their situation. She turned to Grace and said, "Grace, you should leave before things get any worse."

"I know, but why don't you come with me? We can find somewhere for you where I'm going."

"I'd love to, but you need to be on your own and I must find Alec."

"Where will you go then?"

"I'll stay here for a couple more hours before Beatrice's clients start ringing." She smiled and explained, "Beatrice does the day shift, you see – at least she always used to. That's if she manages to wake up, of course." Mel poured herself some strong coffee and then, looking over the rim of the mug, continued, "I just wish I was in your shoes, Grace; just starting out on my first love affair." She looked at her watch. "You'd better go right now, it's getting late and I need to get myself sorted out to find Alec." She searched in her handbag for a pen. "Write to me at this address when you have found Edward. I won't be staying here because Ricard would soon find me, but I'll get Beatrice to send on any post that comes. I'll let you know where I'm staying after I've found Alec and sorted things out with him. We'll have to do something pretty drastic. We could even go to his home in England for a time, I suppose. It depends on how he feels."

"About you, you mean?"

"That's exactly what I mean," she nodded. She hunted around for paper and scribbled down the address, which she carefully placed in Grace's case.

"Are you sure you'll be all right?" Grace asked, putting on her clothes and top coat.

"I'll be surer once I find Alec. I've got a sort of idea where he'll be and it won't be anywhere Ricard would think of looking." She sighed. "It's all pretty bloody, I know, but now I've got away, I feel so relieved. That place was like a fur-lined coffin; there were so many things I loved about it and I may never be as well off again. But it was just impossible; I never knew what mood Ricard would be in. To him I was just a piece of useful furniture for him to crap on. I always knew that one day he would tire of me. I'm getting on a bit now, not like Beatrice, I know, but most of his girls are much younger. He likes them before they are twenty." She smiled as she looked at Grace. "I bet he'd take to you though."

"I don't think he's quite what I am looking for, thank you very much," Grace said, laughing. "But I am glad to see you joking again."

"Thank you, yes. I think you, and even Beatrice in a funny sort of way, have both helped me to deal with whatever is coming my way."

"Whatever I've been able to do is nothing compared to what you've done for me. I shall never forget your kindness, Mel." Grace put her arms round Mel and kissed her. "Please thank Alec for me?"

She picked up her bags, kissed Mel and left quickly to avoid bursting into tears. Mel watched from the window as Grace hailed a passing taxi and sped off.

CHAPTER FOURTEEN

As she boarded the train for St. Antonin, Grace was filled with conflicting emotions; extreme sadness on leaving Mel at a time when she was in so much trouble and extreme elation at getting on with the journey that she felt sure would end in her meeting Edward. Once the train had left Paris, the journey took her through periods of sunshine interspersed with violent thunderstorms. With each change in the weather, her mood altered from optimism in the sunshine to apprehension as storms lashed the train. She began to feel concerned that she was being both foolish and selfish; first of all to have left her mother, and now Mel, when they both seemed to need her most. Many times on the long journey, she drifted off to sleep and her dreams were filled with images of Edward, talking, smiling and dancing in the countryside with her.

After a long journey, changing several times, she finally woke with a jolt as the train pulled into the station in a town not far from St. Antonin. A porter took her bags and hailed her a taxi. She jumped in, asked the driver to take her to a hotel in St. Antonin, and sat back, watching the road as it snaked through terrifyingly steep limestone gorges. At the top of two of the gorges were the small fortified Bastide towns of Bruniquel and Penn, which she had read had been built by the British for defence.

The taxi crossed a bridge across the river Aveyron and pulled up in a square in the town of St. Antonin. Here the driver told Grace that he could not drive down the narrow street she wanted so she would have to walk. She got out and was overcome with the beauty of the mediaeval town, with its stone houses and beautiful church. She worked out where she was from the directions given her by the taxi driver, and set off for the hotel.

At the hotel, she enquired from the girl at reception if she knew where the artist Artemus Ruane lived. The girl herself was unable to help but happily went off to ask the proprietor and, after a few minutes, she returned with the necessary directions.

Hardly able to contain her excitement, Grace went to her room to have a quick bath to wash away the grime from the smoky train journey. Suitably refreshed, and with pounding heart, she finally set off on what she hoped would be the last leg of her long quest. She followed the directions she had been given, and soon arrived in a small square, at one corner of which was a large building. She surveyed the building for a few moments, shivering with excitement at the realisation that she might be at the end of her journey, and that she could well find Edward inside.

The place was quiet with no one around, and her footsteps echoed around the square as she nervously approached the front door. Her face paled and her legs became shaky. She was overcome with a sense of panic and had to force herself to continue walking up to the door.

For several minutes, she just stood there, taking deep breaths, trying to calm her racing heart and summon up enough resolve to knock. With a sudden burst of determination, she raised her hand to the large iron knocker and banged it firmly. For what seemed ages there was no sound from inside the house. She glanced behind her at the deserted square and, for a moment, a feeling of panic made her want to turn back to the hotel, have a long sleep and try again the next day. Instead, she found her hand raised to drop the heavy knocker once more. Her heart missed a beat when a man's voice shouted from behind the door.

"Un instant. Un moment." The voice sounded irritated.

The door was partly opened and, looking into the darkness beyond the door, Grace was just able to make out the stooping figure of an old man.

"Qu'est ce que vous voulez?"

"Pardon, monsieur, mais je cherche Monsieur Artemus Ruane. Est-ce qu'il demeure ici, s'il vous plaît?"

"Peut-être, mais porquoi cherchez vous cet homme?"

"Je suis venu le voir."

"Vous connaissez cet homme?"

"Non."

"Alors, pourquoi voulez-vous le voir?"

Grace was embarrassed because she was unsure of the French words but, after thinking hard for a moment, said "Je pense que je pourrais le savoir."

"Et vous etes…?"

"Je viens d'Angleterre."

"Ah, Angleterre. Angleterre – bien, attendez un instant." The door swung fully open to reveal the older man, dressed in loosely flowing clothes, supporting himself against the wall with an outstretched hand and breathing heavily from the exertion. For some time, he breathed with difficulty, while Grace waited for him to speak.

"You must be Grace," he said haltingly. "I am Artemus." He took her hand and pulled it gently to indicate that she should come in to the hall.

"However do you know my name?" Grace frowned.

"We don't get that many visitors now, you know."

"But, you knew my name!"

"A woman rang me and told me you would be coming today."

Grace walked in to the hallway and waited while Artemus struggled to close the door.

"A woman rang?" Grace queried when the door was shut. "Who was she? Did she give her name?"

"I have no idea who she was, and no, she didn't give her name. She sounded English, though," he replied, panting hard as he walked slowly along the corridor. "Her voice did sound familiar and I've been racking my brains trying to recall where I'd heard it before. But I can't remember who it was. The mind sometimes plays tricks, especially when you get older." He continued slowly down the corridor, leaving Grace standing at the closed door.

"I haven't been in England for some time you see. It's quite a treat speaking English again. Languages are not my forte and I've never been able to speak French grammatically." Noticing Grace still waiting at the door he said, "Sorry, I should have told you to come on in."

"I just can't think who could have called you," Grace pondered. "As far as I can see, no one knew I was coming to this house. Did she sound young?" she continued, thinking that perhaps Mel had called.

"No, she didn't sound young. Seemed to me like an older woman."

"An older woman?" Grace shrugged her shoulders as she stood awkwardly at the doorway to the lounge, waiting for Artemus to catch up with her.

200

Suddenly, Artemus realised her predicament and moving slowly to stand aside, said. "I'm sorry, my dear, I'm forgetting my manners again. Do go in and sit down." She looked back as she entered and saw him struggling back up the corridor to push the heavy lock back into place on the front door.

"You go ahead, Grace, and find somewhere to sit. I'll follow you at my own pace," he called.

Instead of doing as he asked, Grace walked back, took his arm and supported him along the passageway. "Are you unwell?" she asked.

"Unwell? Yes, a little, but not in pain; just some nerve thing, that's all."

When they reached the room at the end of the hall once more, Artemus moved slightly ahead and said, "Do please sit down."

Grace looked round and saw that there were glasses and a jug on the table in the next room.

Following her gaze, Artemus said, "When the woman who rang told me you were coming, I had some drinks made for us by the housekeeper. They're in the studio, which I sometimes use as a lounge."

They walked into the room where the table was laid. It was flooded with sunshine. Grace looked around and saw a half completed painting of a woman on the easel. Before sitting down, she went to it to examine it more closely.

"That is beautiful, "Grace said. "Do you mind if I move it so I can see it better?"

"Not at all, it's only there because it catches the sunlight in the morning." Artemus replied, as he collapsed into the couch. "And when you've done that, please get yourself something to eat and drink and sit down beside me. Could you pour me a glass of lemon, too? Help yourself to anything you want, but nothing for me, as I've had lunch and my appetite is pretty meagre these days."

"Of course," Grace said, pleased to be asked to help and beginning to feel more relaxed. She gathered a few things to eat onto a plate, poured lemonade into glasses and placed them on the small table in front of Artemus. She returned to the painting, picked it up and turned it to catch the sun.

"The paint is quite dry but the image is only part finished, it seems," she commented.

"Yes," Artemus smiled wryly, "like so much in this house." He wondered if he should add 'in my life' but decided that would be too melodramatic.

Grace put the painting back on the easel, picked up their drinks and settled down next to him on the couch. After sipping a little of the cordial, he said, "That woman who rang said you were here looking for someone. I don't know how I can help. My circle of acquaintances is small and gets ever smaller, so I don't suppose I can be of much assistance, but it is nice that you've come to visit from such a long way. You came by train, I suppose. What sort of journey did you have?"

"It was a magical journey, full of light and shade, sun and storms, and I slept and dreamt a lot as well," Grace replied, taking another sip from her glass. She gazed in fascination around Artemus' studio. "This is a wonderful room. It must be marvellous to paint in such good light," she continued, nodding in the direction of the painting.

"I'm afraid my skills are deserting me. I don't paint much any more."

Grace was on the point of asking about Edward but felt that a little more polite conversation was called for first. She looked around and saw that the room was almost empty, except for the one painting and dozens of books lying around the floor.

"Do you read a lot?" she asked.

"I do still read quite a bit, but rather less than I used to," he replied, glancing ruefully at the pile beside him. "But I do love to have books around. The sight of them, the feel of them and most of all, the information they contain, still give me so much pleasure. Sometimes I just rest my hand on one of the leather bindings to feel the power of knowledge inside. "

"You have only the one painting in this room. Why is that? I would have expected you to have the whole house full of your paintings."

Artemus looked around the bare walls of the room. "These walls, this house and my morning studio at the back certainly were filled with my paintings not so long ago."

"So, why not now?"

A look of sadness came over his face. Slowly, he raised his right arm, supported by the other arm and held it out in front of him. When he lowered the left arm, Grace saw that his right arm was shaking uncontrollably. "Can you see why I cannot do it anymore?" he said, with a sad smile. "Painting for me is an addiction, like alcohol is for some other people. But whereas they are able to indulge their craving even until death, I cannot." He raised his hand and put his finger to his temple. "In here, I can still paint. Every day I dream. Every day, a new scene comes into my mind. But it never gets out." He raised his shaking arm again and said, "This is what stops me. I last painted nearly a year ago. When I stopped, it was because my work was appalling. And it had been appalling for at least a year before that. My gallery claimed that I was experimenting with new styles and, for a time the subterfuge worked. They called it my 'Softer Edge Period' and contrasted it with my 'Chiselcut Period'. People still bought 'Artemus Ruane' because they thought they would increase in value and sell as they always had." He looked around at the room and pointed. "You see on the walls, those lighter areas where my paintings used to hang. I suppose I should consider myself lucky. I had every room in this house, and my studio and the attic, filled with my work.

They are my pension, now. Each month, I sell one or more. Ironically, now my regular clients know that I can no longer paint, the old ones have gone up in value." He smiled wryly. "It's what in England they call a double-edged sword."

"How sad," Grace said," I've never been an artist, but I do have a need to create in other ways. If I am prevented, I become desolate, so I understand how you feel." Looking over at the table, she said. "Shall I pour some more drink?"

"I'm sorry," Artemus said. "Once again my bad manners, I'm afraid. There's a flask of coffee or tea as well as the cordial, and you haven't yet eaten any of the things that my housekeeper, Claudine made specially."

Grace picked up the flask and savoured the aroma of coffee. "Would you like some?" she asked Artemus, and when he nodded, she continued, "And how about one of these marvellous-looking biscuits?"

"You help yourself, my dear. They aren't for me. I'm not supposed to eat wheat. The quacks have discovered it's not good for me, so Claudine only cooks them when we have friends in."

"Am I a friend already then?" Grace smiled, glancing over her shoulder as she poured.

"I hope so," Artemus replied, and smiling to himself, continued, "I'm just admiring the way you can pour a drink while looking away. I ceased being able to do that a long while ago."

She passed him his cup and seeing that his hand was shaking, held his wrist while he raised the cup to his lips.

After drinking, he laughed loudly and said, "Well, Grace, that's the action of a real friend. I've had lots of people in here - important people - people with lots of money, as well as some ordinary people. They've all sat in that chair there," he nodded in the direction of an easy chair. "They've sat there and watched me try to drink, and watched me spill drink on my clothes. It was obvious that they were embarrassed but they would look away and say nothing, pretending not to notice."

He drank noisily spilling the liquid. Grace mopped his mouth with a napkin. He nodded his thanks over the shaking cup and spilled a little more.

"Tell me why you've come to see me, Grace. Is it me, or my painting? You must have a very strong reason to come here. Not many people bother now." He looked down at himself and around the room. "Probably because of the messy state I get in," he laughed again, amused at his joke. "I don't care, though. Most of them came because they thought they could make money out of me. And I've noticed that the sort of people who only want to make money never smile and certainly never laugh when I try to joke with them."

"I'll make a point of laughing at your jokes, then" Grace replied with a smile. "I've had little humour in my life so far. There wasn't much of it in Loriston."

"Loriston?" Artemus asked. "Why do you say that name? Is it just a little joke?"

"Oh, I grew up in Loriston and lived there up until a couple of months ago."

"Did you, really? That's quite a coincidence, you see, I once lived there too." His face clouded. "I spent what were probably my happiest times there." With his head shaking as though he was constantly nodding approval, he turned to look more closely at Grace. "What is your family name?"

"Belari."

"Belari? The Reverend Belari? You're his daughter?" he almost shouted. " I'm glad I wasn't told that!"

"Why?"

"I have never found it in my heart to hate anyone but that priest that you would call father was the one person whom I came closest to hating."

"Whatever did he do to you?"

"What did he do? He took away what I lived for; that was what he did."

"How could he do that?" Grace asked, frowning.

"You're probably a little too young to have experienced an all-consuming love, but that was what I had in Loriston." His breath came in ever more laboured bursts, turning his words into a staccato rhythm. "I never expected it to happen to me, but it did and it was the most beautiful experience of my spoilt life." He looked in the direction of the part finished painting. "Your father destroyed it."

"Destroyed your love? I'm sorry, I just don't understand. How was he able to do that?" she asked, "and who it was that you loved so much?" sure that he would tell her that it was Zelda.

206

"I'll show you if you pass me that book on the table," was his response. "Can you reach it for me?"

Grace went to the table, picked up the book and handed it to him. Artemus struggled for a moment with a clasp on the side of the book, but being unable to open it, he passed it over to Grace. When she opened it, she saw that it was not a book after all, it was a box. Inside was a single letter, crumpled with use. She took it out and gave it to Artemus.

"No, I'd like you to read it. I've read it so many times that I almost know every word.

"You don't mind me reading it, it looks like a personal letter?"

"It is personal," Artemus nodded, "but I would still like you to read it. It's a letter from someone I knew, called Zelda."

Grace raised her eyebrows. "Zelda Alleyne?" she inquired.

"You know about Zelda then? How was that?" he said, raising his eyebrows in surprise. "I can't imagine that your father told you about her," he paused to catch his breath, "she meant more to me than anyone else ever has." He looked down at the palms of his shaking hands. "I have been blessed or cursed with a sensitivity which few people understand. Most people filter out sensations, but I don't. It is all there for me; I notice everything, everyone's tear, everyone's smile, the slightest significant movement of a hand, the smallest frown. I wonder about what it all means when I see the dawn bringing new scenes; when I see the sunset, closing up the day, it makes me feel part of the God of Nature. It is a gift that I think few people seem to have, but that gift has meant that there are not many people I can communicate with. They just don't understand. They see the grand picture, not the brush strokes that go into making it." He spread his hands apart. "So it has meant that I have always been alone; there was never anyone I could tell my feelings to, because most people are too superficial and my feelings go from the top of my head to my extremities. I feel them but I can't explain them. That's always the way I was, and it was the way I became after Zelda died. She was the only one who felt sensations as deeply as I do. When I was going through turmoil at the sight of something beautiful, she would see it too. She would put her hand on mine and, without any words passing between us, would make me aware in her silence that she felt exactly as I did. What you have there is a letter she sent me when she was going through a bad time." He raised his eyes and continued, "The letter will let you see the depths of love, and why I feel the way I do about your father."

"But you said that if you had known before I came that I was his daughter, you wouldn't have seen me." Grace looked at him questioningly. "Does that mean you've now forgiven me for being his daughter?"

"Now I've met you, it is obvious that you are not at all like him."

Feeling quite relieved at hearing such an encouraging remark from Artemus, Grace began a careful examination of the letter, and noticed that it had been torn and stuck with tape in several places. She started to read it to herself.

"No, no," Artemus cried. "Read it to me, please."

"You really want me to read it aloud?"

"I do. You see, it has never been read by anyone else." He reached out and with a shaking hand, touched her shoulder. "And in a way, your voice is like hers although she was French and you are English. Please, I'd like to hear you read it to me, if you would."

The paper crackled in her hands as she straightened it out.

"It's from The School House," she read. "'To my Dearest Love...'" She let her eyes run down the page and then looking up at him, said. "Are you sure you want me to read this, Artemus? It is only for you to read, I think."

"And, until now, it always has been. Yes, I do want you to read it, please." He touched her hand again. "She is gone now but I think if she is here in spirit, she would like you to read it."

"Why? I don't understand why you would want me to read what can only have been meant for you."

"I think you will see how we were to each other from her letter. You are the Reverend's daughter; look on it as expiation."

Grace looked puzzled, trying to understand what he was saying but, slowly and in a quiet voice, she began.

'I want to tell you this, dear man.

When we are together and are so happy, all the time I am with you, I can think of no one else and nothing else. At these times, it seems that words are unnecessary. But words are there in my mind and all the time when you smile at me, when you look at me, when you touch me, the words in my mind are saying. 'I love you so. Let this go on forever. I never want to leave you. To be away from you for even a moment is a torment.'

And when you are painting, especially when you are painting a picture of me, my spirit links with yours so that I know what paradise must be like. But this love has suffused me. 'At the going down of the sun and in the morning,' I will remember you. During the night and throughout the day, even when I am in school teaching the children, your mind is my mind and your hands seem to caress me. I am so overcome by the sensation that I wonder the children do not raise their hands and ask 'Please Miss Alleyne, why are you so. Why do you glow and light up the room?'

I have read novels and poetry of the Victorian period when love was never more romanticised, but almost nothing I have read comes even close to the feelings I have when I am with you. Let me quote Elizabeth Barrett Browning. She comes closer than anyone else to my feelings.

'How do I love thee? Let me count the ways
I love thee to the depth and breadth and height
My soul can reach, when feeling out of sight
For the ends of being and idle Grace.
I love thee to the level of everyday's
Most quiet need by sun and candlelight.
I love thee freely as men strive for right;
I love thee purely as they turn from praise
I love thee with the passion put to use
In my old griefs and with my childhood's faith.
I love thee with a love I seemed to lose
With my lost saints, - I love thee with the breath,
Smiles and tears of all my life – and, if God choose,
I shall but love thee better after death.'

I wish Artemus, my heart, that I shall always love thee as Elizabeth loved Robert Browning. Yes, I know *that you are disturbed by my adulation; that your masculinity feels uncomfortable to be so adored. I know that, although your painting is so full of love it is plain for anyone to see, that is where it stays - in the painting! In real life, you do not want to be constantly adored. But I can't help myself and I can't change. Even if you turned away and went back to the other women in your life, Eva, Sasha, Alexei – any of them – I would not mind, because I have shared you in all the places a woman desires, but most of all, in my heart.*

Good night, my dear love. Take me with you everywhere.

Zelda.'

When Grace had finished reading, she was unable to speak, overcome with sadness.

When she could speak, she said in a voice shaking with sadness. "So sad! She died, Artemus?"

Artemus nodded silently, looking at the floor and said, "Before the year was out, only seven months after writing that letter." He cast his gaze down. "She didn't know that at the time she wrote it, she was expecting our child."

"Edward?"

"Edward, yes, you've heard of my son? She died giving him life."

Grace was lost for words, aware that this was certainly not the time to tell him that Edward was her only reason for being there. She had already examined the room in detail, desperately searching for any sign that he might still be around.

"But, Artemus, how fortunate to be loved with Zelda's love; if I can be so fortunate one day, I will die happy." She said, "But what did my father do which made you dislike him so much?"

211

Artemus sighed and slowly shook his head. "It is hard to talk about it to you, his daughter. It may be unfair of me to say this but I think he, more than anyone, was responsible for her death. The 'Reverend'," as he said the name, his face distorted, "was a governor at the school where Zelda taught. It had become obvious that she was pregnant. Your father called her into the office at the school and what he said destroyed her in front of the headmistress. 'This woman cannot stay another minute in this school. She will corrupt the children and infect our community with evil.' The headmistress, who was actually very fond of Zelda, was weak when confronted by the priest who brought with him the wrath of God. She allowed Zelda to be taken from the school. To Zelda, religion was very important, you see and to be rebuked by Belari made her feel so ashamed that she felt herself to be a sinner. She was put on a train with a few things and did not even have time to come to tell me what had happened. Her things were collected from the house she rented and were to be sent to her. But the headmistress was ashamed and sad to see Zelda treated so badly. She personally took Zelda's belongings to the house her sister owned and where Zelda remained until our son was born."

"Did you hear from her, while she was there?"

"I did, yes; the headmistress brought me letters from her, but only on condition that she did not put her address on it. You see, I was blamed for corrupting her. Your Reverend had ruled that I should never be allowed to see her again," Artemus put his head in his hands and in a muffled voice, said, "and I never did see her again, even though I tried. God knows I tried, but I had no idea which town she had been sent to, and even if I had, I would not have known the address." After a while, he looked up and said, "So you can see that I have no love for the man who calls himself your father.

Grace nodded. "Yes, Artemus, I understand."

She put her hand on his. "I know it is wrong to feel the way I do about a parent but it is, and always has been, very difficult for me to love him. And now I have left home, I may never see him again. He is so alien to me that I wonder sometimes if he is my real father."

Artemus looked up quickly, his lips pursed. "Did you mother say that to you?"

"My mother? Did you know her?"

"Yes, I knew her. She helped a lot after Zelda died. It was not easy because your father wasn't away for long but we met whenever possible. She helped me to accept the situation as much as it was possible." He looked up. "She helped me and it also helped her to talk about her own life."

"Did she mention a man, Raphael?"

"'You know about Raphael?" Artemus leaned back in his chair for support.

"Yes, she told me what had happened. Of course, I never knew Raphael but, from what she told me, you are more like him than the man you call 'father'."

"Do you mean you think I might be the daughter of Raphael?"

"I'm not saying that, because I don't know. But what I do feel sure about is that your mother is convinced that you are Raphael's daughter and, from what I have heard of Raphael, you have a lot more in common with him that you have with Belari."

"I'd like to meet Raphael," she said. "In a funny sort of way, I am convinced I will one day, but mother told me that even she had no way of contacting him."

"I think you should accept that meeting him is probably impossible. No one knows anything about him; he could well be dead. He was much older than your mother. Did she tell you that?"

"No, I had no idea. I just assumed that he was about her age."

"No, he was old enough to be her father, probably about sixty, she told me."

"Whatever his age, she loved him more than anyone else she had ever met."

"I think that too, whenever we spoke, Raphael was always part of the conversation," obviously tired, he leaned his head back, "I think it's time you told me what you want here in St. Antonin."

"Edward..." she began hesitantly.

"Edward, yes, what about him?"

"Is he here? I want to meet him."

"Why should you want to meet him? You've never seen him in Loriston, have you?"

"No I never did but I just know I must meet him. Is he here?"

"No, he is not here but he doesn't live far away, why?"

"Could I meet him now?"

"Not tonight. He isn't here and there are reasons why you can't see him, which will become clear to you. Also, he may not want to see you... we never know."

"Why wouldn't he want to see me?" Grace's voice began to shake in her anxiety. "I feel that I know him already. In my mind I've talked to him a lot."

"Imagination is not enough. I would need to be sure that you are ready to meet him. He doesn't meet many people."

"What do you mean? I don't understand. Is he too important to see me or something?"

"He is away for the next couple of days. When he returns, he may see you, but if things go wrong he may not."

"But this is all so strange. Is there some sort of mystery about him that requires me to answer all these questions?"

"Let's say no more tonight, Grace. I'm sorry but I am very tired. This illness, you see. I'd like you to leave me now. "

"I'm sorry, Artemus, it's just that I've come such a long way and it means so much to me but, I will wait. I'll go now. Is there anything I can do for you before I go?"

"No thank you, Grace, my dear. I am able to manage on my own, even though I don't do it very well." He smiled, looking down at his unkempt appearance. "I don't get up very early but come and see me around mid-morning. Claudine will have been in and tidied up by then and gone home to look after her own family."

Grace helped him out of the chair and waited for a few moments as he struggled to move around, before walking back to the hotel.

CHAPTER FIFTEEN

The next morning, Grace went through the same procedure, lifting the big knocker and waiting for Artemus to struggle to the door. When he was settled down she sat in the chair beside him.

"Grace, I must thank you for being so patient yesterday. I know you will have been wondering why you couldn't meet Edward straight away."

"I couldn't sleep at all last night," Grace replied. "Meeting him means so much to me."

"I can't pretend to understand your feelings for him, but I can see that you are anxious to meet him. I just want to make sure you are properly prepared." Artemus placed his hands together, held his fingertips to his lips and thought for a while. "You must know that he is not like other people. He is very different, in ways you may find puzzling and, perhaps, distressing."

"Is that what you conveyed in your painting of him? He certainly does look mysterious," Grace said, frowning thoughtfully. "Do you think that missing his mother has had an effect on him?"

"No, that's not the only reason. I've tried to be both mother and father to him. I've tried everything I could think of but, somehow, I always failed. I could never get close to him as a parent should. He is always silent when I am around. And yet, he looks at me with what seems to me to be affection," he paused. "He is very delicately balanced and you won't be able to see him until I think it is right."

Grace frowned, "I don't understand, why is he like he is?"

"I was told that Zelda was so unhappy before he was born that she went into depression, and the birth was very difficult. The doctor did all he could to encourage her but she was in such pain that he gave her a sedative. I think it was the forceps the doctor used in the delivery that damaged him." Artemus paused as though gathering strength. "She lost so much blood that she never regained consciousness."

"Artemus, I'm so sorry." Grace breathed heavily, holding back tears. "Was… was the doctor at fault?"

"I have never felt there was any value in blaming anyone. He was doing the best he could. After she died, he found where I lived, came to me and wept with remorse. I had never before seen a man weep like that. He put his arms round me and I found myself comforting him. Strangely, his grief seemed to help me to accept her death, at least for a short time."

"Did he bring Edward to you?"

"The headmistress's sister brought him; she had had a big family and told me how to care for him. Edward looked very like his mother, even from a few days old. He was so beautiful, so very beautiful, even as a baby, he looked like Zelda. Without him, I would not have wanted to live."

"He is beautiful to me, too, but does his beauty affect you, a man, in the same way?" Grace asked.

"He is my son, that would be enough, but I am also an artist. I see beauty in faces whether they are female or male." He turned to her. "As soon as I saw you, I knew that I'd love to be able to paint you, but..." He held up his shaking hands. "I know I couldn't."

Grace took hold of his hand and, in a moment of inspiration, said "But I could, Artemus. I could be your hands. Every great artist has his school. I could be yours. I don't know how it would work; I just know we will be able do it by painting together." She placed both her hands on his. "You see, mine are steady. If I hold your hand, it becomes steady. Do you see? You could guide my hand; you could show me the brush strokes you would make. I'd love to paint you. You have a wonderful face. Let's do a 'self portrait' of you!"

"My God, Grace, what an idea, I've never heard of anyone doing such a thing before, but we could try, I think you could be right; I think we might be able to do it together."

"Of course we can do it, Artemus. I don't know how good it will be to start with but, even if it takes ages, we'll do it. Together, we'll do it!" Then, as if to indicate that it had all been agreed, she studied the painting of Zelda carefully once more before saying, "I must get back to my hotel, now. I told them I'd be in for lunch and the owner has been so kind that I wouldn't want to keep him waiting."

"You must go then," Artemus replied, "but tomorrow, Edward is going to be back in St. Antonin. You must come and stay with us here. Pack your things and leave the hotel tomorrow morning. You will really need to be here, so I'll get Claudine to open up the spare room. I'll ask her to buy me some new brushes that we can paint with. There's nothing like new brushes to get you going. They always seem to work best when they're new."

The following day, Grace returned to Artemus's house and told him once more how much she was looking forward to meeting Edward. "Is today the right day for me to visit him?"

"Yes... you can," Artemus responded a little doubtfully. "But you must be strong and prepare yourself. He may not be the man your imagination has produced."

"Doesn't he look as he did in your painting of him, then?"

"Oh yes, of course he is older but he is still the man in the painting. He has been away for some medical attention and it always shakes him up a bit. He doesn't live here in this house now. He is too much for me and he lives with Claudine and her family just a walk away. It's a bigger house than this one and he's better off being with her children. I'll take you to him," he took her arm and leaning heavily against her, slowly led her out of the house. They walked down the road to a much larger house nearby. From within, came the noise of two voices raised in argument. Artemus put his finger over his lips, signalling Grace to ignore the voices.

They entered through the open door without knocking. Artemus indicated a flight of stairs. "You go on up and wait for me. Claudine will have got my brushes from the shop. I asked her to leave this door open."

When Artemus had eventually negotiated the stairs, he needed to pause for breath for a while. Once he had recovered sufficiently, he put a restraining arm on Grace and said with some sadness, "This boy is all I have left of Zelda. I left Loriston to be here, where she was born and grew up, but I've often taken him back to the house where Zelda and I shared such happy times. It was there that I painted him at stages as he grew up. The last time we were there, I painted the picture that you found." As he spoke, he pushed open a door and led Grace into a large, untidy and dimly-lit room. Sitting on the floor was a young man who looked up, suddenly startled. Grace immediately recognised him as Edward. She also noticed that the floor was scattered with toys.

"I've brought a young woman called Grace to see you, Edward. She's from the town where you were born."

Edward did not look up but continued playing with the toys in front of him. Noting Edward's lack of reaction, Grace asked, "Isn't he well?"

Artemus walked over to his son and, with considerable effort, knelt down beside him. Touching his head tenderly he said, "Edward, my son, say hello to Grace. She has spent months looking for us and has come to see you." Still getting no response, he turned back to Grace. "He'll take a while. We need to be patient." He gently ruffled his son's hair and Edward looked up with a look which seemed to be of recognition.

Grace too knelt beside Edward. The young man looked up at her quizzically.

"Now I have seen you, I can see that you are just like the painting your father did of you," she said. She sat down on the floor beside him and took up one of his cars, hoping to create a bond between them.

"Do you mind if I play with your toys, Edward?" Grace asked with a smile. She waited a few moments then tried again. "Do you like talking to your father, Edward?" Again there was no response, but Artemus joined in.

"I'm rather deaf and I cannot always understand him very well, but he does speak to me sometimes."

Grace looked up from her position in front of Edward and asked Artemus, "Do you talk to him very much?"

"Well, I do try but it's so difficult when I get very little response."

"Well, you must keep trying," Grace declared and, turning back to Edward said "We must talk to you, both of us. You have a look of intelligence in your eyes. I can also see that you are uncomfortable with my intruding into your home like this. I know that's because you have no idea who I am." Feeling uncomfortable on the hard wooden floor, she pulled a cushion fro a chair and sat on it. "What do you like doing most?" Edward still did not respond to her.

"I can't walk very far now," Artemus interrupted, "but Edward used to like me to take him into the countryside around here. He loves trees. Stares at them and moves with them when they sway in the wind.

"Dancing with the trees," Grace exclaimed excitedly and turning to Edward, she asked, "You dance like me, Edward. I love to dance too, and I also love the countryside and the trees. Tomorrow we could go for a walk. I saw some beautiful countryside just outside the town on my journey here. Would you like to walk with me?" she inquired and then, with relief turned to Artemus and asked, "Artemus, did you see that? Edward nodded, I'm sure Edward nodded to me. So tomorrow could we go for a walk amongst the trees?"

"Well, I've seen him nod before," Artemus replied, "but I have never been sure if he is doing it because he understands what is being said to him, or if it means anything at all."

"Edward, I want us to be friends," Grace said, placing her hand on his shoulder.

Artemus had forced himself up and was standing with his hand pressed to his back, looking ashen. "We must go now. I am beginning to reach my limit."

"Can I stay with him? I would like to help him play with his cars," Grace pleaded.

"No Grace, you must not."

"But Artemus, I have only been with him for a little while and I've waited so long."

"I said no, Grace and I meant no."

Grace had held her hand up in a plea to stay but Artemus grasped it firmly and, with a grimace of pain, pulled her to her feet. He brusquely directed her to leave and guided her out, closing the door firmly behind them.

When they were both outside and walking back to his house, Grace said, "Artemus, I think that was really cruel and thoughtless both to your son and to me. Don't you see how much I have spent in time and effort to be with him and also, how much I could help him?"

Artemus walked on without saying anything until they had reached his house.

"Something I have to tell you, Grace." His voice was quiet and quavering.

"Something difficult for me to say; he looks so gentle, my son, but, sometimes there comes into his eyes a look..." He paused.

"Yes, go on," Grace said, apprehensively.

"Well, that look means he is frightened, no, terrified is more correct." He stopped with his hand on the door, supporting himself. "And when he is like that, he is sometimes unpredictable in his behaviour."

"Do you mean violent?"

"Not exactly violent but he can strike out."

"And...?"

"I think I saw that look in his eyes just now, when you were talking about him."

"Yes, that was wrong, I shouldn't have talked to him as I did, should I? Now I think about it, I was treating him as though he was a patient."

The following day, having moved in to Artemus' house, Grace continued the conversation about Edward and the painting, as she and Artemus ate one of Claudine's sandwiches.

"In the painting you did of Edward," she began, "he is really beautiful. I have never seen anyone like him. I felt drawn to him right from the first moment of seeing that painting. And I haven't changed now that I have met him in person. You seem to have captured not just his features but his whole personality. It's something I can't describe, but it brings a wonderful feeling of tranquillity to me whenever I see it. If he and I could be together, even playing with his cars I'm sure we could unlock the whole person hidden inside him. One summer, I taught at a school for children who had problems; I found a way to help them, through play." She waited a while as Artemus ate, and then continued, "Artemus, I really want to keep on seeing Edward, but I will need to be alone with him."

Artemus, who was sitting in the armchair, had smiled his gratitude for the snack she had prepared, but his face now clouded over as she spoke. "I told you about his moods. I was serious. He could lose his temper with you, and even hurt you."

"I'm willing to take that risk, but I am sure that won't happen, if I am with him alone."

"Are you saying that I'm a bad influence on him, then?"

"Of course not, that's not at all what I am suggesting." She sat down on the arm of his chair. "It's just that sometimes a parent can unknowingly suppress a child's development. I just think I might see him as he really is, if he and I are alone together."

"I'm not at all happy about that, Grace. I told you yesterday what he can be like if he gets distressed."

"Please, Artemus. I think I can really help him. I am sure that he will respond to me when we are alone together."

"All right," Artemus conceded after a few moments' thought. "What I will do is ask Claudine to stay outside the door to his room. Then, if there is a problem, she will be there. But you will need to treat him very carefully. He likes to be on his own." He paused again, thinking hard. "I'm just wondering if you might be right. You haven't yet met Pierre, Claudine's husband. He looks after Edward a lot of the time now that I can't do so much and I have to admit that he has told me that Edward is fretful whenever I am around."

Grace kissed the top of his head. "You mustn't feel that that is any fault of yours, Artemus. It is just part of growing up and wanting to be able to survive without a parent. I sensed his unease when we were both with him yesterday. He was withdrawn, but I am sure I can get him to relax. We'll get to know each other much better if I can meet with him alone."

"Well, I'm still not sure. He has never been alone with a young woman before. The nearest he's come has been with Claudine. I don't want to be unkind to her, but," he stared at Grace over his glasses, "she is somewhat less attractive than you, you know. Still, I suppose we would have had to try one day. And you never know, you might be right and he could benefit from the relationship. All right, you go and see him. He will be having lunch soon. I sometimes eat with him but today I feel in need of a sleep."

Edward was lying on the floor of his room, playing with his toys, when Grace entered. He glanced up and a slight smile of recognition flickered across his face.

"That's a lovely smile, Edward," Grace said, sitting down on the bed near to him. "You do have some lovely toys; I suppose your father bought them for you. Come and sit with me and tell me about them. I'd love to have a chat with you."

Edward stood up a little uncertainly and then, still holding one of his toys, sat near the bed on a chair which was rickety and bent. He looked at Grace in a manner that she thought seemed welcoming.

"I'd love us to get to know each other. Find out what we both think about things," she said, looking straight into his eyes. After a few moments pause, she continued, "Do you like living in France?"

Edward remained silent for so long that she thought she was failing to reach him but then, almost imperceptibly, he nodded his head. Grace could hardly contain her excitement at this first response. Slowly and quietly, Edward then said, "I like." His words were so indistinct that Grace could not be sure she had heard.

"Did you say 'I like', Edward?" she asked, and again Edward nodded slowly.

"You must tell me more. Do you have any memories of England?"

" 'member England... colder" Edward replied, in the same monotone voice.

"Did you like being there?"

"Liked being there," he said and it seemed to Grace that his speech was becoming clearer.

"Edward, it is lovely to hear you speak."

Edward nodded and a faint smile drifted across his face. Grace continued,

"I have lived in Britain almost all my life. Did you know that?"

"Did not," he replied.

"Well, you listen and I'll tell you about it." She moved along the bed. "Let's sit together on the bed. It will be more comfortable than that chair, which looks as though it might break at any minute. Is that all right?"

"Mm."

"England is very different from France, isn't it?" She paused and waited for him to respond.

"Yes," he said.

"There is less space for people to live, so it is more crowded nowadays, but where I come from, Loriston – you've been there, it's where you were born – it is still very quiet. There are many more sheep than people."

"Mm," Edward responded.

"I expect you are used to answering people like that, but I'd like you to say a little more. Just tell me what you are thinking. Instead of saying 'Mm', you could say, 'I know'."

Edward looked worried and began to breathe quickly and then, with an effort, he said, "I know."

"That is so nice to hear, Edward. Let's keep trying, shall we?"

For answer, he laid his head on Grace's shoulder.

Grace put her arm round his shoulder and said, "I'm so pleased to see you wanting to come close, but you must remember that most people would not like it until you know them very well." She moved back a little so that he sat up again and looked into his eyes.

"Friends," he said.

"Edward, that is a lovely thing to say. Yes, I do think we are friends, but still we have to take a little time getting to know each other." She waited for him to reply but when he said nothing, she continued, "Now tell me, do you like the countryside around here?"

"Like."

"You could say, 'I do'"

"I do," he said and then added, "much."

"'Much'? That is good," Grace said, showing her delight, "because I want to go for a walk in the countryside after you've had your lunch. Or, even better, we could take our sandwiches with us and eat them in the open air. Will you come with me?"

"Will come."

"I'm so pleased to hear you say that. The day is warm and sunny so I'll take you to a place they told me about in the hotel where I was staying. It's here in St. Antonin."

Edward nodded again.

"Now, your father has asked me to leave my hotel and stay at his house. That means we will have chance to get to know each other. Perhaps I might some day put my head on your shoulder." Grace laughed only partly joking. "It seems to me, Edward that you understand what I am saying very well. That's good because I'm a person who likes to talk but where I lived there weren't many people like me. Lots of things and ideas are always going through my head, and I expect they go through yours, too. I'd love to hear your ideas, and then you can listen to mine. People say I am strange because I think and talk about unusual things and they don't understand. But everyone is a bit special you will probably have ideas I'll find surprising." She looked at him and noticed his slight nod. "I'll tell you what we'll do, probably not this afternoon, but soon." She touched his hand. "We'll find a tree and I'll show you a little bit of how I dance. I know my dancing is different but, if we are getting to know each other, you have to know my funny ways as well. Would you like to see my dancing?"

"Would like."

"Edward, that is beautiful. I think you talk really well. Do you talk much with Pierre?"

"Pierre? I talk not," he replied, in his quiet voice.

"Perhaps I can help you with some of the things that Pierre does and get to know you better. Would you like that?"

"Like that."

"You should say 'I would like that'. You spoke in the present tense, but we were talking about the future." Grace smiled, putting her hand on Edward's shoulder. "I will explain these things and you must try to understand, but don't worry if you can't. We'll just keep trying."

"Keep trying."

"Now, I'll go and get the lunch that Claudine has prepared. I'll wrap it up and you can carry it when we go for that walk. We'll see if we can find somewhere nice to sit down and eat."

Grace left the room to collect the lunch. While she was away, Edward sat on the bed, looking at the floor and remained in the same position until Grace came back into the room."

Grace had wrapped the food in a cloth which she gave to Edward to carry. "You can look after our picnic for us," she said, checking that he took the food and held it under his arm.

228

They walked out into the midday sun, along a street shaded by overhanging trees and down to the river where they sat down on steps, leading to the water.

"I think it's time to eat; I'm hungry, are you?"

"Hungry," he replied, as she took the food from him and spread it out on the steps beside them.

"What would you like?" Grace asked. "There are croissants with jam, and bread and cheese. And we have some lemonade. I had some of that with your father. It's very nice. Tell me what you want."

"Will bread and cheese have."

"You mean, 'I will have bread and cheese,'" Grace corrected him.

"I… will… have bread and cheese," Edward repeated laboriously.

"That's good. And after we have eaten, because the weather is so pleasant, we will go for our walk."

Edward picked up the bread, added some cheese and they ate together, watching the water drifting slowly by. The sun was warm and a light breeze blew, causing the leaves on the trees to flutter soothingly. At intervals, couples would paddle past them in boats. If they waved, Grace waved back and seeing what she was doing, Edward waved with her.

When they had finished their picnic, Grace wrapped up the left-overs except for the bread, which she gave to Edward.

"This French bread does not keep well," she explained. "It goes stale quickly so we'll feed it to the ducks over there. You watch them, as soon as we throw bread on the river, they will come rushing over."

Edward broke the bread and threw it high in the air, laughing and clapping his hands as the birds raced over and fought amongst themselves for the pieces. Grace pointed at one of the ducks that was being particularly aggressive, biting all the other birds near him.

"You see that one, Edward? He is very greedy and wants all the bread himself. There are people like that; selfish people who only think about themselves." She stood up and Edward followed her as she began to walk along the river bank. "Often such people become rich and famous. They have houses which are too big for them just to show off their wealth. Often they are not very nice though. Having lots of money doesn't always make them happy."

"Reverend Belari?"

Grace stopped what she was doing, horrified that Edward should be referring to her father, and amazed at his comprehension.

"Why ever did you say that name, Edward?"

"Not nice people."

"Not a nice person, you mean." She wondered how to respond to him for a few moments. "He is my father, Edward, but I know you are quite right about him, even though he is not one of the rich people I was talking about."

The path ended at a boathouse so they turned inland and returned through the town to the house of Claudine and Pierre, where Edward lived.

As they approached, Claudine came from the house and called out in hesitant English, "Oh, Mr. Edward, I have been so worried about you. It is time for your sleep." She turned towards Grace, "I'll look after him now, mademoiselle. He does look well though. He

230

hasn't been for a walk for such a long time. It looks as though you've come from the river."

Edward turned to Grace and said, "You thank."

"No. Thank you, you mean. I'll see you tomorrow," Grace replied, waving goodbye to Claudine.

The next day, she went with Artemus to Edward's room in Claudine's house. He still had his toys spread all over the floor and on some of the furniture. "Would you like to talk, Edward?" she asked. When Edward did not respond, she said, "You really ought to say 'hello' to me."

Edward, without looking up, muttered, "Say Hello."

Grace said, "No, just use the word 'hello'."

Edward continued pushing his cars around and said, "Work to do." He then started laughing quietly to himself and continued to play with his toys.

"We'll leave you to your work, then. We're going to talk with Claudine."

As they went down the stairs, Grace whispered to Artemus, "Your son is so beautiful, isn't he?"

"Yes he is, but he will never pay the rent. He will never have a normal life." He paused on the stairs to get his breath. "I'm pleased at the way things are going with him but, for your own sake, you should think carefully about the future. If you get caught up with Edward, you will give up so much of your young life. I honestly think you'd be best off leaving now and finding someone who can look after you."

"I have not travelled all this way not to stay and get to know Edward. He might reject me, but I want to do what I can for him."

They were standing part way down the stairs, waiting for Artemus to gather breath, when they heard the floorboards creaking behind them.

Edward, in a slow voice, said, "Hear you saying."

"And did you like what we were saying about how you look?" Grace asked.

"He won't answer you. He may have some speech, but he doesn't connect. I think I can sometimes understand what he is thinking, and there are times when it almost seems that he can understand me, but it never gets any farther than that, never what you'd call 'normal'." Artemus said.

"What's 'normal'?" Edward asked.

"Normal is like... well, everybody," Grace replied.

"You normal?" Edward seemed to be asking.

"No, I'm not normal," Grace said and then, going back up the stairs said to Artemus, "you see, he does follow what you say. I want to be able to talk to him. He has intelligence in his eyes. What sort of things does he like doing?"

"Well, I told you that we used to walk together; he loves nature. He stares at the trees and moves with them when they sway in the wind. Don't you, Edward?"

"I love nature too. I'll take him for some long walks. If he likes swaying with the trees, we could dance, too. I'm sure dancing helps the mind develop." Turning back to Edward, she continued, "Do you dance, Edward? I like to dance with the trees. I will take you for long walks with me."

"Not a dog."

"I didn't mean like a dog. You are not a dog. You are Edward, and I am asking you to walk with me."

"Not dog now?"

"You never were a dog. You are a fully-grown man and I have been thinking for a long time about meeting you."

Artemus with considerable effort had reached the door and went outside to sit in the sun. Grace stood on the stairs with Edward at her side. She could see that he was trying to talk and waited for him to speak.

"Seen you before – dreams."

Grace was astonished. "Do you really mean that? You've seen me in dreams? The reason I am so surprised is that I've seen you in my dreams, as well."

"Tired now," he said, ignoring Grace's questions, got up and went to his room, got on the bed and closed his eyes as though going to sleep.

"Edward seems to want to sleep." Grace called down to Artemus

"We must go then," Artemus called back. "He will sleep for at least an hour."

Grace went quietly down the stairs and joined Artemus.

"If he doesn't have his sleep or if he is wakened he will cry, so we'd better go. Let's talk with Claudine about your room. We'll come back later after Edward has slept."

"No, I want to stay, can I please."

"I'm not sure that's a good idea," Artemus hesitated, "but if you do, you will need to treat him very carefully. He does like to be on his own. Don't be surprised if he becomes tearful if he sees you when he wakes."

Artemus struggled to stand up.

"Thank you so much, Artemus. I'll call Claudine, if he does get upset. That is, if I can't pacify him myself. But I'm sure that won't be necessary. Will it, Edward?" she called in a raised voice as though to the sleeping figure in the room above.

Grace went back up the stairs sat herself down in the arm chair and carefully studied Edward and his room. The sunlight shone through the window, making her feel sleepy. After a few moments, she also drifted off to sleep, waking suddenly with a start when she heard a door slam in the wind. She got up and sat quietly on the bed, looking at Edward and, on impulse, stroked his hair. As she touched his head, he woke up and seemed to smile when he saw Grace.

"I do like your smile, Edward," she said. "I want to talk to you and get to know what you think about when you are on your own."

Edward sat up, clutching a toy and looked at Grace quizzically. Then he laid his head on her shoulder for a moment.

"Shall we go out, Edward?"

"Things to think about."

"You are right. Lots of things, but we could do that while we are out. It's a lovely day and not too hot, especially if we went into the forest."

"Will think."

"Good. Shall we go then?"

She saw that he was reluctant to move and realised, from her earlier experiences of children with problems that it was just inertia. She encouraged him to sit up, then collected his shoes from under the bed, laced them up and pulled him gently up into a standing position. She took a blanket off the bed, rolled it up and put it under Edward's are for him to carry.

234

As soon as they began to walk, it was obvious that Edward knew the way. He kept referring to things and commenting on them. "Big tree smile," he would repeat often as they walked. Their path led them through a wood where there were many trees. Edward would face them, raising his arms and imitating their movements as they swayed in the wind. After ten minutes, they found a clearing in the trees with a view across a valley.

"This reminds me of the hills around Loriston, the countryside there is very beautiful too."

"Mm," Edward murmured

"I think you listen to everything anybody says, Edward." Grace said, laying the blanket down on the grass for them to sit on under the shade of a tree. "And I think you understand me." She sat down and Edward sat beside her. "I think you also understand what other people are thinking and feeling."

"Hear you," he smiled enigmatically, "not understand."

"But I feel that I can talk to you and that you do understand."

"Like listen. Like understand."

"Edward, you have beautiful thoughts. Have you ever talked like this with any other girl?" Grace passed her fingers through his hair to tidy it. "Or have you ever known love for a girl."

Edward smiled, but without understanding. "Love father."

"It's nice that you love him, but loving a woman is different."

Grace looked up at the sky through the branches of the tree. "I think that love between a man and a woman is like the branches of the tree above us. When it starts it is like that little tree over there, it can spread and grow and become as strong as the tree we are under now."

Edward stood up and put his arms round the tree. "Love trees."

Grace stood as well and, taking Edward's hands, went close to the tree and formed with him a circle with their arms around the trunk. "I do as well. I think that trees represent the breathing of the earth. Can you feel that energy flowing through us?" She squeezed his hands hard to show what she meant.

Edward laid his head on the tree, closed his eyes and remained there for several minutes. "Feel it," he said, laying his face against it so hard that when they moved away, Grace saw with amusement that the bark had imprinted on his face.

"I am so glad to be here with you, Edward. Will you dance with me?"

Haltingly, Edward followed her steps as they moved together, slowly at first.

"I have waited such a long time to find you, Edward. I wonder if you knew I was coming?"

"Dreamed of you."

Grace stopped dancing and stood still. "You said that when we were in your room. I think it is amazing that I should also have dreamt of you. Am I as you expected?"

"Same... my dreams."

Grace leaned backwards, her hands clasping his shoulders and looked at Edward. "You knew what I would look like, you mean?"

"Knew," he nodded. "Yes, knew." He raised his hand and pointed to the branches above him, spreading his arms in the pattern of the branches. "You there."

"In the sky, do you mean?"

"In tree, my tree."

"It's our tree now."

They danced around the tree until a cloud seeming to threaten rain passed across the sun.

"How sad, Edward, I think it is going to rain."

"Like rain not," he said, taking Grace's arm and hiding his head beneath it.

"I don't like it either, but it is necessary to feed the plants and also to make food for us. We would not be able to live without it."

Slowly they walked back in the drizzling rain. By the time they reached the house, the rain had stopped and the sun's heat was causing the wet road to steam. Artemus was asleep in a chair on the veranda as they walked into the house. Hearing their footsteps, he stirred and opened his eyes.

"Hello, you both look very pleased with yourselves. What has happened?" he asked, sitting up with an effort.

Without acknowledging him, Edward walked past him into the garden and climbed into a hammock which was strung between two trees.

"Yes, I am pleased. Edward is lovely and so interesting when he talks."

"Talks, have you been able to talk with him, then?"

"Yes, I really can talk to him. He listens and I'm sure he understands. Well, he seems to at least." She leaned against the rails of the veranda in front of Artemus. "I've never experienced anything like it, we walked, talked and even danced a bit."

"I'm pleased but…" He eased himself up out of his sleeping position. "I want you to be sure that what

237

you are doing is right for you both. He is vulnerable, and if you change your mind and leave he will be more damaged than ever before."

"Why talk of my leaving? I won't be leaving him."

"You don't know him. Look at him over there; he is tired already from your walk but you are still active. You are young and still idealistic, Grace. The young always feel they can change the world. The reality is usually very different."

"Artemus," she responded firmly, "I am not one of your idealistic young. I am going into this with my eyes open. I know the difficulties and I accept them. Try to understand."

Artemus breathed ponderously and looked over at Edward, apparently sleeping happily in the hammock. "All right, stay a bit longer. Spend time with him and you will begin to see what I mean; you have no idea how difficult he can be. To love someone without getting anything in return is very hard. You'll see the difficulties he has - sudden unpredictable mood swings - days when he will not waken - times when he is inanimate and simply stares ahead without seeing." He nodded his head in the direction of Edward. "I know how he suffers, and how that makes us all suffer in ways which you can't imagine until you go through them. You'll find that tying yourself to him will be a painful commitment..."

"You've had many years since Zelda died and I think you have not seen him as he can be. It won't happen to me, I am already getting something in return."

"I'm so afraid that you will find it becomes like an existence somewhere between living and dying. And it will never get easier. I did not choose what happened and, looking back I can see that for me it would have been better if I had not learnt about that kind of love," he sighed. "And I'm afraid the same could happen to you. The life you are offering Edward is just what I am saying; half living and half dying. I did not choose what happened but you can. Walk away now and find someone who can love you equally. If you don't, you will find you will wish you had in years to come."

"I don't yet know how it can be made to work with Edward, but I do know that I have no choice. I have to try and, what's more, I'm sure there is a way."

"What you are offering is, I think, dangerous for you because in years to come you may well regret that Edward's travails took you over. I know the pain of a love which was cursed, which seemed perfect but which was destroyed by the death of the woman I loved."

"What are you saying? Are you telling me that Edward will die?"

"No, of course I am not, how could I possibly predict that? But there is a chance that he may. Sometimes when he gets into a violent temper, screams and shouts uncontrollably, and lashes out at anyone who comes near him, I fear that he could damage himself or even take someone else's life. You could ruin him or he could ruin you. I can't see any way you could have a good life with him."

"I wouldn't mind that. I just know now what is meant – I was meant to be with Edward. His aggression is probably a result of frustration, a need to do what other people take for granted, but... his problems won't let it happen," she looked up at Artemus to see if she was making sense. "In your portrait of him he is a physically perfect human being. I want to bring out the Edward hidden beneath the surface. I want to direct his energies, teach him to understand himself. I understand what you say about how many people have tried before, but no one will have spent as much time with him as I intend to. You are his father, you and Zelda created him. Don't you feel the same way about him as I do, don't you?" she asked.

"That painting of Edward is very special, just like the portrait of Zelda. When I'd finished them and they were both together, it was like a catharsis for me. But I regret that the portrait has interfered with your life. It would have been better never to have painted it and then leave it for you to find." He pursed his lips; "your life has been changed so much."

"I don't see it as interfering except for the better. Finding it has freed me from my father and brought me to you and Edward. The painting is a force for good. Please don't talk of it being better if you had never painted it. It is part of both our destinies. How else would I have found the feelings I have for him?"

"The love you speak of is a hopeless one. It will hurt you as it has me. Edward is the wasteland of what remains of my love for Zelda. Why don't you go, Grace, please go before you destroy your own life and his as well."

"I want to give him what he has missed. I want to give him a new life. I would never destroy him, Artemus, only your grief could do that."

"Don't be foolish," Artemus said with irritation, "it's not my grief that has damaged him. He was damaged from the moment of birth. He has seen many doctors and not one has been able to cure him or even make any change in him. You are stupid to think that you can do what no one else could."

"Just let me try. All he needs is understanding, someone who will treat him in a different way. It seems to me that he has been placed in a box labelled

'Empty' and the box now needs to be opened. I know I can do it. If you drive me away, he will have no one and he will remain as he is now – alone – and...doomed."

"How can I be sure that you understand what you are letting yourself in for? You are here just because you were attracted to the way he looks, and that's a poor basis for a future. Looks fade. For a time, you will want to mother him, but what will happen later? It is no life for a young woman, Grace. You need to be with other young people. That's where you should be, not here with an old, ailing man with an ailing son."

"I am not leaving Edward or you, Artemus," Grace replied. Hearing a noise coming from the waking Edward in his hammock, she looked over at the sleeping figure. "You belittle yourself when you say I was just attracted by his looks, the painting is more than just an image, it has a life. I came because I needed to meet him," she stood up and went over to Edward, "he needs what I can give him if he is to develop. You have already said no one else has been able help him; at least let me try."

The atmosphere between Grace and Artemus was becoming hostile, and without either of them realising it, their voices were raising in volume. The noise coming from them had roused Edward who sat up and asked, "What you say?"

"Edward, do you want me to stay with you, or go?" Grace asked.

"Want kiss."

"There you see, Grace, see how silly he is? He has never been like that before."

"What's wrong with him wanting a kiss, it shows he needs affection."

"He is a young man who has never had anything to do with the opposite sex." Artemus threw up his hands in horror. "You could unleash desires in him which could be uncontrollable. You don't know the nature of a man's passion."

Grace went white and her hands clenched the veranda rails as she tried to control herself. "Are you saying that your own son should never know what can happen between a man and a woman?" She became more vehement as she spoke. "You're just a jealous old man. Because you lost your own love, you want to deprive him." Turning her back on Artemus, she called, "Edward, do you want me to stay or go? Please tell your father."

"Dance with Grace by tree."

"There, you see!" Artemus said with a note of triumph. "He does not understand, Grace, and what's more, neither do you," he stated coldly.

"With me, he understands, don't you worry..."

Before she could finish what she was going to say, she was interrupted by Claudine from the kitchen asking," Monsieur Artemus, shall I lay the tea things outside for you?" She asked and sniffed as she looked at Grace.

"That would be nice. Please do, Claudine," Artemus answered, grateful for the distraction.

Grace went to help her lay the table but Claudine coldly ignored the offer of help, making Grace realise that she had been listening to what had been said.

When the things were laid out and Claudine had gone, the three of them ate in silence and afterwards, Edward returned to his hammock to watch birds wheeling in the sky. Grace went to sit in the chair next to him but suddenly changed her mind and said.

"Edward, can I come and lie in the hammock with you? It looks much more comfortable than this hard old chair?"

"My hammock."

"I know, and I want to share it with you. Would you let me?"

"Not know."

"Shall we try?" Grace asked, clambering into the hammock. Edward looked at her nervously. When she was in, Grace playfully started swinging the hammock ever more violently until they both fell out on top of each other on to the long grass beneath. They stared at each other intently, as if they were about to embrace. Shaking with emotion, Edward suddenly got up and ran away upstairs, into his room. Grace scrambled to her feet in some confusion and went after him.

"Don't leave, Edward, tell me what's wrong," she called, following close behind him. But before she had reached him he rushed into his room and locked the door. Grace, unable to enter, listened to him kicking his things around the room and at the door.

"Tell me what's wrong, Edward?"

She waited, listening at the door, hearing him sobbing and saying, "Funny hurt."

"Edward, open the door and let me in. I'll be able to help. Where do you hurt?"

Between sobs, he said, "Trousers."

On hearing this, Grace thought she understood what was troubling him.

"Take some deep breaths and open your mouth wide, it will distract you."

"Mouth open."

Grace heard him breathing deeply and said, "I'll go back to Artemus. If you don't want to come down I'll come up and see you later. Is that OK?"

"Can breathe. You go."

She walked down the stairs to find Artemus sitting in the same chair, waiting for her.

"Come into the house, I want to talk to you."

After the heat outside, the house was dark and cool. Artemus mopped his brow with a handkerchief and said. "I am very angry with you, Grace. You've really upset my son."

"He just wants some time on his own."

"You don't understand what you're doing. He is so sensitive. He could fall desperately in love with you, he's not strong enough for that, it would be cruel. I can't allow you to hurt him."

"I do know what I'm doing, there will always be setbacks but he is moving forward all the time, surely you can see that. Why don't you just trust me?"

"How can I trust you? All I know about you is that you are Belari's daughter; you may be like him, for all I know. What have you done to make me trust you?"

Unable to control her growing bewilderment at Artemus's attitude, Grace's voice began to rise. "What have I done to make you trust me? How can you say that, I've travelled more than a thousand miles to be here. In Paris, I got involved in a gangster situation and could have wound up on a cold slab. I've worked hard to make you see that I am the only hope for Edward. Why can't you see that? Just give me time. I'll show you that I am not a silly girl. Let me stay here and work with Edward, you'll find you can trust me. I will do everything I am capable of to make sure he is happy."

"Why don't I trust you? I just don't understand you, Miss Belari, that's all. You are an attractive

244

woman. You could marry someone wealthy or someone very intelligent, yet you want to spend your life with my damaged son. Why?"

"You are wrong to call him damaged. That's part of his problem; he has been put in that empty box and people have low expectations of him. He is just different. Why did I choose him?" she stood in front of him with her hands on her hips. "Because that was what was meant. I have never wanted someone wealthy to keep me in idleness. There is a young man in Loriston who asked me to be his wife and he is all that you describe, well-off, quite nice looking and intelligent. But he does not interest me as Edward does." Grace pulled a chair up to Artemus, put her arms round his shoulders and said in a quiet voice. "It will work between me and Edward. I already have a love for him which I think is something he has never had before."

"I can't believe it." He shook his head. "I know you think I am just being selfish. If it seems like that it is just because I want what is best for Edward. I'm not at all sure you can provide it, but..." He struggled to his feet, went to the window and looked out, marvelling as he always did at the beauty of nature and the sunlight casting shadows among the trees. Slowly he turned, stroked his chin and said, "Perhaps you are right; it is right to give it a try, at least." He pondered a moment longer and then, taking a deep breath, said, "You can stay for one month. In that time, you will have to show me that this can work. If it doesn't, or if it upsets Edward too much, I will have to ask you to leave."

Hearing his words, Grace smiled with delight and rushed over to put her arms round him and laid her head on his back. "I will convince you, Artemus, you

245

will see. You can be sure I will make Edward so happy that you certainly won't want me to leave."

Behind them they heard a footstep. Grace turned and saw Edward, looking red-eyed. "Edward," she called "I'm so pleased to see you."

"Grace stay?" Edward asked.

Grace looked round to Artemus. "She is staying a little longer, yes. She will be with us here," he said.

Edward's face beamed with happiness as he walked to Grace and lowered his forehead on to her shoulder.

During the following days, Grace started reading to Edward from books which were on the bookshelves. Whenever they went for a walk, or just before he went to sleep, she would read a few pages from one of Dickens' novels on Artemus's shelves. Edward was enthralled. He particularly liked 'David Copperfield', always asked for it over and over again, and would act out the scenes. With pleasure, Grace described his reactions to Artemus and he, somewhat unwillingly, expressed his recognition at the change in Edward.

On the following Sunday, Grace took Edward to church to broaden his knowledge. Remembering her own experience of her father's church she went with some trepidation. Her spirits sank as they walked in. The church was filled with people who seemed to her very like those attending the same morning services in her father's church in Loriston. Even the odour of the place, with its damp stones was reminiscent of Loriston and the hard benches and kneelers heightened this impression. But when they were seated and she could see Edward's attention to everything that was happening, she was filled with pleasure. She had put on a smart suit for him and was delighted to see the admiring glances he received both from the matronly women and, particularly, the younger ones. She could not easily follow the service, which was delivered in a local dialect very different from the French she knew. Many of the hymns were sung in the same dialect, but she was able to sing with the congregation by reading from the hymn books. With pleasure, she saw that Edward joined in and seemed to know the songs or to be able to learn them quickly.

After the service, they filed out and shook hands with the priest. He smiled and said something which Grace translated as, "Monsieur Alleyne, c'est un plaisir à vous voir ici."

Overcome with the situation, Grace managed to form the words, "Nous aussi, Père, merci." She, the priest and Edward all smiled at each other. As they walked away, Grace said, "The priest seemed a nice man. Not like my father in any way."

That afternoon, they changed their clothes and walked in the sun to a narrow tributary of the wide river Aveyron to eat their lunch. When they had finished they walked along the bank; Edward found that someone had tied a rope to a tree so that it was possible to swing out across the river. Taking hold of the rope, he launched himself out across the river and swung round in decreasing circles before leaping back onto the bank. Then he passed the rope to Grace. She held tight while Edward pushed her. At the extent of travel, her grip slipped and she fell into the sun-warmed water. Without thinking, Edward leapt in and waded to the centre of the slow-moving river to save her. Finding that the water was only waist high and Grace could easily have walked out, they both laughed. Edward had his arms around Grace's waist ready to help her out. When their laughter was over, they stared at each other and Grace leaned to give a kiss to Edward, causing him to lose his balance and fall over, dragging her with him. So that she could swim more easily, Grace took her top off and did the same with Edward and they swam together semi naked, laughing and splashing each other like children at play.

Grace stood up and embraced Edward who at first appeared to respond but gradually, his smile faded and he scrambled to the bank and ran away looking distressed, pulling his wet clothes on as he ran back to the house. Hurriedly, Grace got dressed too and ran dripping after him.

"Edward, what's wrong with you?" she called. "Stop running away. What's happening to us is only natural. Don't be frightened."

Running as fast as she could, she had almost caught him up when she fell and twisted her ankle. Feeling tearful, she lay on the ground, watching Edward disappear.

When she finally limped back to the house, Edward was in his room, in tears, with Artemus trying to comfort him.

"What's wrong, Edward? What's happened?" he asked.

"Swimming frighted me," Edward replied tearfully.

"Swimming should not frighten you; you've swum many times before. Did Grace frighten you?"

"Frighted self," he replied, just as Grace, still soaking wet dashed into the room and asked,

"Is Edward all right? What's the matter with him?"

"He says the swimming has frightened him. What were you doing?"

248

"We were just swinging on a rope and I fell in. We swam for a while and he was perfectly happy but he suddenly got upset. I am so sorry. It must have been when I was playing with him."

"Being too affectionate, you mean, don't you?" He glared at her. "I was beginning to think things were working, that I could trust you. But I was wrong; you're just making him unhappy. You know what I said about him, if you transgress any more you will have to leave."

"Oh, don't think about me leaving so soon. You said I could stay for at least a month. Things will work out. I'm sure they will. Edward just needs more time to get used to me."

"Look at him. He will never be ready for you. You seem to think that you can make him into a whole person. He can't be what you want. I can see it was stupid to let you even try."

At these words, Edward, who had become calmer, turned to them with a confused look on his face.

"Look, Artemus, he's stopped crying. He'll be all right now," she said, going to him and putting her arm on his shoulder.

"But only until you make him cry again. I am beginning to see the folly of listening to you and your half-baked ideas," Artemus stated firmly.

At that moment, Edward joined in the conversation. "Swim with Grace good," he said.

"So why were you crying, then?" Artemus demanded.

"Feel funny," Edward replied.

Artemus looked accusingly at Grace. "You see," he said to her and, turning back to Edward, repeated, "I think Grace should leave us." When Edward failed to respond, he continued, "Do you want Grace to stay, or do you want her to leave?"

"Say yes, Edward, say you want me to stay. We can have such a lovely time together," Grace pleaded.

"You're bullying him," Artemus accused. "He wants you to leave, I am sure of it."

"Edward, tell your father how you feel. Please tell him," Grace said.

A long and awkward pause followed, as the three of them looked at each other. Finally, Edward spoke.

"Want Grace stay."

"I think you are just saying that because she's here. Why do you want her to stay?" Artemus demanded. He stood up and made the pretence of looking out of the window, in order to avoid eye contact with Grace.

"Want be with her... dance... walk... sing. Sunshine."

"Are you sure that this is what you both want?" Artemus asked, still looking out of the window with his hands clasped behind his back.

"Yes, it is certainly what I want," Grace replied firmly.

Artemus turned back from the window and raised his eyebrows enquiringly. "You seem to me to be so unsuited to each other. But..." he shrugged. "I don't know what to think any more," he frowned. "I suppose you think I'm just a stupid old fool and shouldn't be interfering," he sighed, lowering himself painfully into a rickety chair. "All right, I admit you have changed him for the better. Perhaps I was too hasty, stay for a bit longer."

At his words, both Grace and Edward smiled.

CHAPTER SIXTEEN

One afternoon when Grace had left Edward behind after reading to him, she let herself in to Artemus's house and called his name. She found him asleep in his chair but, hearing her voice he roused himself.

"Yes, Grace?" he said, sitting up. "You look happy. What has happened?

"I am happy, so happy, I feel I could burst. My Edward – our Edward, I mean - is lovely. He is so handsome and he is so good to talk to. He seems to really understand."

"Talk to?" Artemus looked surprised. "Have you been able to have a long conversation with him, then?"

"Not long, no certainly not, but I can talk to him. He listens and I'm sure he understands me more now than he has ever done because his responses make sense."

She sat down on the floor in front of Artemus, her knees raised and her arms around them. "When I am with him and talking to him, he loves it. This afternoon, I took him to the river near here. I wanted him to dance with me because I think that, as the body moves rhythmically, it gets the mind working in harmony with it. It is too early for that to happen yet, but it will. I'm sure he is a natural dancer." She swayed her body to demonstrate what she meant. "Artemus, he inspires me so much, for the first time, I feel I have found what my life was meant for."

"What do you mean?"

"Don't you see? It's as if this was meant to be."

"Tell me why you say that. I'm sorry but I'm still half asleep, my tablets, you see. I don't understand what you mean."

"All this must have been meant to happen, it's as though when you did the painting, fate made you do it." Grace said excitedly. "Finding your house, finding your paintings and seeing your portrait of Edward was in my destiny. At the time, it all seemed accidental to me. But now I am convinced that it must have been fate."

"Fate?" His voice still sounded slightly slurred.

"Artemus, I'm sorry, you are still tired. Shall I leave you to sleep?"

"No, Grace, don't leave. The tablets the doctors prescribe for me are pretty strong. I take a long time regaining myself after I've slept. Keep talking, please. Your enthusiasm is infectious. I am beginning to see that you are just what this house needs." He shook his head vigorously trying to rouse himself, and continued, "I mean that you are what both Edward and I need. It's helping me too, so please go on with what you were going to say."

"I was talking about fate. Why would I have been so impelled to seek Edward if it hadn't been intended to happen? Anyone else would surely have put the painting of Edward back in the cupboard where it had been and forgotten about it, but I could not; it exploded in my mind. I just seemed to lose my reason. Carlton, that friend of mine I was telling you about, tells me I am crazy, and I know I haven't been able to think straight ever since I saw it," she turned her head away and looked into the distance, "I had no choice; I was just driven to leave home and the mother I was just beginning to know. It was something I had no control over. I had to come to France on what was little more than a whim and then happen to be introduced to someone who was able to help me find you both. Without her and her man friend I would never have been able track you down. I was obviously very naïve, I had it in my head that I would find you in Paris. To not only find you both, but then to be able to talk to Edward in a way which, from what you have told me, no one else has. Do you see what I am saying, Artemus?" She waited from him to reply but when he said nothing, continued, "I must have been pre-destined to do this, or is Carlton right and I'm behaving as though I am crazy..."

"I can see that what you did is very unusual," Artemus responded, nodding his head in agreement, and now seeming to be fully awake. "If you are right about this pre-destiny, doesn't it worry you to feel that decisions have been taken out of your hands? To lose free will as though your life is being controlled?"

"I don't see it like that. I see fate as nothing more than a line in the sand which we can follow and, when you do, it is easier to continue but, if you wanted to, you could always travel in another direction. You are always in control." Grace turned to look at Artemus. "Do you know what I am saying? I have always felt in control but I stayed on that line in the sand and it guided me to St. Antonin and you and Edward."

"For me, it has always been different," Artemus replied. "I have never felt in control and it would be difficult to say that anything that happened to me was the result of benign fate. If I see my fate as anything, I see it as malevolent."

Noticing that Artemus was becoming morose, Grace got up from the floor where she had been sitting, sat on the arm of the chair beside Artemus and kissed him on the top of his head.

"Why should my Zelda have had to die?" he continued. "No woman before or since..." He screwed up his eyes as though holding back tears. "I don't want to sound sorry for myself, Grace, but why did she die? It wasn't simply that we seemed just right together. It felt as though we were actually brought into the world to be together. Can you imagine? I had always been a selfish person. We artists are fêted by women, and I was no exception. I was spoiled by them. So many women! And the more they gave in to me, the more I despised them and treated them with little consideration. It seemed right to treat them like that, they seemed to expect it – well anyhow, they never complained." He leant forward, put his elbows on his knees and looked down at the floor. "And, you know, Grace, I hated myself for it, loathed everything I had become. Most men would have given five years of their lives to have what I had. There were women queuing to meet me, happy to serve me in any way they could. That is the funny thing about being human, isn't it? We all have needs but if the needs get satisfied, we get bored and want other things. With Zelda, it was so different. All I wanted after I met her was to give up all the other women and devote my life to her. It is a matter of amazement to me that someone as entirely self-interested and self-indulgent as I was, could change so much that my only pleasure was to give her pleasure. I wanted her happiness so much and I think it was probably the only unselfish thought I had had since my first encounters with women. Zelda was never in good health and there was a time when she had been unwell for almost a week. Not just unwell, she seemed to me to be very ill," he shuddered momentarily and his voice sounded distant, "I can still feel the cold."

"Cold?" Grace asked. "Are you cold on a day like this?"

255

"Sorry, I was drifting." He smiled again. "That probably sounded as though I was talking about the way I treated other women, but that's not what I meant. I'm talking about snow. You know how it snows in Loriston and how it drifts. It was on one of those heavy-snow days; Zelda was with me in that house you found the painting in, and her illness was causing the colour in her face to drain away. She had been ill for getting on for a week. She said it was nothing, and it would pass. But she'd run out of her medicine and I was in a state of terror at seeing her so unwell. She was so ill that I began to think she would die. I felt I had to do something for her to make her feel better - compelled beyond reason to go and get her the medicine she needed. She pleaded with me not to go into the snow, said I might not make it myself. But this selfish man, who would have told any other woman to sleep it off, was driven to go to the town and get what she needed. As soon as I stepped out of the door, I realised why she had tried to stop me. My God, I have never been so cold. On the outside, that is. On the inside I glowed with the thought of her and how the tablets would help make her well again. It probably only took me half an hour to get to the surgery but I returned so frozen that Zelda then became worried for me. She piled logs on the fire and covered me in blankets. I shivered and shook but I hardly noticed because I had picked up the tablets that would take her pain away." He smiled at Grace. "They worked; by the time I was beginning to feel warmer, she told me the pain had gone."

When he had stopped talking, Grace put her arms round him and kissed his head again. "Artemus, that was so kind," she said.

"No, it wasn't kindness. I had no choice; it was as though I was controlled."

"As though fate had taken away your ability to decide for yourself, you mean," she said with a smile, recalling his previous words to her.

"Yes, looking back that was what it seemed like."

"And it was exactly the same with me. I am not a silly young girl. I know what I did would seem foolish in the cold light of day but I had no choice. Everything I did was dominated by that painting of Edward and that's what I want you to understand. Just the thought of Zelda drove you like the thought of Edward did with me." Grace stood up, walked to the partly-finished painting on the easel and picked it up. "This portrait of Zelda must be finished, mustn't it?"

Artemus nodded. "I am doing it from memory. And, oh, how I need to finish it, but these hands won't let me. I have her image so clearly in my mind but the painting has stayed like that for two years. I just can't touch it because I know I would spoil it." He raised his right hand and showed her how badly it was shaking.

"Did you know you left a painting of her in your old house in Loriston?"

"Oh yes, I knew. Somehow, it seemed right to leave it there."

"And the painting of Edward?"

"That too, yes," he nodded. "He was conceived there and I wanted to leave an image of what he had grown into there, with his mother."

"Artemus," she said as she put her arms round his shoulder again. "I took his image away and I've kept it. I'm sorry, was I wrong to do that?"

"Fate, Grace." He turned his head and looked at her. "I'm beginning to believe as you do that you were meant to be here. Fate, my dear, and it was benign fate. Sorry that I blew up just now – my tablets, you know, they make me tired and they make me behave strangely, but that effect is beginning to wear off. Now I can see that I should thank fate for bringing you here." He smiled as though to reassure Grace and continued, "As I said, this house needs you," and, after a pause, he added, "as Edward and I do."

"Like me, you feel that fate sometimes seems to take over our lives?" she asked and, when Artemus nodded, continued, "So do you think you were meant to leave that painting there for me to find?"

"Could I have done that, I wonder? No, that is stretching credulity too far. It was there so that Zelda could be with her son. But, since it resulted in bringing you to this house and to Edward and me it must be the benign fate you talk about."

They remained quiet, each with their own thoughts, before Grace said. "You know, even though I've only been here for a short time, this house feels more like home than the rectory where I grew up and spent most of my life."

"I am so pleased about that, and I think Edward is too. When will you see him again? I have arranged with Claudine that we should all have a meal together tomorrow night."

"So, we will all eat 'en famille'. It will be nice just the three of us, Artemus. I want you to see your son differently. I think you will see that he has more ability than you think. I want us both to talk to him."

"What can we talk to him about, do you think?" Artemus frowned.

"You can talk to him about anything. Painting, music, people you know, anything," Grace replied. "I think he's been considered simple-minded for far too long. That makes him think of himself in the same way. He just needs to be encouraged to see himself as a thinking person. I'm beginning to think that he has a good mind and because it has not been formed by an ordinary education, he says things that would surprise you. This afternoon, when we were walking, he often amazed me with the way he sees things. He said he saw purple in the trees. I couldn't see it until he pointed out the way the light shines through a certain leaf."

"Sees things? Like an artist, do you mean?"

"Like an artist, yes, but not like a conventional, every-day artist," Grace answered, with glowing eyes. "He didn't need to speak. I could tell just by watching where he was looking. I don't yet fully understand what he sees but somehow he seemed to open up my mind. Everything seems so new to him. It was incredible to be with him. It was like looking at my surroundings with the eyes of a child."

"My God, that's amazing," Artemus said. "That's just what I was trying to do when I was able to paint; to interpret what I saw so that the viewer would see things in a new light."

"And you will soon be painting again using my hands," Grace stated firmly.

Artemus sighed and grimaced slightly to indicate his uncertainty.

"Do you really think we could do that? It would be amazing if we could."

"Well, why don't we try – let's have a try now, that's if you've woken up enough?" she teased. "Let's go to your studio - I noticed that you've set up a new canvas. It looked very inviting, as though it were calling to the paint brush, 'Come and write a life on me'"

Slowly, and with considerable effort, Artemus allowed Grace to walk him to the canvas. "I used to feel like you," he told her, as they stood in front of the easel. "If I saw a clean canvas, I was driven to pick up my brush. Cannabis works for some people but for me, it's an empty canvas. You know perhaps, unless I am being too presumptuous, how excited you can feel just before an encounter with the opposite sex. That's what an empty canvas does for me."

Grace gave a slightly embarrassed laugh and countered with, "I can't say I was excited quite like that, but this canvas certainly attracts me. What shall we paint, do you think?"

She seated herself beside Artemus in front of the canvas, picked up one of his brushes and tried some practice strokes on the back of her hand.

"Well, it's been so long since I've had such a beautiful young woman in the studio, I'd like to paint you, Grace."

"How can you, when I am so close and have my back to you?"

"Well now, first of all, you move that long mirror into position." He pointed to the mirror on an adjustable stand. When Grace had positioned it as directed, he continued. "Yes, that will do well. Now I can paint you, because the mirror gives me distance." He smiled and corrected himself, "I mean, we can paint you, in profile. I don't want to finish the portrait of Zelda until we have practiced this new technique together."

"How do we start? I did paint a little when I was in Paris, and the other artists said I was quite good, but I have forgotten all that now. You control the brush, Artemus."

"I think we'll practice on a sheet of paper first," he replied, and attached a sheet of paper to the easel. He squeezed paint onto a palette and Grace pushed the brush into the paint and, guided by

Artemus holding her wrist, tried a series of shapes. At first they were shaky but, by moving his hand to new positions and supporting his elbow on a chair, they found that it was possible to produce shapes.

"No, it's not really working," Artemus said, frowning and becoming annoyed with himself.

"But it will, I'm sure it will. I can sense already that we're beginning to work together. I can feel your hand taking control."

"Can you? I didn't realise that was happening. I've grown to dislike people who want to control others. In my experience, they are usually self-interested and opinionated. I know that is what I was like. Now that I've grown older though, and been more on my own without the shield of success which made me feel dominant, I think I've changed."

Grace turned to kiss him on the cheek and laid her head on his shoulder. "But that's not you, Artemus, not now anyway. You are my benign fate, remember." She put up another sheet of paper and allowed her hand to be guided to form other shapes. "Just let's keep on trying. We'll get there, eventually. And even if between us we produce a style of painting like nothing you have done before, at least you will be painting again."

They worked on for another hour, by which time the light was beginning to fade. Suddenly Artemus burst into delighted laughter.

"Grace, Grace!" he exclaimed, "It's starting to work!"

"I think so too," she replied, her face glowing with pleasure. "I've never known anything like this." She stopped and kissed his cheek again. "It's beginning to feel as though your mind is controlling my movements. Is this 'possession', do you think? If it is, it is an amazing experience, like floating, like I feel when I am dancing, like… " She shrugged. "Oh, I don't know what it's like – perhaps like what you say about drugs. I just know it seems amazing. Do you feel it, too?"

"I do." He turned his chair to face her, its legs screeching on the bare floor. "What you are feeling is akin to love. I don't mean the sort of love you feel for Edward. But it is possible to love the world, to love humanity and, when you experience it, to feel a love for your own self. Some people call it a Pacific feeling. Like being part of an ocean. That is the way I feel when I paint and, I think, it is what you are feeling now." He sighed heavily. "I am just worried about the future for you young people. I don't have much longer in this world but you are going to face the growing storms. I am not happy about Herr Hitler and what is going on in Germany. I saw the war with Germany and I have seen the film 'All Quiet on the Western Front' and I am desperately afraid that we will go through it all again. There is so much hatred in this Continent. You see in the newspaper the assassination in Marseilles yesterday of King Alexander of Jugoslavia, shot by one of his own countrymen. France's Foreign Minister was killed with him. The last war was started by the assassination of Archduke Ferdinand. I pray that this assassination yesterday will not have the same results." He started to raise himself from his chair as he said, "I'm sorry to say, Grace that tiredness is creeping up on me. We'll have to stop for now but there will be tomorrow and more tomorrows, I hope, when we will really begin to work together."

CHAPTER SEVENTEEN

"I am sure you understand everything I say, Edward," Grace declared as she stretched out a blanket on to the grass under the shade of a tree. They had walked to a wood close by and were in a small clearing where trees obscured the sun and stunted the grass. "And it seems to me that you understand a lot of what I am thinking as well." She sat down and pulled Edward down beside her. "Perhaps you understand what other people are thinking." She opened the picnic case, poured a glass of lemonade and passed it to Edward.

"Am I right?" she asked.

"Yes, right. Now, right," Edward replied. "Time right with you."

Grace listened and smiled. "I like the way you speak. You say things poetically. No one else that I know uses language as you do. Your words have a sort of rhythm." She unwrapped the sandwiches and passed one to Edward. While they ate and drank she said, "I feel that I can talk to you. Shall I do that, just talk about anything that comes into my head?"

"So I like," he replied.

"You and I have had very different lives." She paused, gathering her thoughts. "But I think we have both suffered in a similar way. I have had to conform to my father's wishes. Artemus, although he is so much better than my father, has been equally wrong in the way he has treated you. Both he and all those other people who have looked after you decided they knew how to treat you, and having made up their minds, never tried anything different "

"Know that but change I need."

"I know that too, and I want to be sure that the change happens." Grace leaned her back against the tree and pulled Edward down so that his head was in her lap. She looked down at him and said." Edward, you have a most beautiful profile. It's not surprising that your father wanted to paint you so many times." She passed her fingers absent-mindedly through his hair as they lay back and looked through the branches at the sky above them. Edward watched the trees swaying in the wind and smiled with pleasure.

"Artemus did paint," he said. "Times many... painting wonderful."

"Yes, I know, I have one here in France. A painting of you; I suppose I stole it, but it didn't seem like stealing. It seemed that I was meant to have it. It brought me here. Here to Edward." Grace looked up at the swaying branches of the tree. "I am so happy to be here with you, my Edward."

"Also happy, ...my Grace?" He looked up enquiringly.

"Yes, I am your Grace." She leaned forward and kissed him on his forehead. "Now you talk to me."

"With you, my Grace, I like to be. My Grace do bless me now. The tree above branch over me. Tree with arms take us to the sky."

"Keep talking just like that. I love to hear your words."

"To heaven carries me and you et arriverons là."

"Are they your own words?" Grace asked, twining her fingers in his hair.

"My words," Edward replied. "Words not understood?"

"Tell them to me, even if I don't always understand. I still like their sound."

Quietly, Edward started to speak. "The aramusta sang to thee and larsa wes to gather. And in dain malorato thee can wel to me and pleasure." He raised his head and asked, "Grace understand?"

"No," she replied. "I do not understand, but it doesn't matter. Your voice and its rhythms are enough." She bent down and kissed him but very lightly, on his lips this time. "Talk to me again or, if you like, we could sing."

Edward took so long thinking that she wondered if she had upset him. Finally, he began to sing, slowly at first, and almost in a monotone, as if giving voice to thoughts which had never before found release.

"Come with me to exotique

Where we with birds will wing

Where wondrous things with music sound

To make a sad heart sing

The people there have languages

That no one else has heard

And when they speak

They tell of love

That cleanses troubled minds.

Give me your love for me to care

Give me your turmoiled soul

And with my words and with my rhymes

I'll make your spirit whole"

His voice tailed off and he looked at Grace with frightened eyes as though he was fearful that he had said too much.

"Edward, that was amazing and lovely. And it was so different from the first poem, which was in a language all your own, and it's different from the way you normally speak. Perhaps the rhythm of poetry changes your use of words. You must do more of your poetry." She raised his head and lay down beside him putting her head on his shoulder. "I had a 'turmoiled' soul when I lived in my house in Loriston, but it has left me now. Partly it was because I discovered dancing, which helped me a lot. But also I think that just finding you at last has brought me peace, which is something I have never had before."

Edward put his hand on his chest and said, "Me, I have a peace aussi." Then he turned and cautiously kissed the top of her head. Grace put her arms around him so that their faces and bodies were close together. She wrapped her leg around his, ignoring the way it rucked up her skirt. Edward reached down and took her hand. Gradually, they fell asleep.

When they woke up some time later, they gazed up at the tree above them.

"I had a favourite tree in Loriston. I used to dance around it," Grace murmured dreamily. She looked directly at Edward. "Do you think it is strange when I tell you that I loved that tree?"

"Not strange. I love trees." He raised his hand and pointed to the branches. "My tree."

"Our tree," Grace insisted.

"Our tree," Edward agreed.

"I think we should dance around it," Grace said firmly.

She raised herself to her feet and held her hands out to Edward. He stood up and Grace started to sing to music she could hear in her head. She had no idea where it came from, but there was a magic about it.

266

She placed Edward's arms and body in a dancing position and pulled him close to her.

In time with the music she was singing, she started to dance a waltz, pulling Edward gently along with her. At first, he was unsure what to do, but gradually he became more confident and more in tune with her movements.

"A friend of mine in Paris called Mel showed me how to do a ballroom dance like this. It's nice, but not the way I normally dance."

"Dance like you do normal," Edward requested. "I follow you."

"All right, I'll sing something a bit faster and when you're ready you can join in with me."

She now sang more wildly and began to dance around the tree. Edward followed her movements, haltingly at first, but was soon able to dance with increasing confidence. They danced in time with Grace's rhythm, their bodies swaying first one way then another until Grace became breathless and had to stop. Edward stood back, opened his arms, and pulled Grace towards him in an awkward child-like embrace.

Later that day, she walked back with Edward to Claudine's house. "Now you must get some sleep, Edward. I'm afraid I might have tired you out," she said. "I must also go back and look after Artemus."

"Artemus self looks after."

"He always has done, Edward, but he is getting older and is ill, and won't be able to care for himself properly for much longer."

Edward left Grace with a puzzled look on his face as he walked into Claudine's house. Grace continued along the road to Artemus' house where she found him just wakening from his daily sleep.

"Did you enjoy your walk with Edward?" he asked.

"Heaven is in that countryside, Artemus. Yes, we had a lovely time. I discovered more of Edward's mind as well. Did you know that he composes poetry?"

"Poetry? Edward? I've heard him mutter a few words, that's all. They're usually too jumbled up to make any sense."

"He has a language which uses words which I've never heard before – 'maloration, - 'aramusta' -, but he also recited a poem using the words you and I use in a most beautiful way."

"Good Lord, that's astonishing. He has never been to a conventional school but I had a tutor for him for many years. Eventually, I asked her to stop because she seemed to be getting nowhere, and Edward didn't like her; he was always sulky with her and stayed that way sometimes for days."

"It's almost as though he has three parts to his personality, the one we see every day, the other where he uses this strange language which appears to have no meaning, and the third in which he composes poetry using normal English."

"Remarkable - my son, my dear boy, able to compose poetry and think in words which are only his."

"That's his charm. Everyone who met him under-rated him. It's not your fault, but I can see that you have been influenced by the people around you and the things they have said about him. They don't understand him properly and can't be bothered to make the effort to see what there is beneath his quiet exterior. Because of that, he has been treated wrongly. He thinks deeply about things but has been given no opportunity to express his thoughts. I just sense that he has a mind not yet matured, but one which will be capable of great creativity."

"Grace, I never realised. He always sat quietly and seemed happy with just being a child."

"Did you ever try to talk to him?"

"Well, the doctors said he had been seriously brain damaged at birth and would never be able to talk properly. I suppose I have always accepted that they were right."

"That was wrong. Can you imagine having a mind full of ideas but with no one to talk to. It must be a torment for him."

"But what you do not know, Grace, is that he can have a violent temper. If I ever try to push him, he yells and throws himself around in a frightening way. I always thought it best to just leave him alone when he was like that."

"He has never been anything other than gentle with me, but because of frustration, you can understand him being aggressive. He needs kindness and a lot of attention. And that's what I intend to give him."

"I want to be a better father to him too, Grace. What should I do?"

"We'll talk about things like that when we have dinner together. You'll see a great change in him if you are gentle and talk to him. It'll be just the three of us."

"Ah, but we may also have a guest with us."

"Oh yes, Artemus, a lady guest is it?" Grace teased. "I've only known you for a short while, but I'm beginning to see what you're like. I suspect you still have a soft spot for the ladies."

Artemus laughed with undisguised pleasure but said nothing.

CHAPTER EIGHTEEN

Artemus, Grace and Edward sat at the dining table that evening. A meal had been prepared by Claudine, and four settings had been laid. Grace started to serve the food and jokingly said

"Your lady guest has not turned up then, Artemus."

"I didn't say it was a lady, did I?"

As he spoke, the door behind Grace was opened quietly. Grace heard nothing because she was absorbed in mixing the salad. A figure passed her in the candlelight and pulled the chair back beside her. Grace glanced up and her mouth dropped open in astonishing.

"Mother!" she practically shouted and knelt down by the chair in which Elsa was sitting, to bury her head in her mother's breast. She looked up at her mother in amazement, "how did you get here?"

"I came here to see you all," Elsa replied, hugging Grace tightly against her. "I no longer live in Loriston."

"What?" Grace leaned back. "Do you mean you have left Loriston altogether?"

"I do"

"Does that mean you have left...?"

"Yes, I shall no longer be living with the Reverend Belari."

Grace looked bemused, her hand to her mouth as she stared at her mother. "The Reverend Belari?"

271

she repeated. "You've never called him that before. Why do call him that?"

"We must not forget that we are in company now, dear. We'll talk about him later. Tonight is Edward's night."

"Sorry, mother, it's so lovely to see you that I forgot Edward and Artemus." Grace put her hand on Edward's arm. "Tonight, we are all here because of Edward." She filled glasses around the table and said, "Let us all drink together to celebrate your return." Before raising her glass, she said. "Mother, you look wonderful. You look so well, and you seem... happier."

On that note, they all stood, raised their glasses and called out a toast to Edward. He responded with a smile of pleasure and said in a quiet but clear voice, "Thank. All...you."

They sat down to continue the meal, but before long Grace stood up again and declared, "And now, I'd like to drink to you, mother. You look amazing. Better even than you did that time I helped you with your make-up."

So, once more, they drank a toast and clinked glasses, which made Edward laugh out loud.

Artemus said, "She's right, you know, Elsa. When I last saw you, you were under that cloud called Belari. The cloud has lifted, you do look a different woman. And we are all so glad to see you here." He raised his glass shakily to Elsa. "Thank you for coming."

"Thank you, Artemus," she replied teasingly, "but it wasn't just you I came to see. We have Edward to thank for releasing us from what has been a pretty empty life. Edward is the real reason we are all here, isn't it?"

Seeing Edward laugh in delight, Artemus quietly said to Grace, "You know, I have never seen him..."

and then, correcting himself. "I've never seen you laugh like that, Edward," he continued in a louder voice, addressing his son directly. "Is it having all these nice ladies around that's making you so happy?"

"It . . . is," Edward replied, his speech still a little uncertain. "Nice ladies."

"Tell them what we did this afternoon, Edward," Grace said.

"Walk," he answered. "Went walking."

"And we danced, didn't we. Not much, just for a little while," Grace added. "You see, Edward isn't used to dancing, so I started; he just watched at first and then I dragged him in to dance as well. Isn't that so, Edward?"

"It is so," he replied.

"But, the most surprising thing was when we walked back. A deer came out of the woods," she continued. "In England, deer are scared of people and, as soon as they see someone, they dash away. But this one came right up to Edward, nuzzled his hand and lay down in front of him. It was amazing to see."

"Like animals," Edward said.

"St. Francis," Artemus said, smiling at his son. "That's the name I've given him." He looked at his son with pride. "I don't know how he does it but he has always been able to charm animals. You're right, Grace, he does have an air of peace, doesn't he? I've never been properly aware of it until you said that. Animals can sense his peace, I suppose. Do you remember the dog that was growling at me and biting my trousers, Edward?" he asked, still addressing him as adults do children. "When you came along, he stopped and just sat down."

"I do bring memory." Edward replied. "Then he became friend to me." Artemus nodded in agreement, his mind far away.

"I think it's time to eat, now," Grace said briskly, standing up and serving the food onto plates.

Artemus took his plate and started to eat, but suddenly decided to get some more wine from the kitchen. Grace followed to give him a hand and Artemus spoke to her in a quiet voice that only she could hear, "I'd like to say something to you, Grace. I think you have created a miracle. I don't think it is saying too much to call it a miracle. I have never heard Edward talk like this. He has occasionally said odd words but now he's making sentences."

"Yes, but we must never talk around him, Artemus."

"How do you mean?"

"Edward has a thinking mind and he needs to take part in the conversation, not be just the object of a sentence."

"But you see I have to get used to a new situation. It's all so very different with him."

They carried the wine back to the table and sat down. Artemus filled everyone's glass and turned to Edward who was still hungrily eating his food.

"Grace wants me to paint again, Edward. She will be my hands. I haven't painted for...," he shrugged, "well, I can't really remember for how long, but it must be at least two years."

"Two years, two months, three days," Edward replied.

Artemus looked stunned. "My God, you are probably right! I painted you with a dove held in your hands, holding him up to the sky. It was a marvellous subject, but that was before my hands were shaking too much." He fell silent then for a few moments of reflection. "That painting was actually so bad that I burnt it."

"Saw fire eating the painting."

"I didn't know that you were watching. It was the first time I had ever burnt any of my work. Paintings are like people. They have personalities and they express themselves." Turning to Grace, he said. "That was why I left those paintings in my house in Loriston. Their personalities made me feel that they wanted to remain there."

Artemus finished eating and sat back, wiping his mouth with a napkin. Grace poured him another glass of wine, which he drank before saying regretfully, "Will you all excuse me? I'm sorry but tonight I am dreadfully tired. I must leave you now."

"Oh, Artemus!" Elsa exclaimed, "I am so sorry, I hadn't noticed. Let me help you up."

"You two have a lot to talk about. I'm sure Edward can give me a hand. The old bed he used to sleep in is in the next room. Can you help me, Edward?" He stood up carefully and held his arm out. Edward took it, said, "Goodnight. I go bed too." He supported his father as they both left the room.

"Nice that he's staying here tonight. Normally he goes to the housekeeper, Claudine. I don't get on too well with her. I think she sees me as an intruder." Grace went to the door and called out, "Edward, tomorrow, if the weather is fine, we'll take another picnic into the country and we'll walk much farther and do some dancing. Don't forget, now."

"Not forget," he called back.

Both Grace and her mother watched them go, closing the door behind them.

"Now tell me, mother. Tell me what has happened. Is father all right?"

"The man you call father is out of my life."

"Whatever happened?"

"When you left, he was in a dreadful temper, and he sulked for days on end. You know the way he could. And then, one day, when he returned home, I don't know if he had been drinking but he became violent. I'd only ever seen him like that once before."

"Raphael?" Grace asked.

Elsa nodded. "Yes, like he was when he found out about Raphael. He terrified me and blamed me for what he called my 'wanton ways'. He hit me, just once," Elsa added. "Once was enough. As I fell, I picked up a poker from the grate and, when he started to come for me again, I raised my arm to hit him. Thank the Lord that he backed off. I was in such a rage that I would have killed him. All those years when he had pushed me down; when he convinced me I was useless and ill, suddenly welled up and put such strength in my arm that I would have killed him with one blow."

"Mother, how could you? It would have been a dreadful thing to do," Grace said anxiously. "You must have been terrified; otherwise I just can't imagine you doing anything like that. You've always been so gentle."

"That moment of rage changed me. I finally realised that I had strength and I could also see that that strength really terrified him. In a strange, almost frightening way, it thrilled me to see that I was in charge of the situation. While I held the poker in my hand, ready to strike, he ran out of the house in fright. He jumped into his car and drove off." She put down her drink. "That was the last time I saw him. I called for a taxi, collected a few things together and left the house for good."

"But, mother, you could hardly walk when I last saw you. How could you leave the house?"

"Doctors call it mind over matter, I think. I just forgot any difficulty I had had walking and . . . well," she raised her hands, "I just walked, quite awkwardly at first because I was in a hurry, and I almost fell over several times. You know when you left and we got the money from the bank for you, I drew out a lot more than you needed and hid it in the house, I must have thought even then that I would leave him. I also have a cheque book. I managed to pack some bits of clothing and the jewellery which had been given me by mother – I left anything which he had given me."

"What about the things you loved - the ornaments and the paintings, all those things?"

"As I was driven away in the taxi, I could feel a sensation I had never had before, Grace. Freedom for the first time, intoxicating freedom, and it made me realise that all those things which I thought I loved were just snares holding me to a life which was not mine. I looked back at the house and it seemed to me I was looking at someone else's life. Isn't that odd? For over twenty years I had been there and it had left no mark on me. I suddenly saw that those things you thought I loved were just substitutes for real love. They were like hands - no…, more like chains, holding me, holding me in that house of his, trapping me in that dark sunless room."

"But, where did you go - to Harrogate, to grandfather's old house?"

"I couldn't go there, he would have found me and, anyhow, there are tenants in it now. Funny, isn't it? When I got into the taxi I didn't know where to ask him to take me. I had my address book with me. You had given me that telephone number. I had wanted to ring many times, but I knew you needed your freedom. I didn't want to follow you, but I couldn't think of anything else I could do. The taxi took me to the station and I went into the Station Hotel, ordered myself a drink, can you imagine that, I'd never done it before then I rang the number on their phone. I was surprised when Dusty answered." Elsa wiped her eyes. "I had once known her quite well, because we both had Artemus as a friend. The sound of her voice took me back to those times and made me realise the enormity of what I had done." She shook her head. "I just couldn't stop myself crying even while I talked to her. It seemed to me that I had opened the gates to the tears I had not shed during all those years that I had been married. The receptionist looked at me very strangely but I didn't care, I just paid and left."

"What did Dusty say when you rang her?"

"Isn't she a wonderful person? She just said, 'Come to me'. Just those words, 'Come to me'. I wrote down her address and caught the next train. That journey was a revelation. I felt like a young girl again. I had had so many years when I was just an adjunct to him and here I was, free of him at last. I stopped the night in London and caught a morning train. When I met Dusty, she took me to a nice restaurant. I was able to order a meal and I was served by a nice young man. Very handsome too, Grace."

"I must have left for Paris by then," Grace said.

"Yes, you'd already left a couple of weeks earlier. I would have loved to have seen you, of course, but I was also glad that you were not there, because you would have felt constrained by me. That was the last thing I wanted. Above all, I wanted you to be free of both him and me."

"Did he try to get you found?"

"No. I rang his verger. I had become very friendly with him, you know. He used to bring me flowers from his allotment and, even without my saying a word, he had understood the situation between the Reverend and me for a long time. I was afraid that if I sent a letter, the Reverend would be able to find me from the postmark, so I asked the verger to scribble a message from me saying that I would not be coming back and he was not to try to find me."

"Oh, mother, I am so pleased for you." Grace stopped, struck by a sudden thought. "Of course, it was you who rang Artemus, you must have spoken to Mel, found out where I was going and told Artemus I was coming."

"Yes, I rang Artemus, but I didn't tell him who I was and I don't think he guessed."

"He said he didn't know who had rung, but he did think he recognised the voice as someone he had known."

"I didn't announce myself, but I expect he guessed and he just wanted you to have a surprise."

"Wonderful surprise it was, too."

"Artemus and I got to know each other after Zelda died. Not all that well, of course, because the Reverend would have been furious. But we did become friends, and he tells me I helped him over a very difficult time. I'd met him off and on when he visited Loriston, but I'd lost touch with him until Alec told me where you were going."

"So you spoke to Alec and Mel? That's good. They must still be together then. But how did you get Mel's number? Surely she hasn't gone back to her apartment?"

"No, she'd rung Dusty and left her number. She and Alec are in England somewhere. They are not telling anyone where, but they are buying a shop, so they must be settled."

"I'm so glad. I have been concerned about her and had no way of finding out where she was. But what will you do now?"

"I only know I shall never go back to Loriston. I may stay in France, at least for a while. I like it here in this town. I may buy a house. Even if I don't stay, and return to England, I could use it for holidays. Or you could use it."

"Edward and I could use it."

"Dusty told me how you felt about him. Do you still feel the same, now that you have seen what he is like?"

"No, I don't feel the same. The intensity is the same but the feeling is different. I can't explain it really but perhaps he makes me feel maternal. Whatever it is, I know that I want to spend my life with him." Grace's face glowed with pleasure.

"I don't think you should make that sort of decision until you have had more time with him. You are still young and things could change. Have you thought that you may end up as just a nurse to him?"

"I have and I don't mind." Grace shrugged her shoulders. "Many people wonder what life is all about, and why they have been put on this earth. I am lucky because I know why I am here. If I have to devote my life to him, it's what I was intended to do. Time I spend away from him just feels like time lost to me."

"You should see as much of him as you can, then. What you are saying is important and you need to be absolutely sure of yourself and of Edward. When do you see him tomorrow?"

"In the morning, we're going to go for another walk along the river, but for longer this time than we have done before. When we're alone, he's a very different person from the one everyone else sees."

"I'll just say this, Grace," Elsa took Grace's hand in hers, "that was exactly how I felt about the Reverend Belari before we married." She picked up her glass and thoughtfully sipped her drink. "If you are seeing Edward tomorrow, I shall spend the day just lazing around. I have a good book and I'll enjoy a day's rest, I'll probably come here to keep Artemus company. I'll catch up with you the day after. I'm so enjoying being free to do what I want, it's a luxury I never had in Loriston."

They finished the bottle of wine, talked until it began to get dusk then walked together to the hotel where Elsa was staying.

"I want you to be very sure about Edward, Grace. He is not at all like other people. Think long and hard about what you are taking on?" Elsa queried putting her hand on her daughter's shoulder.

"I don't even want to think about it. I am sure, completely sure," Grace replied. "I don't think I have ever been more convinced about anything in my life."

"Have you had any thoughts about Carlton? I met him in Loriston and have spoken to him on the 'phone several times."

"Yes?"

"Well, he just seems such a nice boy and he is so fond of you, you know."

"As you say, he is a nice 'boy'. He has a lot of growing up still to do."

"I can see that, but you could help him."

"No, mother, Carlton needs a different type of person from me. You said he is very fond of me but his

281

fondness is suffocating, when I am with him I just have to get away. I just find it, well, irritating."

Elsa looked hard at Grace. "There is something I have to tell you, Grace."

"Yes, what is it? Something about father?"

"That as well but, first of all, it's about Carlton."

"Yes, go on." Grace looked puzzled and then her frown cleared. "You are not saying that he is here with you, are you?"

"Not yet, but he will be."

"Here, do you mean? He is coming here?"

"Not just him."

"Not just him?" Again Grace had frowned momentarily. "What do you mean? Has he got a girlfriend at last?"

Her mother laughed. "You'd like to see him settled, wouldn't you? No, he is not bringing a girlfriend. He is still pining for you. He's bringing Dusty or, rather, she's bringing him. She's on a buying trip for her gallery. When she heard how Artemus was, she decided to see if she could buy some more of his work. When she told Carlton, he asked her if he could come along too." She looked at her daughter's face, for signals of the way she felt. "Do you mind?"

"I haven't much choice, have I? It'll be nice to see him, I suppose. He is a nice boy, but that's all he is. I want to get on and help Edward and I don't really want to have Carlton here with him. Carlton was always very dismissive about what he called my 'painted boy'. He thought I was just being stupid. I know I will have to see him, but I don't really want to." She pursed her lips. "Do you think I am being too hard, mother? He has been very kind to me..."

"You're your own woman now, Grace, so you must make up your own mind. I'm not going to interfere. Neither I, nor the Reverend Belari, can hold you back now," Elsa said as they arrived at the hotel. "I am going up to my room now."

"Can I come into the reception with you? You did say you wanted to tell me something about father. I've had such a strange day, a little more talk may help me sleep."

"All right, let's walk for a while. I've a few more things to tell you. We can walk past the little house I have looked at. You'll like it, I'm sure."

The house, built of stone in mediaeval times, delighted Grace. "Mother, it looks marvellous, you must buy it."

"I will buy it. It belongs to Artemus. He wanted me to stay there and, even when we spoke on the 'phone, he suggested it would be ideal for me. He even offered to give it to me, but I shall pay whatever it is worth."

"I'm so pleased. If you come to live here, we could have lots of time together. It would be a real help too because I shall have so much to do, what with Edward and getting settled."

"And Artemus, don't forget Artemus. He is going to need looking after as well."

"Artemus?" Grace put her hand over her mouth. "Oh, dear, I was so wrapped up in my own thoughts that he slipped my mind. You are right. He is going to need a lot of care as well."

"Well so long as I'm here and I stay as strong as I feel now, I'm sure I'll be able to help. I'll get to know his needs. You will have your work cut out with Edward and he will respond best to you." They had returned to the hotel by now. Elsa kissed her daughter goodnight and said. "I think I shall stay here, dear; it does seem to be very beautiful, and quite hilly like Loriston. I'll go back to Harrogate occasionally and Artemus might like to come with me. It would do him good to get away and out of his house. I can see that he has become lazy and he doesn't look after himself properly. That was what happened to me in the Rectory. Now I want to be doing things and making up for lost time."

"What were you going to tell me about father?"

"The Reverend Belari is suing for divorce. He...," she stopped and pushed her hand through her hair distractedly, "he says you are not his daughter."

On hearing this, Grace screwed up her eyes to hold back tears and then put her arms around her mother. The two women embraced each other. After a few moments, Elsa pulled away and brushed her eyes with the back of her hand and they started to walk back to the hotel.

"I don't know why it makes me tearful. I ought to be happy," she said. "I am so glad to be away from him, and from that depressing room he wanted me to stay in. I've done what I knew I should have done even before you were born. Now that you and I are both free and I have caught up with you, I can start living again. Do you remember I once said to you that I thought I wouldn't live long?"

Grace nodded and said, "Yes I remember. You told me I should leave the vicarage and I was worried because that meant leaving you there with him. It nearly tore my heart out when I did leave, to think of you in that dark room and in that house which I had grown to hate." She put her head on her mother's shoulder. "But now, mother, you look so well, you look like a different woman."

They had reached the hotel. Elsa kissed her daughter and held her hand for a moment before parting. As she went in, she told Grace, "Dusty and Carlton will be here in a few days. I'm going straight to bed. It's so warm here. Loriston was never like this. I hope I can sleep in this heat. It seems even hotter now than it was during the day."

CHAPTER NINETEEN

The next morning was overcast, and it looked as though it was going to rain. Grace had donned her raincoat and a hat and walked excitedly to Claudine's house where Edward always had his breakfast. She was disappointed to see that he was not outside waiting for her as usual.

Claudine came to the door when Grace knocked.

"Oui?" Claudine inquired without smiling.

"Monsieur Edward, s'il vous plait," Grace answered, noticing that Claudine was speaking French.

Wordlessly, the housekeeper stepped back and allowed Grace to enter.

"Où est il, s'il vous plait?"

The older woman sniffed and indicated with her thumb that Edward was in his room upstairs.

Grace went up the stairs slowly, wondering what she would find. As she pushed open the door to his room, she saw Edward curled up on the bed sucking his thumb.

"Edward, how lovely to see you, are you ready for our walk? We'll have a lovely time walking in the rain."

Edward did not respond, except for turning on his other side to face the wall. Grace went to the bed and put her arms across his body. Edward shrugged his shoulders in an effort to push her arms away.

"Edward, please don't treat me like this. I'm your friend." She kissed the back of his neck. "Your father told me that you sometimes feel sad and that you don't want to get up. Shall we go out and see if a change of air might help?" Still he shrugged and moved away from her.

"Edward, can you tell me what's wrong?" Grace tried again. "If we are to be together, I must try to understand how you are feeling, but when you are like this, just lying there without speaking, well, it worries me. I feel helpless, useless, as though I am shut out of your life."

Edward turned on his back and stared at the ceiling, but still made no response.

"Edward, speak to me, please, say something – anything, it doesn't matter what, just speak," Grace said, her voice becoming agitated.

When Edward still did not respond, she bent over him, took his face in her hands and, in attempt to get through to him, almost shouted, "What is wrong? Is it something I've done? You were happy to see me last night but this morning I don't know what to think."

Edward's eyes were still cast down but he muttered, almost inaudibly, "Sun gone."

"Sun?" Grace repeated. "You don't mean you are silent just because the sun isn't shining?"

"Sun mean day is good."

"Yes, all of us like the sun. I always feel better when the sun shines, but rainy days like today can be nice as well. We'll go for our walk and it will be just as enjoyable as a sunny day because we'll be together. That'll be nice won't it?"

Edward remained silent for a moment and then with a look of defiance said," No sun, day will be bad."

On hearing this response, Grace nearly exploded again. She grabbed hold of his shoulders and shook him. "Can't you see I'm trying to help you?" she said, her voice becoming louder, "there are many days when there is no sun. It doesn't matter. You must see that."

"Sun good," Edward slowly insisted.

"I KNOW THE SUN IS GOOD!" Grace yelled directly into his face. "BUT WE CAN'T HAVE SUN EVERY DAY." She was breathing heavily with emotion and then took several moments to calm herself as she realised that she was making things worse. "Do you want to walk with me or not?"

Edward shook his head and replied, "Unlucky. Day not right. Don't want walk, will be unlucky day."

"Unlucky! Unlucky, walking with me! How can it be unlucky?"

"Will be unlucky."

"Unlucky! Don't you know any other word?" Grace shouted at him again and, when he still remained silent, she began to weep with frustration, turned on her heels and ran down the stairs. She returned to her room in Artemus's house and put her head in her hands, staring first at the ground and then unseeingly through the window into the distance. Unable to think clearly, she lay down on her bed, her mind revolving around what her mother had said to her the day before.

The next morning, Elsa got up very late, having not slept well. She breakfasted in the hotel, then returned to her room to read and rest from the after-effects of her long journey and a poor night's sleep. She continued to think about Grace and Edward. Throughout the morning she dozed fitfully. After a late lunch, she continued reading for a while, before deciding to see how Grace and Edward had got on with the walk. Before leaving, she changed her clothes and put on some make-up. It was mid afternoon by the time she knocked on the door of Artemus' house. She heard him muttering to himself as he walked unsteadily up the corridor. When he finally opened the door, he exclaimed, "Oh, Elsa, I'm so glad to see you! Is Grace with you? I didn't see her this morning, so I went to her room and she wasn't there."

"I assumed she was with you."

Artemus frowned. "She seems to have taken her bag with her, and all her clothes, which is very strange. Things are in such a state of change that I thought she might have taken things to the hotel with you for some reason."

"No, I left her outside the hotel last night," Elsa replied, and then her mouth dropped open. "Is she with Edward, do you think? I do hope not."

"Why do you say you "hope not"?"

"She has no experience with men and Edward is…" she stopped speaking and looked confused.

"Edward is what?" Artemus demanded. "Do you mean he is dangerous? Is that what you mean?"

"Well…," she hesitated, "Edward is strange, isn't he?"

"Grace herself says he is different, that's all. And what's more it's that difference which makes him interesting to her. Her actual word is 'fascinating'. But even she finds she cannot always understand the way he thinks and the way he sees things; but if you are saying that Edward may have harmed her, I can tell you he has never harmed any one or any thing in his life. He is the gentlest of creatures, sometimes he does get very angry, but he has never done anything." He put his hand to his chin and pondered. "In any case, she can't be with Edward, Claudine has been and said that he hasn't moved from his room. He doesn't like these rainy days when the sun doesn't shine. He'll probably be happier now that the clouds have passed over. It looks like we're going to have another hot day."

"But what about Grace? I left her happy last night and now you are saying that she's taken her case and gone off somewhere." Elsa's voice was rising. "Where can she be, then?"

As she spoke, they heard a noise and turned round to see Edward walking towards them.

"Edward!" they both shouted.

"Have you seen Grace?" Elsa asked anxiously.

"Grace?" Edward said looking puzzled. "Come to see her with father."

"She's not here," Artemus replied. "Has she been with you during the night?"

"Been with you?" Edward frowned.

"No, but she seems to have gone off somewhere. When did you see her last?" Elsa asked

"Saw her night last. Where Grace now?"

"We don't know. Wherever she can be?" Elsa asked.

"In house?" Edward nodded at the door.

"No, she isn't. She's nowhere in the house. I've looked in every room, and in the garden as well." Artemus replied.

Edward looked blank for a while and then said, "Tree."

"What do you mean, 'tree'?" Artemus asked.

"A tree; sit by; dance by. She teach me to dance," Edward answered.

"Well, she did have a tree in England," Elsa mused. "She told me that when she was feeling confused, she would go to her tree and dance. Dear God, I hope that is what she's done here." Turning to Edward, she asked. "Can you take me to that tree where she dances? Artemus, you'd better go on in and rest. I hope that we'll find Grace there and can bring her back with us."

Edward and Elsa walked along the path which Grace had taken him though the woods. When they reached the clearing, Edward stopped and said,

"Music. Hear music?"

"No, I can't hear any music. You must be imagining it."

"Hear music. Music of Grace."

"Music of Grace," Elsa asked. "Are you sure it's not just music in your head?"

Edward put his hands over his ears and replied, "Music here."

"Does that mean we are near the tree?"

Edward nodded. "Near, tree near."

"Please be there, Grace," Elsa said to herself, her voice shaking.

They followed a track through the forest and just as they entered a clearing in the woods, Edward began singing quietly to himself:

'Dance in an empty room

To music of our minds

To air and wind and wild-torn skies

And evanescent lines

Believe in me

I know your soul

I know that flight-thrown guise

Where you and I in tournament
Begin to see beyond
This always present emptitude
When we shall find our song.'

Elsa stared at him in amazement. "Is that your own song?"

Edward nodded his head. "My song. Yes, my song. Song of Grace."

"It's beautiful, Edward. I didn't know you composed songs.

"Mm. Like songs," as he spoke, he stopped and pointed, "tree," he said.

Elsa followed the direction in which he pointed. "But Grace is not there," she said with, disappointment in her voice.

"See! Fire!" Edward suddenly exclaimed, pointing at wisps of smoke rising into the air.

"What does it mean? Is she there?" Elsa asked as she began to go towards the smouldering ashes.

On the embers she saw the partially burned remains of several sheets of paper. Elsa snatched them away from the heat and stamped on the smouldering remnants. Sitting down, she tried to make out the writing on them. Edward came and sat beside her and resting his head on her shoulder said. "Where Grace are you?"

"She's been writing a letter, starting it many times and crumpling the paper up, I suppose, when she wasn't happy with what she had written." Elsa said

"To Edward?" he asked.

"Some may have been to you, but I can't read them clearly, because they are blackened by smoke

292

and burned in places. This one she must have written last and thrown it on when the fire was dying down because it is only a little bit marked."

"Say?" he asked.

"It's hard to read because some of the words have been destroyed. But what I can make of it says, 'To you all. I thought I could, but now I think I cannot.... I thought it was my destiny to look after Edward and all of you in your different ways, but I realised this morning that there is not enough strength in my mind to...' Then there is something else I can't read but it goes on, 'I shall not be here when you get this.' Then there is another burned bit, 'I feel happier there; music and dance always helped me but this time it is not able to help enough. I thought it would make me see things better, but I am still confused. I don't think I am strong enough to take it all on. I want to find peace in myself... Please try to understand. I... I'll be away for a few days so that I can think.' It's all burned from there so I can't read anything else. But, Edward, she is still safe!" She covered her face with her hands. "I was so afraid...I ...Reverend Belari...Sorry, I'm confused...I just didn't know what she would do. Thank God she is all right. But where can she be?"

As she spoke, Edward, who had sat up to listen to what Elsa was reading, leaned his head against Elsa's shoulder again and whimpered quietly.

"Grace is where?" he asked, his voice muffled in Elsa's shoulder.

"I don't know, but now I know that nothing has happened to her, I feel much happier," Elsa replied. "Come on, we'll go back and tell Artemus."

"See Grace," he whimpered.

Elsa put her arm round his shoulders.

"We can't see her, I'm afraid." She said, "She has always been an unusual girl. Many times when things were difficult at home, she would go off, sometimes for days. Her father would do nothing. He used to say she was just playing - to get attention and he wouldn't give her that satisfaction."

Edward stared at her, looking baffled. Elsa looked around for other signs that might suggest where Grace had gone. When she found nothing, she said to Edward, "Come on, my dear, we must hurry back and see if we can start a search for her."

Back in her hotel, Elsa found a note in the slot where her key was kept. She opened it with shaking hands and then, with a beaming smile, saw that it was from Grace.

Dear Mother,

I have found everything so confusing since. Meeting up with Edward was like walking into a dream. He is not well but somehow that made it seem even more right for a time. It seemed to make me even more necessary to him. But things are going wrong and I am so glad that you are here. I have needed someone to talk to. Even though he is so kind, I cannot talk to Edward about things that concern us both. Artemus is also kind but he is not able to understand how I feel about Edward. When you asked me if I was sure about Edward, I realised that deep down I did have doubts, and they were so deep that I hadn't allowed myself to admit to them, even to myself. I've decided to have some time to think (and dance as well) so I've taken a bag with clothes and some food, and I'm just going to wander in the woods for a couple of days. Don't worry, I will be all right.

My love to you, mother, I am so delighted that you are at last happy and here with us all.

Grace.

As soon as she had read it, Elsa felt like weeping with joy. When she had become settled, she took the letter round to Artemus and read it to him.

"Thank God she's coming back," Artemus responded. "I think I might have been too hard on the girl. Edward is so different now, and I realise that, more than anyone else, Grace is responsible. I would like to see them together."

"Let's hope that she comes back feeling the same, then," Elsa replied. "I'll go and tell Edward that Grace is safe and will be coming back."

That night the weather turned and it became cold and windy. Elsa lay awake for a long time, convinced that Grace would return. She slept only fitfully until dawn when she finally fell into a deep sleep of exhaustion which lasted most of the rest of the day. When she eventually woke up, she found a note had been pushed through the door. With shaking hands, she opened it and read:

Dearest Mother,

One night was enough; even with what I thought were warm clothes it was very cold. I'm back now and am going to Artemus's house to sleep in my room.

I have decided that my destiny is with Edward. I don't think I will ever mean anything without him.

Grace.

When she had read the letter, Elsa collapsed on the bed, weeping with relief.

CHAPTER TWENTY

The following day, the screeching of brakes announced the arrival of Dusty as she raced through the village in her MG sports car and pulled up outside Artemus's house. As Grace watched, Dusty emerged, slightly larger and more billowy than when Grace had last seen her, and walked purposefully round to the other side of the car where Carlton was struggling to open the passenger door.

"Carlton, I do wish you were good at things. There's something wrong with this door, as I told you. I'd get it fixed locally but nobody in this part of the country seems to have any idea about anything mechanical."

After much fiddling with the key, and pushing and pulling, the door finally sprang open and Carlton slowly clambered out, obviously just waking from sleep.

"Where are we?" he asked.

"If you open your eyes, Carlton, you'll see that we are here."

"Here?"

"Yes, here, in the village where your Grace lives, of course."

Artemus came out of the house. Walking slowly with the aid of his stick, he raised a hand in greeting to Dusty and she flung herself at him, almost knocking him over.

"Sorry, Dusty, I am just a little unsteady these days," he said.

"The old problem - alcohol, is it? Bit early in the day though, you old soak."

"Wish it was alcohol, I'd be able to do something about it then."

"Well, try taking more of it. That's what I always do. If I'm a bit unsteady from the night before, I take a 'wee dram' of whisky and I'm right as rain in no time." She stood back and gave Artemus a long appraisal. "But, my dear old soul, you don't look at all well. You've got a new agent back London who told me that you were suffering from some illness or other." She started fumbling in her hand bag. "I've got some gin here and more in the car. It's the sort you like, you know, the sort that you can't get over here. Reckon that'll soon put you right." She looked over his shoulder and saw Grace coming out of the house.

"Ah, there you are young woman. Come and see. I've brought this love-sick ninny to see you."

Grace responded to Carlton's open-armed greeting by walking to him but she could only smile weakly at this man now part of the life she was trying to forget.

Noticing her coolness, Carlton took her arm and walked with her to a seat in the square.

"Aren't you glad to see me? I've had an awful drive in that cramped MG to get here to see you."

Grace sat down beside him and looked long at the hills in the distance before she responded.

"Thank you, Carlton. I am sorry that you had to put up with an uncomfortable journey." Momentarily, she put her hand on his. "I am touched that you should come all this way but I must tell you that I am not the girl you knew. I told you that I would only be happy when I met Edward."

"Yes?" Carlton said expectantly.

"Well, I have found him."

"And...?"

"And... I am happy here with him."

Carlton's head dropped with a groan. After a few moments, he looked up.

"But how can you be? Dusty has told me she spoke to your mother and Artemus on the 'phone and she told me what they said about Edward." He looked up at the sky and frowned. "He's almost a loony, isn't he? You'll have to look after him for the rest of his life. What will you do for money? Surely you want a man who can care for you - a real man like me. Come home, whatever you have done wrong, all you'd need to do is go to confession and your father would forgive you. In England I can look after you."

At his words, Grace frowned and, was about to speak when Carlton continued. "Everybody's talking about war. If you stay here, you will be English in a foreign country. If there is a war, you'd need a real man to fight for you."

"I don't think anyone wants a war so I'm not going to even think about it."

"Don't be too sure, in any case, you'll be better off in England with me. I'd make sure you had everything you wanted. Your paint boy certainly won't be able to do that, will he?"

"Don't use expressions like that," she said angrily, "no, Carlton, I am sorry, but Edward is all I want. As for money, I shall have more than enough for him and me."

"But you can't just moulder away in this isolated place; it's way out in the sticks - taken us forever to get here."

"I don't intend to moulder."

"What else is there here? Will you do labouring on a farm, there doesn't seem to be anything else going on here from what I hear?" He grimaced, "I can't imagine anything more depressing".

"If I tell you, you will only laugh," she replied, and then, after a moment, continued, "But I will tell you, all the same. Dancing like I used to do in Loriston has helped me so much and it has also helped Edward. He is different now from when I first met him." She stood up and, with Carlton following, started to walk back to the house.

"So?" Carlton asked, raising his eyebrows and feigning bafflement.

"So, I will make a life with Edward here; set up a school of dance to help other people who have problems. Edward will be good as a dance teacher."

"Dance teacher, how can a loony do that? Why can't you see it? Admit to yourself that it's a stupid idea and it always has been. He'd be better off in a home where he can get treatment. Come back with me, Grace." He said as he tried to take her in his arms.

Grace pushed him away so violently that he almost fell backwards. "No, Carlton, Edward is not a 'loony', he is a sensitive man, it may surprise you to know that he and I have a lot in common, something I have never been able to say about you." She turned and walked back into the house.

Later that day, Grace was in her room, trying to read when there was a knock on the door and Dusty came in.

Grace stood up and threw her arms round Dusty's ample figure.

"What is wrong, Grace, your eyes are all red, you look as though you've been crying?" Dusty asked as they both sat on the bed.

"It's Carlton again."

"Don't I know it, I've had to put up with him for three days. Every time I showed any interest in a waiter or the gorgeous concierge at the hotel, he treated me like a pariah. I began to think he was turning into a prig like your father, Belari. He told me they have been meeting a lot, I sometimes wonder if Carlton is going to become a priest, he talks a lot about the need for a faith, keeps badgering me to go to confession." She huffed, "me – can you imagine? I'd be there for a week, I've got twenty years to catch up on, probably enough stuff there for ten D.H. Lawrence novels."

Grace frowned, "Carlton and my father getting together, whatever for, I can't see what they would have in common."

"Don't kid yourself, honey, as the Americans say; Carlton always had a pious side but now forgiveness of sin is almost all he talks about."

"But he always tells me that at university, he lived a wild life."

"Just talk. I suspect he had a couple of glasses of cider and kissed a girl behind the bike shed. Ever try anything on with you?"

"We didn't have that sort of relationship. But he kept making suggestive remarks."

"That's probably why he complains about me so much," Dusty grinned, "envy that I've had all the pleasure and he has all the piety. He and Belari have got that to talk about and there's you, of course."

"Me! How do you mean?"

"Apparently, Belari is full of regrets about you - wants you to go back. Between you and me, I suspect that's one of the reasons Carlton asked to come when he heard I was planning to visit Artemus."

"I don't understand, do you mean Carlton is just my father's messenger?"

"Oh, not entirely, Carlton is as jealous as Hell about your Edward. Aside from piety, that's what dominates him." Dusty got up and sat on the chair beside the dressing table. "Sorry," she said, "my back's killing me after two days in the MG, I need to lean against something."

"Father really wants me to return, I can't believe it, he's never shown any interest in me," Grace said, "but what about mother?"

Dusty pursed her lips, "he told Carlton that Elsa has hurt him so much he never wants to see her again."

"Poor mother," Grace said, leaning back on her arms to stretch her own back, "well, I say 'poor mother' but I don't think she would ever want to go back to the rectory, no more than I could. I'd as soon lock myself away in a nunnery; I'd get more freedom there."

"What were you crying about when I came in then?"

"Carlton made me so cross with his stupid remarks about 'paint boy', which is what he calls Edward. He just can't see any farther than his jealousy – even calls him a 'loony' – he'd never understand what I can see in Edward – that he has far more creativity than Carlton will ever have." Grace began to look tearful again, "But he's still a very good friend – he's done a lot for me and I don't want to repay him by treating him badly."

"You don't know him as well as I do, there's a lot of the martyr in him."

"I don't follow you."

"In medieval times it was called flagellation – whipping your own body to expiate a sin. Carlton would've been a master masochist if he had lived then."

Grace sat up and put her hand to her mouth.

"What is it, Grace, what are you thinking?"

Grace looked at the floor and said quietly. "Am I like that? Is that why I want to give my life to Edward when everyone tells me it is stupid and, deep down, I know that it is."

"I don't know, it's too deep for me but, what I do know is that you have no choice. You may be blessed, you may be cursed, but you have to do it."

THE END